A DELIG

Vaguely Bethia [...] terrified at being alone in this room at a country inn with Mr. Digory Rendel—but terror seemed to be the last thing in the world that she was inclined to feel.

In his stockinged feet, he came toward her as silently as a cat. Pulling her unresisting to her feet, he untied her cloak and lifted it off her shoulders. When he hung it on a hook by the door, she found herself watching with delight the way his muscles rippled beneath the thin fabric of his shirt.

So this is seduction, she thought. This is what poets write about—this feeling of fires igniting in every vein when he looks at me—this desperate longing to have him touch me—this aching need to feel his arms around me.

But Mr. Rendel showed no sign of wanting to hold her. "I shall, of course, sleep in the chair," he said, moving past her to resume his place by the fire.

Clearly Rendel meant to try to be the gentleman that he most emphatically was not. Clearly he meant to resist the temptation that a female as beautiful as Bethia presented. And just as clearly he would fail—if Bethia had anything to do about it. . . .

The Counterfeit Gentleman

The Counterfeit Gentleman

by

Charlotte Louise Dolan

A SIGNET BOOK

SIGNET
Published by the Penguin Group
Penguin Books USA Inc., 375 Hudson Street,
New York, New York 10014, U.S.A.
Penguin Books Ltd, 27 Wrights Lane,
London W8 5TZ, England
Penguin Books Australia Ltd, Ringwood,
Victoria, Australia
Penguin Books Canada Ltd, 10 Alcorn Avenue,
Toronto, Ontario, Canada M4V 3B2
Penguin Books (N.Z.) Ltd, 182–190 Wairau Road,
Auckland 10, New Zealand

Penguin Books Ltd, Registered Offices:
Harmondsworth, Middlesex, England

First published by Signet,
an imprint of Dutton Signet,
a division of Penguin Books USA Inc.

First Printing, August, 1994
10 9 8 7 6 5 4 3 2 1

This book is dedicated
to
Mardy and Eddie LaForge.

Friendship knows no bounds
of
time or place.

Chapter One

May 1818

"There, what'd I tell you," a voice out of Bethia Pepperell's nightmares said. "This place is deserted."

A second voice that had also come and gone like a will-o'-the-wisp through her dreams replied, "So you say. I say there could be an entire regiment of preventatives not a hundred yards away."

Forcing her eyes open, Bethia discovered she was half sitting and half lying on the seat of an unfamiliar coach. Its interior was grimy, its squabs stained and frayed. Moreover, a cold fog was insinuating its damp tendrils through the door and reaching out for her with ghostly fingers.

"If we can't see them, then they can't see us. Stands to reason."

"Well, it's still making me nervous, so hurry up and bring her along before the fog lifts."

Vague memories slipped and slithered through Bethia's mind—memories of a man who'd held her while a second man forced her to drink wine made bitter with laudanum—and instinctively she shut her eyes and feigned unconsciousness.

Unseen hands caught her and dragged her out of the coach. Then the man slung her over his shoulder as easily as if she were a bag of meal.

There could be no doubt that they were somewhere on the coast, for the scent of the sea was all around her. After they had gone only a few yards, the footsteps of the two men began to echo hollowly. Opening her eyes just for a minute, Bethia saw heavy wooden planks, and in the cracks between them she could glimpse dark, murky water.

Even with her wits befuddled, it was not hard for her to deduce that she was now being carried the length of a dock.

Her thoughts gradually became clearer, and by the time the men lowered her into a small boat, she remembered the way the larger man had burst into her bedroom and abducted her. What a fool she had been to think herself safe behind a locked door.

Oars rattled in oarlocks, and when she felt the boat begin to move through the water, she risked opening her eyes the merest crack. The dock had already been swallowed up by the fog, and there was nothing to be seen but the dark form of a larger boat.

Soon even that ghostly shape was no longer visible, and still the man with the pocked face rowed on.

More than likely they were taking her out to a yacht where her wicked cousin was waiting, ready to carry her to France where she could be forced to marry him even against her will.

Or so he doubtless thought. None of her three cousins knew her very well, or they would have realized just how obstinate she could be when someone tried to bend her will. Moreover, although she had never thought of herself as vindictive, she was quite determined to make the cousin who had instigated this abduction pay for every indignity he was causing her to suffer.

Before she could decide the best way to thwart his intentions, the rocking of the boat destroyed what little control she had over her stomach. With a moan, Bethia leaned over the edge of the boat and cast up her accounts in a most unladylike manner.

"The devil take her, she's awake," the larger man said, leaning on his oars. "We'd better give her some more laudanum."

"I left it in the coach," the smaller man said, "but it doesn't matter—she doesn't have enough strength to try anything."

"Then we oughter tie her up proper, so she can't get away."

"Get away? Don't be daft. There's nothing she can do, so hold your tongue and get on with it. This fog is making me nervous."

After a moment's hesitation, the larger man began to row again.

"How much longer?" the smaller man asked, voicing the same impatience that Bethia was feeling.

"If we don't go far enough south-southeast, the current won't bring the body back to shore tomorrow."

"Sometimes I don't know why I was fool enough to think you know what you're doing," his companion said, peering intently ahead, as if by sheer will power he could see through the mist and discover how close they were to their destination.

"You may know London like the back of your hand, but you'd be as helpless as a newborn babe out here on the water 'thout me. Why, you don't even know how to row a boat. You'd prob'ly end up going in circles, and then when the fog lifted, you'd find yourself sitting right by the dock—and the next thing you'd be seeing would be the hangman's noose."

Much of what had happened in the last few days was still unclear to Bethia. But one thing had now become all too obvious: The body they were referring to was hers, and unless she could come up with a quick and effective plan, then when this boat was returned to its mooring, it would be carrying two people rather than three.

If only she were strong enough to overpower one of the men! If only she could swim! She wished, in fact, that she were a man—wished she knew how to shoot a gun—wished she had a gun to shoot or even a sharp knife.

But wishing was pointless; her grandfather had always told her that. Facts must be faced squarely and difficult situations met head on had been his guiding principles since he had left home as a young man, out to seek his fortune . . .

Oh, if only he had not made such a vast fortune and then died and left it all to her!

Fiercely, she banished such unproductive thoughts. She would not—could not—meekly accept her fate. With her last breath, she would fight for her life, even knowing it was doubtless a futile effort.

It was a perfect morning for a smuggling run. The sea was calm, the light fog showed no sign of lifting, and Digory Rendel knew the currents along this section of the coast well enough to be sure that any cask of brandy he might be forced to throw overboard would come ashore in Carwithian Cove with tomorrow's tide.

Having retired from smuggling the previous year, however, he had no casks of brandy sharing the space in his rowboat. Ostensibly spending the day fishing, he had been on the water for over an hour and had not yet bothered to bait his hooks. Instead, he was simply allowing his boat to drift with the current while he contemplated the way his life was now drifting just as aimlessly.

He needed another goal—something to challenge him—something to . . .

There was a faint sound of oars splashing, and for a moment his muscles tensed, before he reminded himself that he was now completely respectable, with nothing to fear from any excise man. More than likely it was not government men anyway, but other smugglers, who were now plying their trade in what used to be his territory.

An imp of mischief made him decide to remain still. If he timed it just right, he might be able to scare the smugglers into tossing their entire load overboard, which would be good for a laugh later over a pint of ale in the Blue Gull, especially if it was his former partner, Jem, in charge of the crew.

It was not Jem's baritone that came across the few feet of water separating the two boats, but rather a female voice, forced unnaturally high by fear.

"Please, please, do not do this. I will pay you any amount you require if you will only spare my life."

"We've already been paid well enough," a man replied—a Cornishman by his accent, but not someone whose voice Digory recognized.

"However much it is, I will double the sum—triple it even."

"Aye, and then where'd we be if 'twere known that we'd gone back on our word? Out of a job is where, because who'd trust us with their dirty work if it got about that we took bribes? We're honest criminals, and we've our reputation to think about."

"You are cold-blooded murderers is what you are."

"But not double-dealers; that is a distinction I value. Moreover, I've never taken orders from a woman, and I don't fancy starting now." The second man's English was more cultured, as if he'd had at least a smattering of education.

Suddenly, there was a sound of scuffling, and Digory took advantage of the men's temporary distraction to remove his boots and jacket, slide a knife under his belt, and roll as noiselessly as possible over the side of the boat and into the water, where he clung to the gunwales and waited for his next opportunity.

"Blast it all! I tol' you she oughter be tied up proper like."

"That's not a matter for us to decide. The gentleman who hired us was most specific. It must look like an accidental drowning, and ropes might leave suspicious marks on her skin."

"Then you oughter've given her another dose of laudanum this morning, 'cause she's marked me right and proper—scratched me like a little she-cat. I've a mind to teach her more respect."

"None of that, now. There'll be no shortage of wenches for a man with the kind of money you'll be getting."

"So you say, but I got a hankering to try out a real lady. More than likely she's a virgin, too. Seems a pity to send her to the devil 'thout even—Owww! She bit my hand!"

There was more scuffling and then the sound of a loud slap, and without letting his arms break the water, Digory swam the few yards separating him from the others. As their boat emerged from the gloom, he was relieved to see that the men's backs were turned toward him.

Staying low in the water and as close as possible to the boat, which nudged against his shoulder every time the oc-

cupants shifted position, he could only hope that the girl
would keep the men's attention firmly fixed on her.

Each of the men had a pistol stuck in his belt, and if even
one of them glanced over his shoulder, there would be two
bodies washing up on the sand with tomorrow's tide.

"I'll take a whip to you myself, Jacky-boy, if you don't
settle down to business. That's always been your problem—you let yourself get distracted at the damnedest
times. If I had it to do over, I'd leave you in the gin shop
where I found you."

"Don't forget who knows the currents and who don't,"
Jacky-boy said with a sneer. "Fact is, you need me more
than I need you, so maybe I should have more than half the
earnings."

For a moment it looked as if the two men were going to
have a falling out, which Digory planned to use to his advantage. But as luck would have it, the girl managed at precisely the wrong moment to get one hand free. She
immediately began pounding her fist on her captor's arm,
which distracted both men from their quarrel.

Ignoring her ineffectual blows, Jacky-boy lifted her off
her feet and swung her out over the water.

Taking a quick breath, Digory dived under the boat and
came up on the other side, almost directly under a pair of
shapely legs surrounded by billowing petticoats trimmed
with lace.

Carefully keeping the girl between himself and the men
in the boat, he grasped one trim ankle firmly. At the touch
of his hand the girl began screaming hysterically and kicking wildly, but Digory only held her more tightly, knowing
that if he even momentarily lost his grip, the weight of her
clothing would pull her down, and he would have to be
lucky indeed to find her once that happened.

"Get on with it and throw her in before someone hears
her."

"The devil take her! She's clinging worse than a barna-
cle."

All at once the girl stopped struggling, as if she had finally realized it was a human hand holding her ankle, and a

moment later her full weight came down on Digory, pushing him deep under water.

Precious seconds were lost before he could untangle himself from her skirts, but after what seemed an eternity, he had one arm firmly around her waist. His other hand was covering her mouth and nose, and his legs were straining to get them both as far away as possible from the murderers' boat before he was forced to come up for air.

The girl was a dead weight in his arms, which made his task easier while at the same time making him afraid he was wasting his efforts. She might already have inhaled a fatal amount of seawater, but if he came up too soon, the fog would not conceal them adequately and both of them would be at the mercy of the paid assassins, who did not appear to be the slightest bit merciful.

When his lungs could stand it no longer, Digory kicked his way to the surface, praying that the fog would conceal them. The girl's head lolled on his shoulder, but he was relieved to hear her taking great gulps of air through her mouth. He pressed one finger to her lips, and she nodded weakly, indicating she knew what he meant, but it was a moment before she was able to moderate her gasping.

"She must've sank like a stone. Strange."

Jacky-boy's voice sounded too close for comfort, and it brought back too many memories of other occasions when Digory had escaped from dangerous situations with his skin intact—more or less.

Very gently, so as not to make the slightest sound, he began kicking with his feet, not actually swimming, just trying to put a bit more room between the two of them and the men in the boat.

"What's strange about it? She couldn't swim, and besides, no one could stay afloat long wearing as many clothes as she had on."

To be sure, the girl whose head was now supported against his shoulder was decidedly prettier than any of Digory's former comrades had been. The water seemed to give her dark brown hair a life of its own, and it swirled caressingly around his neck.

"Still and all, I'd've expected her to thrash around at

least a little," Jacky-boy said, sounding quite aggrieved. "There's no sport in it this way."

Digory wondered idly if the two men in the boat included swimming among their skills. He would have found it amusing to see how long they thrashed around before sinking, but his first priority must be to get this girl ashore. And even when she was safe, he needed the two men alive so that he could persuade them to reveal the name of the man who'd hired them.

"She's drowned, you lummox, and that's all there is to it. And tomorrow, just as soon as we 'discover' the body, we can collect the rest of our money. Now get us back to shore."

The girl had her arms around Digory's neck now, and their bodies were so close in the water, his legs kept bumping hers with every kick. Looking down, he saw she had dark brown eyes, which appeared too large for her face. The salt water made her lashes cling together, making her look as if she'd been crying.

But he'd heard her in the other boat, and she had not been weeping piteously. She must have known how slim her chances were, and yet she had bargained for her life, her resolution never wavering.

Finally, Digory heard the welcome sound of oars rattling in the oarlocks, and he uttered a silent prayer of thanksgiving that today of all days he had followed his whim and gone fishing. It was appalling that a person's life could depend on such a chance event.

Gradually, the noise of the other boat became fainter and fainter until nothing could be heard but the cry of a lone sea gull.

"Who are you?" a dulcet voice whispered in Digory's ear.

"My name is Rendel. I am a . . ." He hesitated briefly, then said simply, "I was fishing when I first heard you."

"You have a boat? Oh, thank goodness."

"I am afraid it can do us little good now since our chances of finding it in this fog are remote. But that is no great matter. We will simply swim to shore and leave my boat to follow in its own good time."

"Oh."

A wealth of disappointment was in that one word, but there was little that Digory could say to reassure her. "I am a strong swimmer, and I have lived in this area all my life, so I am quite knowledgeable about the currents and the tides. And if I had to guess, I would estimate that we are only a half mile or so from shore."

"But how can you tell which way to go in this fog?" the girl asked, and he was pleased that she was managing to keep almost all the fear out of her voice. She was no coward, this one, and in spirit, although not in looks, she reminded him of his half sister, Cassie.

"I was born with a natural sense of direction, and the tide is with us, so we have nothing to worry about," he said without adding that if the tide turned before they were safely on shore, even he might not be a strong enough swimmer to save them.

But he had no intention of saying anything that would shatter the girl's self-composure, which he suspected was hard won. "We will make better progress if you could dispense with your petticoats."

If she had been a girl from the village, he would have bid her take off her skirt also, but such a demand would not do for a lady, especially when their situation was not yet dire.

"I shall do my best to untie them," she said, and while she struggled to undo the knots, he did his best to keep both their heads above the water.

Finally, she gave up her efforts. Once more wrapping her arms around his neck, she whispered, "I am afraid the saltwater has made the knots too tight."

"Then I shall have to cut them," Digory murmured, sliding his hands up under her skirt.

She gasped and stiffened in his arms, but she neither jerked away nor cried out.

Moments later she was free of most of the sodden fabric, and pulling her around behind him, Digory showed her how to hang onto his shoulders so that he could have both his arms and legs free. Then keeping his head above water, he began an easy sort of breaststroke. It was slow, but he could maintain it for hours without tiring.

The girl was silent at first, and then she whispered, "There is something over there in the fog—to our left and a bit ahead of us."

Digory's crew had frequently told him he had the luck of the devil, and apparently they spoke the truth, for his boat was bobbing peacefully about fifteen feet away.

Changing direction, he moved to intercept it. "If you can hang on to the gunwales while I get in, then I can help you climb in."

A few minutes later they were safely on board, and Digory unshipped the oars and began to row with a steady rhythm toward Carwithian Cove, the only place he could be sure the kidnappers would not go to—at least not until the next day.

His thoughts were less easy to control, and when he looked at his passenger, his pulse began pounding in his ears.

Her arms were covered with gooseflesh, and her lips were quite blue, and she should not have been in the least bit appealing. Perhaps it was because her wet garments disguised none of the feminine curves of her body and legs, or because he had just been in intimate contact with her that he felt an unexpected surge of desire.

Even knowing she was too far above his station for him to have such thoughts did not prevent him from wanting to take her in his arms and warm her in the way men have warmed women down through the centuries.

If only the circumstances had been different—if only she were a village girl and not a well-born heiress—he would have cheerfully stolen a few moments of pleasure.

"I have always disapproved of ladies who dampened their dresses," Miss Pepperell said, beginning to shiver violently. "Now I am even more inclined to think them fools, for in truth I am finding it most uncomfortable."

He could tell the very moment when she realized how her remark had served merely to direct his attention to her womanly curves, because hot color rose swiftly to her cheeks, and she immediately lowered her eyes.

"My jacket is folded up there behind you—feel free to make use of it," he said.

Of course it was possible that it was not her own words, but rather the carnal desire she had seen in his eyes that had shattered her composure.

Once she was adequately clothed, she regained her poise, which only made his own wayward thoughts seem more despicable in comparison.

Looking up, she met his eyes squarely and said calmly, "I am afraid that I do not know the proper thing to say when someone saves your life. All I can say is thank you."

"You needn't thank me," he said curtly, annoyed with where his thoughts had led him—and angry with himself for not being able to ignore the tension between them. "But I would appreciate some explanation of what is going forward. Since it is obvious that your recent companions were not interested in catching fish this morning, could you perhaps tell me how you came to be with them in that boat?"

"It is a long story, and it is hard to know where to begin." She paused, then continued, "My father was Baron Pepperell. I do not remember much about him because he died when I was three years old. A distant cousin inherited both the title and the estate, so my mother and I went to live with her father. She passed away less than a year later, leaving my grandfather to raise me. And he died two years ago in August, leaving me in the care of Aunt Euphemia, Lady Clovyle, that is. She is my father's sister."

Although Miss Pepperell did not say so directly, it was obvious from her voice that she had been much more attached to her grandfather than to her aunt.

"Is she the only relative you have still living?"

"On my father's side. On my mother's side, however, I have cousins galore, but only three who are likely to be implicated in the plot you have just spoiled. Or I should say, any one of the three had a motive for hiring those two men."

"Three cousins, each with a motive," Digory said, stopping rowing for a moment so that he could listen for the sound of the buoy marking the reefs by Penistone Head. Reassured by its bass voice that he was still on the proper course, he resumed both his rowing and his questioning.

"I suppose money is involved somewhere in your story."

"A great deal of money," Miss Pepperell said, her voice bleak. "My grandfather, James Granville, was the younger son of the Earl of Granwood. In his youth grandfather quarreled with his father and older brother and left home. Years later he came back to England with a fortune in his pocket and married my grandmother, who was herself the granddaughter of a duke.

"They had only one child, my mother, who had but one child, me, which means I am the sole heiress to my grandfather's estate. Unless, of course, I die unmarried before I reach the age of one and twenty, in which case Wilbur, Gervase, and Inigo Harcourt will all inherit equal shares. They are the sons of my grandfather's only sister, who married the Reverend Percival Harcourt." She was quiet for a long moment, then she added what was only too obvious. "Apparently one of them has decided that a third part of my grandfather's estate is worth committing murder for."

Digory considered what she had told him. "It would seem to me that the easiest way to circumvent whichever cousin is plotting against you would be to marry. Surely you have had ample suitors?"

"Indeed," she said, and there was a touch of bitterness in her voice, "with both beauty and fortune, as well as the proper family connections, I have been quite the belle of the ball. But how can I determine which, if any, of the young men courting me love me, and which ones love only my grandfather's money?"

"A common, yet not insurmountable problem with heiresses, I believe."

"If it were only that, I would take my chances and hope for the best. But suppose . . ."

She was quiet for a moment, and then he finished the sentence for her. "Suppose one of your cousins is conspiring with one of your suitors, do you mean?"

"Oh, I am so glad you said that. After the number of apparent accidents that have befallen me, I feared I was inventing danger even where there was none. But if you see the precariousness of my position also, then I am not simply being hysterical."

"Accidents? Tell me about them."

She hesitated. "I feel so foolish mentioning them. Aunt Euphemia—she is my guardian and is sponsoring me this Season—insists that I have been making a fuss about nothing. To her way of thinking, the accidents were the result of mere happenstance, and if my imagination had not been overly stimulated by the reading of too many lurid novels, I would never have indulged in such flights of fancy."

Miss Pepperell scowled and thrust out her lower lip. "She went so far as to tell me that if I continued to cast aspersions on the character of such honest, upright, God-fearing men as my mother's cousins, who are in every way respectable, then I myself belonged in Bedlam."

"I would say that being thrown overboard by two men who openly admit that they were paid to kill you rather refutes any suggestion that you might be imagining things. But tell me more about the other supposed accidents."

There were now subtle differences in the sound of the sea, which meant they were approaching the shore.

"Well, to begin with, after one evening party I became quite ill. Tainted oysters, my aunt said. But no one else was the least bit indisposed, and even though I knew it was farfetched, I suspected poison."

"Were your cousins present at the party?"

"Yes . . . and they each, at one time or another, brought me something to drink. I was sick for several days and weak for quite some time afterward. Then, only a sennight after I began to go out in society again, I rode out to Hampton Court with a group of friends. On the way home, the cinch on my saddle broke, and I was saved only because my escort was right beside me when it happened, and he managed to catch me as I was falling."

"And had the cinch been cut?"

"No, it was merely old and rotten, so there did not appear to be anything sinister about the accident. But our groom insisted it was not the same cinch that had been on my saddle when I left our stable. I believed it to be a second attempt on my life, but Aunt Euphemia insisted that the groom was fibbing in order to protect himself from being turned off for failing to do his job properly. She discharged him over my objections."

"And your cousins? Were they at Hampton Court when you were?"

"Who is to say? We spent an hour or so wandering through the maze, and anyone could have come and tampered with my saddle and still been well away from there by the time we emerged from the shrubbery."

"And were there any other suspicious incidents?"

"Not only suspicious, but nearly fatal. A few days later, when I was shopping with my maid, someone tried to shove me under the wheels of a heavily loaded brewer's wagon. My aunt insists someone merely jostled me accidentally, and of course I have no evidence—nothing to prove that she is wrong in her opinion. And yet in my own mind I have not the slightest doubt that the blow was deliberate . . . and that the attempt came within a hairsbreadth of being successful."

"Has it ever occurred to you that your aunt herself might be aiding and abetting one of your cousins?"

Miss Pepperell laughed. "If you knew my aunt, you would know how preposterous that idea is. To begin with, she is my father's sister, and so could not, under any circumstances, inherit anything from my grandfather, who was my mother's father."

"One of your cousins might be paying her."

"She does not spend all her income as it is, and she has frequently told me that I am her heir. She has been most generous to me in the past, and I see no reason to doubt her on that score. But the real reason I cannot suspect her is that the rules of etiquette do not cover the subject of ridding oneself of a superfluous niece. As a child, my aunt learned how one should comport oneself in society, and I do not think she has ever deviated from the proper path."

Digory had met similar people, not only among the *haut ton*, but even in the little village in Cornwall where he had been raised, and he was forced to conclude that Miss Pepperell was undoubtedly correct in her assessment of her aunt's character. Which was indeed fortunate, since her aunt was living in the same house.

"In any case, after the last supposed accident, I could not stop looking over my shoulder, and I began to notice two men who seemed to be loitering in my vicinity much too often. I begged my aunt to let us retire to Sussex, where I have an estate, but she refused to consider leaving London in the middle of the Season—or rather, until I have acquired a husband. Last week I became so afraid, I resolved not to leave my room until my birthday. Despite my aunt's scoffing at such extreme—and to her way of thinking, unnecessary—measures, I felt there was nothing else to be done."

"And?"

"And on Monday last—I am not entirely sure how long ago that was, because those horrible men kept dosing me with laudanum whenever I woke up enough to swallow it. What day is it today?"

"Thursday," Digory said. The sound of the surf was louder now, and the fog was becoming lighter.

"Then it was only three days ago, while my aunt was at the opera, that the larger of the two men who had been following me gained entrance to my grandfather's house. How he managed that, I have no idea, although my cousins have each had ample opportunity over the last several years to make copies of the house keys.

"In any event, the man called Jacky-boy came into my room while I was reading, and before I could cry out, he had gagged me and trussed me up and was lowering me out the window to his waiting henchman, whose name I never heard. They brought me here to wherever we are."

"The south coast of Cornwall," Digory said. "They were the men in the boat?" he asked, needing to be sure they were dealing with only two hired assassins and not four.

"Yes," the girl said bleakly.

The bottom of the boat grated on the sand, and Digory shipped the oars, then climbed out and dragged the boat up onto the shore, well above the high-tide mark.

Since it was virtually in his own backyard, Digory knew this cove well, and many a night he had helped haul kegs of brandy up from the beach to assorted hiding places. Quite isolated from passing traffic, both on land and at sea, it was perfectly designed for smugglers . . . and for ambushes.

A great many rocks and boulders lay scattered at the base

of the low cliff, and some were sufficiently large to provide cover for a troop of preventatives intent upon seizing an illicit cargo—or for the band of smugglers who would be waiting tomorrow to capture a pair of would-be murderers.

Holding out his hand to Miss Pepperell, Digory said, "Come now, we are almost home."

She was too chilled to walk well, and he had to support her with an arm around her waist. He led her along the base of the low cliff until they came to the narrow path, which they climbed, leaving behind them the sea and the fog.

Chapter Two

The man sitting in the darkest corner of the Double Anchor was not one of the London gentlemen who thought it amusing to frequent low dives in Soho. On the contrary, he was a man who appreciated elegance and luxury, and he was, moreover, a man who was determined to become accustomed to a great many more of the finer things in life.

At the moment he was feeling especially pleased with himself. His scheme for removing the only impediment between himself and a vast fortune was proceeding in every minute detail precisely as he had planned it.

Although the earlier fog had prevented him from actually witnessing his cousin being rowed out to sea, the mists had cleared enough by the time the boat returned that he had been able to see it held only his two hirelings.

They were a nasty pair, and they had made assorted threats as to what would happen to him if he failed to keep his end of the bargain. But he trusted them no more than they trusted him. Only a fool believed that there was honor among thieves. Unlearned and unlettered they might be, but they were not too stupid to understand the basic principles of extortion.

What had obviously never occurred to them was that he might not only be willing but also quite capable of shooting them through the heart rather than submitting to blackmail. At Manton's he was adjudged to be a fine marksman, and as to scruples, his desire to cut short his cousin's life should have made it clear to them that his conscience was obligingly flexible when money was at stake.

What made this moment all the more amusing was the knowledge that the two scoundrels had no idea that he had followed them to Cornwall. It would never even occur to them that the red-haired, unshaven sailor watching them guzzle brandy might be the same person as the fastidious London gentleman who had daintily held a scented, lace-trimmed handkerchief to his nose to protect himself from the odoriferous fumes of Soho.

The wig had been a veritable inspiration, but then every element of his plan was so well thought out, it was a pity more people could not admire the beauty, the sheer perfection of it all. As a strategist, he was without equal, a veritable nonpareil, a master of the art of intrigue and no small hand at disguises.

No one could ever have the slightest suspicion that things were not as they appeared to be, which meant his success was assured.

Jenny Cardin had seen an odd assortment of customers come and go at the Double Anchor, but something about the one now sitting in the corner with his hat pulled well down over his face bothered her.

" 'Tisn't that he don't look like a sailor, and he talks coarse enough," she said to her husband, Tom, "but all the same there's something disturbing about him, and I'd be willing to wager good money that he never sailed before the mast."

"You're not one to spook easily; doubtless he's a bad'ne." Her husband slid a pint of ale across the counter to her. "Take him another drink on the house and see if you can't figure out what's havey-cavey about him. Then if it looks like he's going to cause trouble, I'll have him out of here so fast his ears will still be ringing come Michaelmas."

The stranger said nothing when she set down the drink, not even so much as a word of thanks. But when she went back to the bar, Jenny was able to tell her husband what had aroused her suspicions. "It's his hands; they're as pink and soft as any lady's," she reported. "You s'pose he's one of them white slavers, come to steal some of our Cornish maids away?"

"He's got no eyes for the girls, that one don't," her husband replied. "I've been watching him since you pointed him out, and all he's doing is sitting there staring at them other strangers." With the merest nod of his head, he indicated two men who were already well to go, although the sun was not yet high in the sky. "But whether he's working with 'em or agin 'em, it's too soon to tell."

"Suppose they're all three meaning to rob us?"

"Well, if they're fixing to catch us off guard, I'd say they're the ones what will be surprised."

The sunlight not only warmed Bethia, it also promised her life and safety. Her horrible nightmare was over at last ... or was it? Mr. Rendel was looking worried again. Could they still be in danger from the kidnappers? Might one of them be hiding behind that tree? Might they be creeping along on the other side of the low stone wall, waiting to jump out and grab her?

"Do you think they will come after us?" she asked, her voice no more than a breathless whisper.

"Who? Oh, you mean the men in the boat. No, they are doubtless celebrating in some tavern, dreaming of the wealth they think they will soon be collecting from their employer." Mr. Rendel voice was calm, but his forehead was still creased.

"Then why are you frowning? If it is not those villains, then what is worrying you?"

His expression lightened. Smiling down at her, he said, "My worries now are quite mundane. The first one is that we need to get you safely back to my cottage without letting anyone see us together, lest you be compromised."

"You are worried about my reputation?" Bethia asked in astonishment. "After I have just escaped a watery grave?"

"To be sure I am worried. Most people do not truly comprehend how important a good name can be until they have damaged theirs," he replied. "I would not be doing you a good turn if I saved your life only to ruin your reputation." Turning left where the path divided, he continued, "And the other thing that is bothering me now is how we shall arrange for you to have a bath."

At the word *bath*, Bethia could feel the heat again rising

in her face, and she quickly looked away from her companion in hopes that he would not notice.

"I know from experience that dried salt on one's skin is not particularly comfortable. For my part, I am accustomed to sluicing myself off behind my cottage with cold water from the cistern, but I can hardly expect you to do likewise."

Turning in at the gate of a little cottage, he stopped with one hand on the latch. "And therein lies the problem. As I see it, we have only two alternatives, neither of which is without drawbacks."

"Well, an hour or so ago my kidnappers were not willing to offer me any choices at all," Bethia said, trying not to look at Mr. Rendel, whose wet clothes were every bit as revealing as hers undoubtedly were . . . and trying also not to think about Mr. Rendel standing naked in his garden.

Opening the door for her, he said, "Somewhere around, I have a hip bath, and I can heat water over the fire. But I am afraid I have neither maid nor housekeeper in my employ to assist you."

Bethia started to enter the little cottage, but then the significance of what he was saying struck her, and the prohibitions of a lifetime froze her in her tracks.

Ever and again her aunt had warned her that all men were alike—no matter how honorable they might appear, not a single one of them could be trusted alone with a young, unmarried female. Despoiling a maiden's innocence, so her aunt insisted, was every man's chief goal in life.

"If it is not feasible for you to manage without help, I can ask my neighbor to come over. The widow Pollock lives but a short distance farther along the lane, and she would doubtless be willing to act as lady's maid for an hour or two," Mr. Rendel said calmly. "Unfortunately, gossip travels as quickly in the country as it does in London. Even if she tells no one you are here, people will be curious as to why she has been in my cottage. And once someone begins asking questions, it is always possible that the wrong person will hear and become suspicious."

Although he did not come right out and say it, Bethia had

the strongest feeling that Mr. Rendel was no longer talking about her reputation, but about the wicked men who had tried to drown her. And thinking about them made her realize that she was already far outside the small, safe world that was governed and firmly bound by her aunt's rules and strictures.

There was no way to discount what Mr. Rendel had done. At great risk to his own life, he had saved hers. If either of the men in the boat had seen him, they could have shot him through the heart, or simply bashed him over the head with an oar. Considering that he had given her back her life, she would be a small-minded person indeed if she balked at trusting him now.

"I feel sure I can manage by myself, so I think we can refrain from asking your neighbor to become involved." Without further hesitation, Bethia ducked her head and crossed the threshold.

As soon as she stepped through the doorway of his home, Bethia knew that the man who had dragged her from the sea was not—could not be—a simple fisherman.

"Sit by the fire where you will be warmer," he said, and as chilled as she was, she needed no second invitation.

She started to seat herself in the large wing-backed chair that was placed conveniently close to the fire, but it was upholstered in silk brocade and remembering her damp dress, she sank down instead onto a small, three-legged stool.

Mr. Rendel appeared to be quite accustomed to wearing wet clothing, since he made no attempt to warm himself by the fire. Instead, after throwing a few pieces of wood on the fire, he took two tin buckets from their hooks by the back door and began carrying in water to fill the large black kettle hanging from a pot-chain.

With part of her clothing beginning to give off steam while the other half still felt as if it were woven out of icicles, Bethia looked around in growing puzzlement.

From the outside the cottage had appeared to be quite bleak and primitive. Built of rough, undressed stones with a thatched roof, it was no different from any of the other cottages they had passed.

Having frequently paid calls on the tenants residing on

her grandfather's estate in Sussex, Bethia had expected to find that one end of the crude building was used by Mr. Rendel and his family, and that the other end of the building was occupied by their livestock.

But if ever any animal that mooed or neighed or cackled had lived under this roof, it was in the quite distant past, because no trace of them remained, not even the faintest, lingering odor.

Moreover, although this one room served as kitchen, living room, and dining room, and the fireplace was obviously intended both for heating the cottage and cooking the meals, the furnishings were not the crude homemade benches and table she had expected.

On the contrary, the floor was polished wood rather than packed dirt, and was covered with an Oriental carpet rather than strewn with rushes. In addition, the clock ticking on the mantel above her was ormolu, and the round table with four matching chairs had to have been designed by none other than Sheraton.

Indeed, if it were not for the fact that the room had a rather low ceiling, she could have believed she was in a manor house rather than a cottage.

Watching Mr. Rendel, who had finished filling the kettle, and was now climbing up a ladder into the loft, Bethia noticed another discrepancy. In the far corner of the room were several bookcases filled with leather-bound volumes, which belonged neither in a laborer's cottage on the south coast of Cornwall, nor yet in a manor house. Country squires, in her experience, were not inclined to muddle their brains by too much reading.

No, the extensive collection of weighty tomes in this room would be more suited to a vicarage. But from the oaths she could hear accompanying the numerous thumps and bumps coming from overhead, she rather doubted Mr. Rendel was a member of the clergy.

By the time he came back down, dragging with him a tin hip-bath, she felt as if she were bursting with questions she wanted to ask him, but she had been too well brought up to pry into another person's private affairs.

No, that was not quite correct. Propriety and impropriety

were not what mattered here. What was making her rein in her curiosity was much more fundamental than the rules of etiquette that she'd had drummed into her head since she was a small child.

Mr. Rendel had saved her life, which gave him the right to know anything about her he might wish to know. But the reciprocal was not true: Owing him more than she could ever repay him, she had no right to ask anything more from him than what he freely offered.

In fact, sitting by his fire, doing nothing while he was doing all the work was beginning to make her feel guilty. "Is there anything I can do to help?" she asked.

Digory looked down at the bedraggled figure hugging her arms in front of the fire and tried very hard to think of her in the same way he had always thought about the poor wretches he had helped drag from the sea in the past—the victims of storms or poor seamanship or vessels that were simply unseaworthy. There seemed to be an unlimited supply of fools who underestimated the power of the sea or who overestimated their own abilities.

Miss Pepperell was, or so he had been telling himself, just another scrap of humanity temporarily needing his help. Soon she would vanish from his life, leaving no more trace of her presence than had all the nameless others who had sat where she was now sitting, and who had shivered as she was now shivering.

And who had *not* looked up at him with soft brown eyes filled with concern for his well being.

"I can manage," he said, wondering if he could actually manage to forget the courage she had shown in the face of imminent death. And likewise the absolute trust she had given him, despite the fact that he was a total stranger and not what anyone would call a harmless-looking man.

It was even more unlikely that he would ever forget her face, forget the softness of her skin, forget the way her arms had felt around his neck.

Or forget the feminine curves her dripping garments had been unable to hide—forget how acutely he had wanted her there on the beach—how a single glance at her now was enough to rekindle his desire, to heat his blood.

What he wished he could do was to carry her into the other room and share his bed and his passion with her.

What he was going to do was fix a bowl of mulled wine.

Mr. Rendel had made it very clear that he wanted neither her help nor her conversation, so Bethia did not ask what was in the cup he handed her. From the smell of it, it was some sort of spiced punch. She would have preferred tea, but politeness dictated that she drink what her host had prepared.

At first she was not at all sure she liked it, but then she felt a warmth begin to spread through her body, and she decided to try a little more. This time she could actually taste the cinnamon and cloves, and she rather thought she might become used to this beverage.

Which raised the question of how long it would take for her to become accustomed to being alone with a man—for her to be able to look at Mr. Rendel without having her heart decide all on its own to speed up.

Watching Mr. Rendel pour steaming water into the hip bath was not precisely the same as observing a pair of footmen carry buckets of water to fill the enameled tub in her own dressing room back home, Bethia realized, feeling heat rise once again to her face.

It should have been no different; a tub is a tub and a bucket is a bucket.

But it was in truth vastly different.

There was an unshakable feeling of intimacy about the entire situation. She knew she would soon be naked in that tub . . . and she knew he knew she would be naked . . . and he was not a footman.

Who was he?

Watching the practiced way he added cold water to the tub and tested it until the temperature was precisely right, it would appear that he must have spent time in service, perhaps even been employed as a footman.

But everything about him—the way he walked, the way he talked, the way he took charge—made it impossible to believe that he was a man accustomed to taking orders. Indeed, anyone could see in his eyes that he was used to giving orders . . . and that he would also expect to have them obeyed.

Bethia knew her aunt would be scandalized at the mere thought of a strange man preparing her niece's bath, and she would doubtless have a seizure if she knew that Bethia was alone in a cottage with no maid or chaperone in attendance.

Last Monday Bethia herself would have found it unthinkable, but she was not the same person she had been three days ago. Being only moments away from death and then being given back her life made her look at ordinary, everyday things in an entirely different manner—made her reappraise things she had previously taken for granted.

Mr. Rendel was still apparently concerned with propriety, however, because as soon as her bath was ready, with soap and washcloth and towel laid out for her use, he strung a rope between two hooks and then draped a quilt over the line to give her some privacy.

That was not actually needed, because with only a brief word of assurance that he would be close at hand if she needed him, he disappeared into the room at the opposite end of the cottage, shutting the connecting door firmly behind him.

Setting down her cup, Bethia stripped off her garments and with a sigh of pure pleasure, stepped into the tub and sat down.

She managed to shampoo and rinse her hair without spilling too much water on the hearthstones, and indeed she encountered no problem until she was done bathing and had dried herself off. Then she discovered that the efficient Mr. Rendel had forgotten to provide her with any dry clothing.

Her first thought was to call him, but then it occurred to her that he himself might not be done with his cold bath. And she knew that however much she might think herself ready to dispense with propriety, she was not quite willing to summon him to her side while she was naked.

Beginning to shiver again despite the nearby fire, she decided that the only thing to do was use what was already at hand, namely the quilt.

With a heartfelt prayer that her host would not choose that precise moment to return, she pulled the quilt from its line and with much fumbling, managed to wrap it around herself. Then hobbling as best she could, she dragged the upholstered chair closer to the fire and sat down to wait for her host to return.

But she could not stay seated long. The smell of the spicy drink was too tantalizing, and she decided to finish her drink. Freeing one hand from the confines of the quilt, she retrieved her cup and took another sip and again felt the delightful warm glow begin to spread through her limbs, heating her veins to the tips of her toes and the ends of her fingers.

A few moments later she began feeling the slightest bit light-headed, which surprised her until she thought about what she had just been through. In the last few hours she'd frequently had the unpleasant sensation that events were proceeding at too fast a pace to be fully comprehended. She had felt herself being dragged along at breakneck speed, as if she were in a curricle behind a pair of runaway horses.

Was it any wonder that there were moments, like the present one, when she could not be completely, absolutely, positively certain that she was awake? That she was not still caught up in a laudanum-induced nightmare?

Well, perhaps nightmare was not the proper term for the situation she now found herself in, but it was in truth a most peculiar dream.

To begin with, Mr. Rendel had appeared quite simply out of nowhere. Indeed, at first she had thought he was some horrible monster rising up from the deep to wrap a tentacle around her ankle and pull her down to the bottom of the ocean.

Some might scoff at the idea of a sea monster, but was the truth any more plausible? That by a sheer fluke of luck a fisherman had happened to be near where her abductors intended to drown her—a fisherman who had not only heard her cries, but who had also felt compelled to do all he could to save her? Even though by so doing he had risked his own life?

It was almost easier to believe that he had been conjured

up by her desperate longing for someone to help her. Or perhaps it was the gods on Mount Olympus who had heard her pleas and sent one of their own to save her?

Bethia raised the cup to her lips and discovered it was empty. The bowl was right beside her chair, but she quickly discovered that if she held the cup in one hand and the ladle in the other, then there was no hand left to keep the quilt from sliding down around her waist.

In the end she solved her dilemma by simply dipping the cup itself into the brew. It was really a delicious concoction, and it seemed much more efficacious than tea, which was her aunt's remedy in times of crises both large and small.

This brought to mind the question of whether Aunt Euphemia was correct. There was a possibility, Bethia had to admit, that she was actually suffering from disordered mental faculties. It could be that everything she thought had actually happened—the abduction, the murder plot, the rescue—was nothing more than the wild fantasies of a deranged mind. Perhaps even now, when she thought she was sitting here by a fire, drinking a most delicious punch, it could be that she was in actuality ranting and raving behind bars in Bedlam.

Unfortunately, Mr. Rendel was not making it easy for her to believe she was awake. She had done her best to convince herself that he was no figment of her imagination— that he was exactly who he claimed to be: a fisherman who had fortuitously been in the proper place to hear her cries.

Sitting there all cozy and warm, assuaging her thirst with a most delightful concoction, she brooded over the contradictions in Mr. Rendel's person, in his home, and in his actions.

All things considered, was it any wonder that she was not completely sure she was awake and not dreaming?

After all, if this were not merely a dream, would she be naked—except for the quilt, which was even now surreptitiously trying to slide off her left shoulder—would she be naked in the presence of a man? Not even her grandfather would have felt comfortable sitting beside her when she was dressed—or rather, undressed—as she was.

Perhaps before Mr. Rendel rejoined her, she should put on her gown, although as wet as it was, it was quite an immodest garment—less modest, in fact, than the quilt. Which in turn brought up the most interesting question of whether or not modesty was in any way logical.

Taking another sip, Bethia considered the question of propriety. It would be highly improper, she knew beyond a doubt, for Mr. Rendel to see her in her nightgown, although that garment actually covered more of her than most of her walking dresses did. But her dresses were designed to be seen, and her nightgown was not designed to be worn outside the privacy of her own bedroom.

Which was all very well and good, but that did not answer the question of the quilt, which was neither a garment designed for public view nor a garment designed to be worn in private. A quilt was not actually a garment at all, in fact, which thus left unanswered the question of whether or not she was properly attired.

A quilt was neither a dress nor a gown, so she was definitely not clothed . . . but on the other hand, she was also not naked, because she was completely covered—at least all but one of her arms was—by the quilt.

Perhaps her host, who seemed to know about everything else, had read sufficient philosophy to answer the question of whether or not a lady was dressed or undressed if all she was wearing was a quilt.

She heard the door behind her opening, then Mr. Rendel asked, "Are you dressed?"

Stifling a giggle, she answered in her most solemn voice, "That, I am afraid, is a question I am not at all capable of answering."

After a pause she heard his footsteps crossing the room. Swiveling around to greet him, Bethia was so amazed by his transformation, she lost all power of speech and almost lost her grip on the quilt as well.

Gone were the rough homespun shirt and breeches of a fisherman. Dressed now in a black jacket, burgundy waistcoat, and fawn-colored unmentionables, Mr. Rendel was in every way the proper country gentleman. To be sure, the jacket he wore could not completely disguise the extraordinary breadth of his shoulders or the powerful muscles of his arms.

And despite his sartorial elegance, she could not quite forget what this man had looked like in his shirt sleeves and wet breeches. When they had emerged from the water, she should have modestly averted her eyes. Why she had not done so was a question she did not feel up to coping with at this moment.

"Are you warm enough?"

"I am quite warm, thank you," she murmured, lowering her glance lest he read her thoughts, which were becoming even more brazenly improper. She felt heat rise to her face, and she could only pray he would think her high color was due to her proximity to the fire.

One other thing she had noticed even while trying to pretend that it did not matter one way or another—it would seem that Mr. Rendel lived here quite alone.

Not only did he lack a maid or a housekeeper, but he seemed to be in other ways similarly unencumbered. No wife or children had greeted him upon his return, and there was no sign that any woman shared his abode. There was no loom or spinning wheel, no butter churn, no wifely shawls hanging on the hooks by the door . . .

"Your hair is not drying fast enough," he said, coming up behind her and taking a strand between his fingers.

At the touch of his hand, her heart gave a lurch, then speeded up of its own accord.

"If you wish, I can brush it dry for you."

For a brief moment modesty warred with desire. Despite her the thoroughly improper path her thoughts had been wandering down, she knew quite clearly where her duty lay.

It was, of course, totally out of the question to allow any man—other than a husband, which she did not at the moment have—to touch her so intimately. Especially since she had not even settled the question of whether or not a quilt constituted proper attire for an unmarried lady visiting a bachelor in his abode, which in and of itself was a totally unforgivable breech of decorum. Quite scandalous, in fact.

And despite knowing that even *thinking* about allowing

Mr. Rendel to brush her hair would scandalize the old biddies who were her aunt's friends, if she were to be honest, Bethia had to acknowledge a strange longing to feel this man's hands touching her again.

In the end—could she blame it on her fatigue?—desire easily overcame good sense.

Looking up into gray eyes that betrayed no emotion, Bethia nodded mutely, and without speaking, Mr. Rendel vanished once again through the doorway at the other end of the cottage. When he returned, her cheerful mood vanished, for he carried in his hand an elegant, ebony-backed brush. Unfortunately, there could be no doubt that it was a lady's brush.

It would appear that Mr. Rendel did have a woman in his life. Was he married after all?

Or perhaps it did not belong to a lady? Might the brush have been left here by his mistress?

Or perhaps the owner of the brush, be she lady or otherwise, no longer belonged in his life?

While Bethia was still considering the implications of the brush, Mr. Rendel began to untangle her hair, and Bethia had to bite her lip to prevent a sigh from escaping.

Knowing she was being a fool did not prevent her from feeling jealous at the thought of another woman in this man's arms, and she surreptitiously used the quilt to wipe a tear from the corner of her eye.

As irrational as it was, she felt that she belonged somehow to Mr. Rendel. Which meant he must also belong to her, did it not? Or did saving her life involve an obligation only on her part?

Mr. Rendel was as careful as her dresser would have been, first working out all the snarls, then pulling the brush in long, soothing strokes through her hair.

But his touch was like a lover's caress, and his very gentleness sent shivers up and down her spine. She could not forget that he was not her maid—that he was every inch a man.

Maybe he was a gentleman . . . but then again, maybe he was not. At this moment she felt so odd, she was not at all certain in her own mind which she wished him to be.

Were these strange feelings natural after one had narrowly escaped death? Were they merely a kind of hysteria brought on by having almost been murdered? She disremembered hearing about other people's near escapes from death—coming a rasper on the hunting field being something altogether different.

No, she was the only person she knew who'd had a near fatal accident—in her case more than one. On the way back from Hampton Court Palace, Lord Keppel had saved her from what could have been a fatal fall from her horse. But now that she considered the matter, she felt nothing more for him than the same gratitude she had felt for the unknown merchant who had prevented her from falling under the wheels of the brewer's wagon.

Which could mean that the intensity of emotion she was now feeling was not—or at least not entirely—the result of Mr. Rendel's having saved her life.

Unfortunately, the longer he brushed her hair, the more difficult it was becoming for her to keep her thoughts in order. "I think you shall have to marry me," she murmured, not aware of what her words would be until it was too late to call them back.

Chapter Three

"And I think you have had quite enough to drink," Mr. Rendel said, laying down the brush and lifting the empty cup from her hand.

Bethia knew it was not the punch talking, but a strange lassitude was making it difficult to debate the matter properly. She did not utter any objections when Mr. Rendel picked her up, quilt and all, and carried her through the doorway into the next room, which turned out to be a reassuringly masculine bedroom.

He laid her down between sheets that smelled of sunshine and lavender, then pulled more blankets around her, tucking her in as if she were a small child.

Only when he did not lie down beside her on the bed, which was wide enough for two, did she try to protest. "Don't leave me alone," she said, her tongue feeling rather thick in her mouth. "Please stay with me."

"I will be close at hand," he said, "and I will come at once if you need me."

"I need you now," she said, feeling no surprise or shame at her own boldness, but he merely chuckled and went out, leaving the door slightly ajar.

She was too tired to climb out of the bed and follow him . . . too tired to insist . . . or perhaps she had indeed imbibed too much of the spicy punch.

Still and all, marrying Mr. Rendel was a remarkably good idea, and she felt proud of her cleverness at thinking of such a thoroughly splendid solution to her problems.

She had no doubt at all that she would like being married to him—to this man who had emerged like the god Neptune from the sea to save her from a watery grave.

Not only was Mr. Rendel singularly attractive, but she knew beyond a shadow of a doubt that she could trust him with her life. And once they were married, she would no longer be in danger of assassination.

Curled up in his bed, her head on his pillow, she tried to stay awake to plan what had to be done—what arguments she might use to convince him—but it became harder and harder to fight against her fatigue.

Finally giving up the losing battle, she allowed herself to drift off to sleep, and just before consciousness faded completely, it seemed to her that she could feel his arms around her . . . but she was too tired to open her eyes and see if he was really there or if he was merely a figment of her imagination.

It had been a mistake, Digory realized, to have given her any punch. Hot tea would have doubtless been adequate to warm her, although in truth he could not have foreseen that she would help herself to several cups of the spicy beverage.

Stone sober she would never, of course, have proposed marriage with a total stranger, nor would she have invited him to join her in bed.

Scruples were a damnable burden at times, and never more so than when she had looked up at him, her eyes and her voice both pleading with him to stay with her.

But there were murderers abroad tonight, and there were few enough hours left to prepare a trap. Checking one last time to be sure his guest was still sleeping, Digory let himself out of his cottage, locking the door behind him.

It had been nearly a year since he had given up smuggling, and when he sent word that there would be a meeting tonight, Jem and the others would all be quick to say, "I told you so."

None of them had actually believed Digory was serious when he'd announced his retirement, but he minded not that tonight would bring their ridicule down upon his head, so long as they were willing to help him.

It was a measure of how much distance he had put between himself and his former subordinates that he did not even know if they were here in Cornwall. They could easily be in France, purchasing a boatload of kegs filled with brandy. Or given that it was the dark of the moon, they might be planning to move a load inland tonight.

On that point, Mrs. Pollock was able to reassure him. Jem, who was her sister's son, and the other smugglers were presently between trips, and she offered to send one of her boys to pass the word that Digory wanted to see them.

Although she invited him to join her family for a bite of supper, Digory could not completely stifle the feeling that something unforeseen might have occurred in his absence—or even merely that Miss Pepperell might have awakened and found him gone, which would have been bad enough—so he declined his neighbor's offer and walked as quickly as possible back along the lane to his own cottage.

Entering it, he found everything precisely as he had left it, and when he peeked into the bedroom, his guest did not appear to have moved a muscle during his absence.

The dress she had left hanging before the fire was dry, but when Digory examined it, he found it would need more than a good pressing to set it to rights. Luckily, his guest was approximately the same size as his aunt had been.

Opening a small trunk that served double duty as a window seat, he extracted one of his aunt's dresses. It was not at all modish, but at least Miss Pepperell would have a choice come morning.

Tiptoeing into the bedroom, he placed both garments on a chair where she would be sure to notice them when she awoke.

He was not as quiet as he might have wished, but his guest did not even stir. Seeing her lying there so peacefully, Digory was again sorely tempted to crawl into bed and spend the rest of the night holding her in his arms.

If he were a gentleman, he would have the right to marry her and share her bed. But he was no gentleman. That being the case, why should he be expected to act like a gentleman and leave her untouched?

There was no answer to that question, but in the end he

tiptoed out of the room, this time closing the door firmly behind him.

The tedium of sitting in a waterfront tavern for an entire day and what looked as if it would be an entire night made it necessary for Mr. Harcourt to remind himself repeatedly of the rewards that would soon be his if only he used sufficient patience at this crucial point in his marvelous scheme.

Fortunately, what he had most feared—that one or both of the two men he had hired might be cursed with a loose tongue—did not seem to be the case. Unfortunately, they both seemed to have hollow legs, which the bar maid was doing her best to fill.

Several times he had almost made up his mind to leave his hirelings alone—to risk having one of them say something untoward, which might later make someone suspect that the accidental drowning was no accident. But the possibility of losing the fortune he had pursued for so long— no matter how slight the risk might be—had kept him there.

After what he had endured this day, it would be a genuine pleasure to start both Jack Williams and Dick Fane off on their journey to Hades. But first they had to finish the task they had been hired to do. Once they discovered the body, then he could appear on the scene in his rightful identity— the distraught, grief-stricken cousin who had known the unfortunate child was depressed after her grandfather's death, but who had not thought she would be driven to suicide.

He would not, of course, try to persuade the magistrate that Bethia had killed herself. Rather he would try so hard to persuade everyone that she had *not* killed herself, that they would, of a certainty, be brought to believe just that.

With luck, the body would come in with tomorrow's tide, or so Williams had asserted. If not tomorrow, then the next day for sure.

It had better be tomorrow, Mr. Harcourt decided, for he did not have the stomach to sit a second day in this tavern.

Within twelve hours—thirty-six at the outside—he would be an extremely rich man. Perhaps before he removed Fane and Williams permanently from his life, he should consider if there might not be some way he could arrange to divide his uncle's money up two ways instead of three.

One unfortunate accident, and he could have half again as much as he now stood to inherit. And if there were a pair of unfortunate accidents? But then again, one must take into account that too many accidental deaths might arouse suspicion.

In any event, there was no need to decide right at this moment which of his brothers it would be easiest to dispose of. First he must do his utmost to see to it that poor little Bethia would be allowed the benefits of a Christian burial, even though everyone would believe that she had taken her own life.

Digory's former crew came shortly before midnight, and although none of them actually said, "I told you so," their smirks made it obvious that was exactly what they were all thinking. And never had retirement seemed so pointless as now, when Digory looked around the circle of men—Jem Caravick, who was well endowed with common sense plus the instincts he needed to be a successful smuggler; Harry Tankyn, who had no ambitions to be anything more than he was; and Big Davey Veryan, and his cousin Little Davey Veryan, who were the two largest men in the parish.

His crew—for a dozen years they had been with him through innumerable dangers, and the bond that had been forged between them was unbreakable.

But it was only their companionship that Digory missed; he could do without the smuggling. For him the excitement—and with it the enjoyment—had gone out of the trade long before he had actually retired.

"Just like old times," Harry said with a grin. "So when do we sail, and is it kegs we'll be smuggling past the preventatives, or is it men?"

"This time," Digory replied with an answering smile, "we do things backward. Today we are going to play the role of preventatives and hide on the beach."

It was not the wisest way he could have broached the subject, because the circle of eyes around him instantly became hostile. It would seem, after all, that the friendship between them could indeed be broken.

Abandoning any further attempts at humor, Digory quickly told them what had happened earlier that day, and how the hired ruffians intended to finish the job at high tide and collect their reward.

The sound of men's voices woke Bethia from a deep sleep, and for a moment her mind was filled with the terrible need to remain completely motionless so that her abductors would not notice she was awake, else they would force more laudanum down her throat.

But as soon as the muzziness cleared from her mind, she remembered clearly the events of the day before, when she had awakened from a drugged stupor filled with hideous dreams, only to find herself trapped in a waking nightmare that was worse than anything that had come to her in her laudanum-induced slumber.

Hearing Mr. Rendel's voice in the other room, she remembered how he had magically appeared to save her from a watery grave. And she remembered also how his hands had felt on her waist—remembered how safe she had felt in his arms.

Her suggestion of the previous day had apparently not been totally inspired by the punch, because even now, stone sober, she could not think of any better solution to her present dilemma than to marry him.

The only problem was that Mr. Rendel had not taken her proposal as seriously as she had meant it. But that was a minor matter and soon remedied. Once he understood what a wonderful opportunity she was offering him, he would not be slow to seize it. She was, after all, an heiress, and she knew from experience that gold was a more powerful lure for men than a pretty face and a dainty ankle.

With difficulty she fought her way free from the tangle of quilt and bedclothes and stood up, wrapping the quilt around her again for want of anything else. Remembering her mental debate of the previous afternoon as to whether or not a quilt constituted proper attire, she realized that Mr.

Rendel had had good reason to think her more than a trifle bosky.

The room was dark now, the only illumination coming from a single candle, and tiptoeing over to the door, she opened it enough that she could peek out and see who was there.

At the sight of the large men filling the other room, she had to fight off the urge to scurry back to bed and hide herself under the covers. But gathering her courage around her like a second quilt, she noiselessly shut the door and looked around for something to wear.

She discovered that her dress, which she had left drying in front of the fireplace in the other room, was now draped over the back of a chair. It would seem that Mr. Rendel had come in while she was sleeping.

Her face grew hot just thinking about him standing beside her, looking down at her lying in his bed. What had he thought? Had it been difficult for him to resist the temptation to slide under the covers and take her in his arms?

Or had he been a gentleman and kept his eyes carefully averted? More than likely he was too much in love with the owner of the ebony brush to feel the least bit tempted by a stranger he had dragged out of the sea.

Holding up her dress, Bethia found it was little more than a rag, which was hardly surprising after the rough treatment it had received. Made of delicate lawn trimmed with velvet ribbons, it had been designed for activities no more strenuous than sitting and sipping tea; it had certainly not been intended for use as a bathing costume.

Fortunately, there was another, less tattered dress folded neatly on the chair. Mr. Rendel had not been able to provide her with a lady's gown in the latest mode, but she could hardly fault him for that. The garment of homespun linsey-woolsey was at least clean and not the least bit revealing.

And it was also vastly warmer than her own gown had been, she discovered once she had dressed herself. Until this moment she had not realized how much comfort a lady sacrificed in order to be stylish.

Fighting off an unexpected timidity at the thought of seeing Mr. Rendel again—and feeling especially bashful about facing a large group of strange men—Bethia opened the door, but did nothing to call attention to herself.

"I only hope they try to fight," Harry said, raising balled fists. "I wouldn't half mind cracking their skulls together."

"Remember, our purpose is to capture them alive so we can find out who hired them," Digory said sharply.

"A little pain will only loosen their tongues," Harry pointed out with a shrug, and no one in the room saw any reason to contradict him.

Briefly, Digory outlined his plan, which was quite simple, and when he finished, a soft voice from the doorway said, "When is high tide? Do we need to get started soon?"

Digory turned and saw Miss Pepperell standing in the doorway, her eyes still soft and heavy with sleep. How long she had been listening, he had no idea, but apparently she had heard most of their plans. "We? You are not coming with us. You are staying here where you will be safe."

"Alone?"

Her voice betrayed her fear, and looking around, Digory saw to his great displeasure that his colleagues were not blind to her charms. They had all risen to their feet as soon as she had spoken, and now they looked ready to fall at *her* feet in rapt adoration.

But he was in charge here, and his orders were not to be disregarded as blithely as were the King's laws. "You are in no danger alone in my cottage," he said firmly, "and it would be extremely foolhardy for you to come with us, so I shall not listen to any objections."

His crew thought different. For the first time since he had brought them together, they did not immediately accede to his wishes. Despite his having made it perfectly clear that the matter was closed, they began trying to persuade him to change his mind. He should have realized that after a year under someone else's leadership, their unquestioning obedience, which he had once taken for granted, was no longer his to command.

"It just don't set right with me to leave the young lady

alone here," Harry said, looking at Jem instead of at Digory.

"Suppose they've already discovered that she didn't drown? Then what?" Big Davey asked.

"And suppose they come skulking around here while we're down at the cove and find her alone?" Little Davey added.

"The chances of that happening are most unlikely," Digory pointed out, holding back his temper only with difficulty.

"But not impossible," Harry said. "Someone may've seen the two of you yesterday climbing up the path from the beach, and people gossip, and you can't say for sure those two villains have been sitting in a pub with nothing more on their minds than their next mug of ale. They may have been nosing around on their own, sniffing out dangerous information."

Miss Pepperell chose that moment to leave her post in the doorway and join the group, and seeing the fatuous smiles on his companions' faces made Digory realize he was only wasting precious time by arguing.

In fact, given the way they were looking at her, if she even mentioned wishing to marry him, his formerly loyal men would probably fall all over each other in their rush to drag him before the vicar. "Turncoats," he muttered under his breath, but none of them paid him the slightest attention.

Not daring to meet his eyes, Miss Pepperell smiled sweetly at the others and seated herself at the table. Looking up at them, she said, "I have been thinking that if I put on my own gown and lay down by the edge of the water, those horrible men would—"

"No!" came in unison out of five masculine throats.

"You are not going to be the bait," Digory said, and this time his men sided firmly with him.

"A decoy ain't a bad idea, though," Harry said. "My wife could take the dress you was drowned in and stuff it with straw and rig it up to look as if it was you."

Then another thought relative to Miss Pepperell's clothing popped into Digory's mind, and he made an even stronger effort to divert that young lady from her purpose. "Speaking of ladies' gowns, has it occurred to any of you that if those men see a female with us, they may forget their orders to have Miss Pepperell's death appear an accident and shoot her down on the spot?"

There was dead silence, as the men, and Miss Pepperell also, recognized the validity of his objection.

Then Jem spoke up traitorously, "Do you know, she's about the size of my littlest brother, and wearing a suit of his clothes and with her hair tucked up under a cap, she could easily pass for a boy. Besides, I'm sure she'll promise to stay out of sight behind the rocks until the fighting is over."

There were murmurs of agreement from the other men, and a rapturous smile from Miss Pepperell for Jem, and Digory realized that if he did not get things under control quickly, someone would next be offering to arm her with a dirk or a brace of pistols.

Bowing to the inevitable, he finally agreed that Miss Pepperell could accompany them. With a rapturous smile that was enough to break a man's heart, she hurried to fetch her old dress and give it to Harry.

With the eagerness of a young lad in the first throes of calf love, Jem promised to drop off a suit of boy's clothing before dawn, but even with nothing left to discuss, neither he nor the other men made any move to leave. Instead, they all showed every sign of hanging around until dawn just so that they could bask in Miss Pepperell's smiles, which she was dispensing all too liberally. In the end Digory virtually threw the besotted men out of his cottage.

Alone at last with Miss Pepperell, who did not look the least bit repentant, Digory forced himself to be stern. "When did you first suspect that one of your cousins was attempting to enrich himself by foul means?"

Bethia's mind was instantly flooded with all the horrible memories, which for the moment she had been able to push out of her thoughts. Staring into Mr. Rendel's eyes, she found herself quite unable to speak.

Or was she tongue-tied merely because his gray eyes were so bewitching? As desperately as she wanted to turn

away from his penetrating gaze, which seemed to be looking into her very soul, she could not break free from the
spell he had cast over her.

Was he experiencing the same thing she was? Could he
feel this bond that connected them—the powerful force that
linked her fate with his? Or was it only in her imagination
that they were forever bound together?

He got up from the table, and turning away from her, he
added another log to the fire, then stood looking down into
the flames.

With his back toward her, she found herself able to talk
quite normally, her voice steady and casual, conveying no
trace of her inner anxieties and confusion. "Actually, all
three of my cousins tried fair means in the beginning. Although none of them had previously paid me the slightest
note, after the reading of my grandfather's will, they began
vying with each other quite openly for my attention. I was
quite bombarded with flowers and other small tokens of
their esteem, and as soon as the period of mourning was
over, they appeared on our doorstep one after another and
asked my aunt's permission to address me."

Bethia suppressed a shudder at the memory of how unpleasant and distasteful it had been, then continued, her
voice growing more and more wooden as her emotions became more and more heated. "Cousin Wilbur hastened to
assure me that since we are only first cousins once removed, there is no problem with consanguinity. Cousin
Gervase felt my only possible objection might be the difference in our ages—he is twenty-two years older than I am—
but he explained that being around me made him feel quite
youthful. And Cousin Inigo actually gave me his word of
honor as a gentleman that he would give up all his mistresses once we were married."

Instead of returning to his place at the table, Mr. Rendel
sat down in the upholstered chair by the fire. "I am surprised that you were able to resist such impassioned pro-
posals," he said with a smile.

Although at the time she had not been able to find any
humor in the situation, Bethia now found the corners of her
mouth turning up of their own accord. "My aunt was like-

wise of that opinion and felt it was clearly my duty to accept one or the other of my cousins, since their breeding was impeccable, their manners—at least when she was present—were beyond reproach, and in addition, I would thereby be keeping my grandfather's wealth in the family. Taken together, these were, in her opinion, irrefutable arguments in favor of such an auspicious alliance. She did, however, give me leave to decide for myself which of my three cousins I would marry. She was quite put out with me when I insisted upon having a Season first."

It seemed to Bethia that her ears still rang with her aunt's recriminations, which over time had grown from gentle reprimands to scathing denunciations of Bethia's character. "Due to my grandfather's ill health and then his death, I was not able to be presented at court until I was nineteen, and for all of last Season, my cousins paid me such marked attention, at times it felt more like persecution."

Turning to look into the fire, which seemed to be radiating less heat than Mr. Rendel, Bethia added, "With the wisdom of hindsight, I can see that I should never have made it clear to them at the beginning of *this* Season that I was absolutely adamant about refusing them. It would have been safer to have played them off against each other and kept all three of them dangling after me until I was of age."

"And when will that be?"

"Not until the end of September," Bethia said, her voice little more than a whisper. Surely he must see how much she needed him to marry her?

"A good four months," he replied thoughtfully, and then his glance caught and held hers, and once more she was unable to look away.

Could she survive four months without this man beside her? Could she survive a month? A week? Even a day?

Although it had not been mentioned, her proposal of that afternoon hovered between them. *I think you shall have to marry me.* Silently, she pleaded with him to take her offer seriously.

"It was not the punch talking," she said finally. She knew she was blushing again, but she met his gaze squarely, trying with her eyes to communicate what was so difficult to say a second time.

When he did not reply, she said, "You yourself pointed out that the easiest way for me to be safe was to marry."

"But I was not proposing myself as the bridegroom."

"But—"

"I cannot marry you," he said, and his voice carried such conviction, the room at once became colder and the darkness outside the cottage seemed to ooze in through the very stones.

"I s-see," she said finally, feeling quite sick at heart. "You are already married. I had not considered that."

Looking at the entrancingly beautiful young girl standing so near him, Digory fought a battle with his conscience. How easy it would be to let the falsehood stand—to let her go on thinking that he was a married man.

It would be even easier to take what Miss Pepperell was offering—to accept her proposal and thereby acquire a well-born wife and a great fortune.

He cared nothing for her grandfather's money—he had enough of his own, safely invested in government consols. But it had felt so right to see her lying in his bed, and he knew that if he made the slightest effort, he could undoubtedly turn her gratitude into love.

A few hours ago he had risked his own life to save hers, and in a few more hours he would do it again. Yet he could not in all honor claim that she owed him anything.

"I am not married," he said, knowing that only honesty was possible between them.

"Betrothed?" she asked, as persistent as a gnat.

"I have no previous attachments," he said bluntly, and his honesty was rewarded with a dazzling smile.

"Then why do you say 'cannot'?" she asked, her voice as low and seductive as that of the most practiced courtesan. How she had managed to arrive at the age of twenty without having been married—or seduced—he could not for the life of him fathom.

"Because I am not a gentleman," he said fiercely, attempting to use anger to blunt his growing desire. "I am a smuggler." Retired now, but he did not tell her that, knowing it would only serve to weaken his argument. Honesty, he was coming to realize, was a risky business. While he could not lie to her directly, it occurred to him that it would be prudent to conceal much of the truth from her.

"Some people call smugglers 'the gentlemen,'" she said with another of her smiles, this one as innocent as a child's.

"Only those who are foolishly romantic."

"I do not see that your occupation should stand between us. Once we are married, you will be able to give up smuggling and become a gentleman of leisure."

It was obvious that he was going to have to tell her the whole truth—or at least more of the truth—in order to make her understand why marriage was impossible. "I am also a bastard, and marrying you will not make that stigma go away."

Miss Pepperell blanched, as if he had struck her, and even knowing he'd had no choice, Digory felt pain that it had to end this way.

But she surprised him yet again. Closing the distance between them, she laid her hand on his cheek and, looking down into his eyes, said, "I care not whether you are well-born or base-born. Your actions tell me better than your words what kind of man you are. I believe you are an honorable gentleman, and I find you more to be admired and trusted than most men who have ancient titles and endless pedigrees."

Then she showed herself to be a merciless opponent, for she bent and brushed her lips gently against his. The scent of her filled his nostrils, and so difficult was his struggle not to respond, that he was unable to push her away when she slid her arms around his neck and settled herself on his lap.

Chapter Four

"I have been alone and frightened for so many weeks," Miss Pepperell said, pressing herself so close to Digory that her tears wet both their cheeks. "And I cannot believe the danger will be over in a few more hours."

Her fear tore at him, but if he accepted what she was offering, he would only pull her down to his level, which would, in the end, cause her additional pain. Yet despite his noble resolve, he found himself here and now holding her close, as if determined that nothing and no one would separate them.

Rocking her back and forth, he tried unsuccessfully to persuade himself that he was only comforting a hurt child. But her kiss, innocent though it had been, had heated the blood in his veins, and her body was too softly curved for him to succeed in maintaining that illusion. What made it even more difficult to stay where he was, was the clear knowledge that she would not offer even a token resistance if he carried her back to his bed, where he knew he could take her far away from all her troubles.

But the respite would be temporary. In the end he would only be adding to her problems. No matter how he might try to justify it—and he was trying desperately to do so— seducing her was the worst harm he could inflict on her.

"You will be safe soon," Digory explained with a confidence he did not actually feel. "Despite their claims to being honorable thieves, I am sure that once we have caught them, it will be easy to persuade those two blackguards to tell us who hired them. With their sworn statements we can have your villainous cousin thrown into jail, after which you will be free to marry a proper gentleman."

He started to lift her back onto her feet, but she immediately tightened her arms around his neck.

"I am sorry," she said, a world of misery in her voice, and he knew she was apologizing for being so frightened. She continued to cling to him, and he did not have the heart to refuse her the little comfort she could find in his arms.

Feeling her terror as if it were his own, a fierce anger burned in him, and he would have willingly paid out every penny he had earned smuggling in return for half an hour alone with the man who had driven her to this state—who had done his best to destroy her.

Realizing that they had only this night to be together, and accepting that the longer he held her in his arms, the harder it would be to part with her when the time came, he stayed where he was and made no further effort to put a safe distance between them.

After what seemed an eternity but was probably only half an hour or so, he realized she had fallen asleep on his lap. Carefully, so as not to wake her, he carried her back into the other room and once again laid her down on his bed and pulled the covers up around her.

Sleepily she stirred, stretching out her arms as if reaching for him. Knowing she would not object if he crawled under the covers beside her only made it harder to leave her untouched.

But he was an honorable man even if he had no right to call himself a gentleman. He might don the clothes of a gentleman and provide common clothing for his guest, but that could not alter the fact that she was a lady and he was a bastard.

What perverse vanity had made him want to have her see him finely dressed? And what twisted desire had made him want to see her dressed as a woman of his own low social standing?

Feeling quite disgusted with himself, and knowing how weak was his own resolution where this girl was concerned, he quickly left the bedroom. This time he closed the door firmly behind him, but he was quite unable to close his mind as easily to thoughts of what might have been—and what could never be.

Despite Miss Pepperell's fears, by tomorrow night the identity of her wicked cousin would doubtless be known, and in two more days, information could be laid against him in London. Which meant that in less than a sennight, just as soon as the miscreant was safely incarcerated, Miss Pepperell would no longer have any need of his protection . . . or any reason to be sleeping in his bed.

Glancing around the room, he realized that he was not well equipped for company. With only one bed in the cottage, he had but two options, the floor or the chair. Neither promised him a good night's sleep, and his only consolation was that he had passed many a night under far worse conditions. At least the cottage had a good roof, and he had ample driftwood for a fire.

In the end he decided upon the chair, but sleep was a long time in coming and was troubled by unpleasant dreams, in which he searched in vain for Miss Pepperell, whom he could hear crying to him for help.

Bethia was not sure what woke her early the next morning, but all at once she was wide awake, her ears straining to hear the slightest sound. Everything was quiet—too quiet.

Sliding noiselessly out from under the covers, she tiptoed over to the door, opened it a crack, and peered into the other room. She fully expected to see Mr. Rendel's reassuring form, but he was not there.

Immediately the desperate terrors of the day before flooded back, turning the little cottage into a place of fearful danger, of frightening shadows, of unseen perils lurking in every corner.

The clock on the mantel began to strike the hour. Automatically she counted the chimes—five times they sounded. She had not slept too late and missed the rendezvous with the other smugglers, so why then had she been left alone? Had the murderers returned and done something horrible to Mr. Rendel?

Frantically Bethia struggled against the waves of panic that washed over her, threatening to pull her down, to drown her. Desperately she fought against the desire to let loose her hold on sanity, to melt away into the darkness, to shrink down into nothingness.

Then she heard footsteps outside, and she would have screamed if she had been able to take a breath.

The door was slowly pushed open while time stretched out into an eternity of heartbeats. Then Mr. Rendel stepped into the room, his arms filled with wood for the fire, and at once everything returned to normal. The shadows retreated, and the room became a cozy place again, filled with warmth and the mouth-watering smells of food cooking, which made her realize how ravenously hungry she was—as if she had not eaten in three days, which indeed she had not.

The only remnant of her terror was her heart, which still raced wildly in her chest. But perhaps it beat so quickly not from the residue of fear, but because the man closing and bolting the door behind him was altogether too attractive?

"I am surprised you are awake already," he said, dumping his armload of wood into a bin by the fireplace and then crossing to the table and pulling out a chair for her.

Feeling as if her legs might give way at any moment, Bethia walked the few steps to where he was waiting and sat down. Unexpectedly, bitter memories intruded. She was not supposed to be here. Someone had intended that she should never see the light of another day, never eat another meal, never . . .

"I was going to let you sleep another half hour." Taking a bowl out of the cupboard, Mr. Rendel filled it from the iron kettle hanging above the fire, then set it down in front of her, the very casualness of his manner dispelling the dark thoughts from her mind.

The kedgeree he offered her was not what she was accustomed to eating first thing in the morning. She was used to hot chocolate and a shirred egg and two slices of toast lightly spread with marmalade, not rice cooked with lentils and smoked fish.

But although the food was peasant fare, the bowl Mr. Rendel handed her was fine bone china and the spoon he gave her was sterling, as were the candlesticks on the table. And the candles were wax, not tallow.

While they ate in silence, she wondered again at the incongruities and inconsistencies of this man, whose polished ~~manners were also more~~ suited to a London drawing room than to a peasant's cottage.

When she finally pushed her bowl away, feeling remarkably restored in body and in spirit by the simple repast, there came a knock at the door—a sharp rat-tat, which immediately destroyed all her hard-won equanimity.

"Stay here," Mr. Rendel ordered her, as if he thought she could actually have forced her legs to move. She waited, trembling in her chair, while he opened the door a crack and spoke to someone outside.

A few moments later, he returned to the table and tossed some articles of clothing down on it. Boy's clothing, she saw, and somehow the sight of it made her realize just exactly what she had gotten herself into.

"I think you are being remarkably foolish to insist upon coming with us," Mr. Rendel said, and it was no more than she herself was thinking.

With the hour for action at hand, Bethia could not find the same reckless courage she'd had in the middle of the night. But weighed against the fear she now felt at the thought of confronting her two abductors was the even more paralyzing fear of being left alone.

Doing her best to show more determination than she was actually feeling, she said, "Since it is obvious that I have become an intolerable burden to you, I will not trouble you any longer. If you will but loan me some money, I shall take a stagecoach back to London and pick one of my eager suitors at random and marry him."

Digory cursed under his breath. Apparently, Miss Pepperell had had a better night's sleep than he'd had. Her spirits were greatly restored even if her common sense appeared to be still woefully deficient.

With an effort Digory kept his own voice calm. "I have no wish for you to leap blindly into marriage with a stranger, especially one who may turn out to be a villain, and I have never even hinted or implied that you should do such a foolish thing."

Grudgingly, she nodded her head.

"The only thing I am objecting to this morning is taking you along on this expedition. You will have to be patient with me if I do not appear overjoyed at the prospect of putting you back into danger. Having saved your life once, I confess I am not looking forward to doing it a second time."

Miss Pepperell bit her lip and looked as if she were about to burst into tears, which only made Digory feel like a miserable cur, deserving only of a kick.

"I do not mean to be a burden," she said. "It is just that I feel safer when I am with you."

A single tear escaped to run down her cheek and past her quivering lips, and Digory would have liked to take her in his arms and comfort her. But there was even more danger in that direction, so instead he left her alone to finish her breakfast while he changed out of the ridiculous clothes of a gentleman.

Once again wearing the smock and breeches of a smuggler, he emerged from his bedroom, and the sight of his guest sitting there looking quite bereft and dejected made him feel like some sort of monster. Wholly against his better judgment, he said, "I must own, I will undoubtedly be easier in my mind if I have you where I can see you. So you might as well see if those clothes fit."

They fit, but did little to disguise Miss Pepperell's charms. She looked, in fact, like a very pretty young woman dressed in boy's clothing. But after she tucked her hair up under one of his caps, Digory had to admit that from a distance her disguise would probably be adequate.

Even so, he could not entirely shake off the feeling that he was making a mistake.

Although she would never have admitted it to her companion, Bethia needed all the courage she possessed to follow Mr. Rendel out of his cozy cottage and into the chill air of a Cornish morning. Not even the roosters were awake yet, and the only things moving on the horizon were the thin columns of smoke rising lazily from the chimneys of the cottages they hurried past.

Any pride she might have felt in her own fortitude deserted her when they arrived at the top of the path leading down to the beach. If there had been no fog obscuring the sea, she might have managed alone. But staring down into the soft white obscurity, she knew she could not reenter that world of terror. Before she could prevent it, a soft cry of despair escaped her lips.

Mistaking the cause of her fear, Mr. Rendel turned back and held out his hand. "The path looks steep from above, but it is not really dangerous. If heights bother you, you can hold onto me."

She wanted very much to run back to the cottage like a craven coward, but instead she took the hand he was offering her and discovered she had enough courage—barely enough—to follow him down the path into the formless world waiting below.

Even when the other smugglers appeared noiselessly out of the fog, she did not even shriek with terror . . . but then she did not let go of Mr. Rendel's hand, either.

"There's a boat down at the other end of the beach," a man she identified as Little Davey said in a low voice. He was, in her opinion, not the size of man anyone could call little, except that he was slightly smaller than Big Davey.

"It's mine," Mr. Rendel said. "You'd better take care of it, or it will make the murderers wary."

Harry appeared next, carrying the hastily constructed dummy over his shoulder. To Bethia's way of thinking it would never fool anyone. But once the fog lifted, an hour or so after they had finished all the arrangements and hidden themselves behind assorted boulders, the dummy looked entirely too real. Harry had weighed it down with concealed rocks, so that although the waves tugged at it, the "body" did not float away.

Even knowing it was nothing but straw and old sheeting with seaweed for hair, Bethia could not help shuddering every time she caught sight of the gruesome object. So easily might she have been the one lying there; just so would her body have looked after the tide carried it in.

Unable to look at the dummy without trembling, she shut her eyes. But she could not close her ears to the waves breaking with monotonous regularity on the beach. They sounded like the ticking of an eternal clock that never winds down, counting . . . counting . . . counting the ever decreasing minutes of her life. And with each passing hour, the sun beat down with increased intensity.

She was just beginning to think that they were waiting in vain—that the two villains had forgotten all about retrieving the body—when above the sound of the surf she heard voices. As they grew louder, she recognized them, and instinctively she moved closer to her rescuer, only with difficulty managing not to clutch Mr. Rendel's arm in panic.

His muscles taut, his body coiled like a spring for the attack, he did not look at her, but only murmured out of the corner of his mouth, "Remember, you gave me your word that you will stay here behind the rocks until it is all over."

Too frightened of the approaching men to speak, she could not force even a single word of acknowledgment out of her constricted throat.

Mr. Rendel turned to look at her, and the devil was in his eyes. For a moment she was more terrified of him and his wrath than she was of the kidnappers.

Then he smiled and touched her cheek lightly with his hand, and her fears—all of her fears—subsided, and she felt safe again.

As if from an immense distance rather than just a few yards away, she heard Jacky-boy cry out enthusiastically, "There's the body, right where I told you it'd be. Now'll you admit I know my job?"

The two men speeded up their steps until they were almost running, and as soon as they were past the waiting smugglers, Mr. Rendel gave a low whistle. With a suddenness that astounded her, the small cove erupted with violence.

Bethia could not bear to watch the pain that the men were inflicting on one another, and yet she could not tear her glance away. To her astonishment, some of the smugglers were grinning, as if they were enjoying the fray.

Her ears were filled with the sound of men shouting, and the thud of fists striking flesh and bone, and Bethia winced with each blow, as if she herself were being battered.

Then with the same abruptness with which it had begun, the fight was all over. From her hiding place behind a boulder, she saw that Big Davey was holding one of the villains with his arms twisted behind his back, and the large man named Jacky-boy was lying motionless on the sand.

Using his foot, Harry turned the man over, then said, "He's dead. 'Twould appear he fell on his own knife."

Mr. Rendel nodded his head once, and then, as if it were commonplace for him to have dead bodies at his feet, he turned his attention to the other kidnapper.

"We want a name," Mr. Rendel said, and Bethia heard a world of power and arrogance in his voice. The captured man should have been intimidated, for surrounded as he was by five strong men, he had to realize how effortlessly he could be dispatched to join his companion, who was surely feeling the unremitting fires of hell by now.

"'Tis you who need to explain yourself," the man said quite brazenly. "My companion and I were merely taking a walk and enjoying a bit of brisk sea air when you fell upon us like savages."

"We want the name of the man who hired you," Mr. Rendel repeated, and Big Davey gave a jerk on the man's arms for added emphasis.

But even with his face contorted in pain, the man persisted in his denials. "I do not know . . . what you are talking about," he managed to say with visible effort. "I am innocent of whatever it is . . . you think I have done, and I demand the right to put my case before a magistrate."

"You are lying," Bethia cried out, springing to her feet and dashing out onto the sand. "You and your partner admitted quite openly that you were paid to kill me."

The man looked at her as if she were a ghost returned from the grave, and his face became bloodless.

Confronting the man who would have murdered her without a qualm, Bethia was amazed to discover that he was much smaller than she remembered him. "You will tell me which of my cousins paid you to drown me, or these men will not hesitate to force the truth from you."

Goggle-eyed, whether from pain or from thinking himself confronted by an unearthly spirit, the man could only stare at her, his mouth agape.

Bethia was about to repeat her demands when a shot rang out and Big Davey let out a yelp of pain. The captured man instantly wrenched himself free and was off down the beach with the smugglers in hot pursuit.

Before Bethia fully comprehended what was happening, she was thrown down onto the sand and a heavy weight came down on top of her, squashing the breath out of her body.

The voice cursing steadily in her ear she recognized as belonging to Mr. Rendel, and she was about to demand that he let her up, when he caught her under her arms, dragged her to her feet, and shoved her toward the cliff, which offered them protection from the assassin or assassins above them.

Only half the curses, unfortunately, were directed toward the man on the cliff who had shot at them. The other half of the imprecations were aimed at her, and it was not hard for her to grasp the basic idea that Mr. Rendel would have infinitely preferred it if she were safely back in his cottage, or failing that, if she had followed his explicit orders, which were simple enough for an idiot to comprehend, and not taken a step away from the boulder behind which he had told her to conceal herself.

Mr. Harcourt's hand shook as he aimed the second dueling pistol. Shooting at a man, he had discovered, was much more difficult than making a perfect score at Manton's Shooting Gallery. And if he missed this time . . . but he could not miss. His very life depended upon it.

Lying flat on his stomach on the top of the cliff, he waited, his sights trained on Dick Fane, who foolishly thought he was running toward freedom, but who was actually hurrying toward his own death.

Harcourt knew he would have but this one opportunity; there would be no time to reload either of his pistols. Should he aim at Fane's head? It seemed at this moment a very small target. But if he aimed at the chest, though he might fatally wound Fane, still the man might live long enough to speak a name—to betray who had hired him.

But on the other hand, the path Fane was now struggling up was narrow, so that even if the bullet did not strike a vital organ and kill him instantly, he would surely lose his footing, and the rocks below would guarantee that he died quickly.

Taking a deep breath, then letting it partway out, the man with the gun slowly squeezed the trigger.

Fane crumpled and fell, and even before his body struck the rocks, Harcourt was up and away, running toward his horse, more acutely aware of his own mortality than he had ever been before. The back of his neck prickled, as if a gun were even now being aimed at him—as if at any moment a bullet might slam into his back, throwing him to the ground.

Jerking the reins free, he sprang into the saddle, kicked the horse into a gallop, and was a good quarter of a mile away from the cove before he finally managed to get his left foot into the stirrup.

Bethia peered around Mr. Rendel's broad shoulders and saw that two of his men were returning. The slump of their shoulders and the scowls on their faces made it obvious that the assassins had escaped.

Even so, it was singularly obtuse of them not to notice that their leader was in an unreasonable frame of mind.

"We should have left a man topside," Big Davey said gruffly, and Harry added weakly, "It appears the third murderer came on horseback."

"So you let them both get away?" Mr. Rendel's voice was so fierce, Bethia was amazed that either of his men had the nerve to reply.

"Not exactly," Big Davey said, glancing sheepishly at Harry, as if expecting some help from that quarter. "Apparently the man on the cliff was not aiming at me, which is probably why I'm still standing here with only a nicked arm."

There was blood on his shirtsleeve, which in Bethia's opinion should have elicited sympathy rather than censure.

One could hardly expect a wounded man to chase down an assassin, but apparently smugglers didn't worry about such trivial things as bloody arms.

"He was aiming at his hireling," Big Davey said, and with a terrible premonition, Bethia knew what he was going to say before he actually said it. "The poor fool was halfway up the path, doubtless thinking he was running toward someone who would save his worthless skin, when the second shot took him right through the heart." He gestured down the beach to where a second body now lay broken on the rocks. "He'll not be naming any names now, no matter how politely we ask."

Despite their careful plans, death had found them there on the beach—not her own death, but it could easily have been. If her hat had fallen off and her hair had tumbled down around her shoulders, would her cousin—for she strongly suspected he had come in person to supervise his minions—would he have sent the second bullet through her heart?

Or through Mr. Rendel's heart since he had thrown himself down on top of her?

"There's still a chance Jem and Little Davey might be able to track him down," Big Davey said, but his words did not hold the weight of conviction.

"At least I can give evidence that this was not your fault," Bethia said, and both of the smugglers looked at her with strange expressions on their faces. "I am fully prepared to swear under oath that you did not kill these men in cold blood," she explained. Then she realized that what she saw in their eyes was amusement.

Confused, she turned to Mr. Rendel for an explanation, which he was not slow to give her. "There are certain currents that carry kegs of brandy"—or dead bodies, his eyes added—"in to shore. And there are other currents that carry whatever is tossed into the water far, far out to sea."

That was all he said, but in his eyes Bethia could read a smug, masculine satisfaction that he had shown her irrevocable proof that he came from a different world than hers, and that he could thus never marry her.

"In that case, I shall be . . . happy to do my part to dispose of the bodies," she said, grimly determined to hide her squeamishness.

For a moment she thought she saw a spark of admiration in Mr. Rendel's eyes, but then he said flatly, "No," and without another word his men left them and retrieved the rowboat, which they had hidden out of sight behind some rocks.

With an efficiency that amazed her, Big Davey and Harry set about loading the dead men into the boat, and soon the beach was empty of all but a few pieces of driftwood, and the tide quickly smoothed the footprints from the sand and washed away all traces of blood. The little cove was as peaceful as if there had never been any violence to mar its serenity.

For a second time in less than twenty-four hours—so little time?—Mr. Rendel helped her back up the path to the top of the cliff. Had he been this alert the last time also? Had his muscles been this tense, ready at any moment for an ambush? Had his glance continually darted from bush to stone wall to thicket, always searching for any would-be attacker?

She dared not ask him. But then she did not need him to tell her that there was no way of knowing if her cousin—whichever one of them was trying to kill her—had fled back to London to avoid detection, or if he was perhaps lurking in the shadow beside that little stone barn across the way, or if he was waiting around the next bend in the road, his guns reloaded . . . or if he was behind them, slinking along to see where they were headed.

Chapter Five

The overwhelming relief Bethia felt when they reached the little cottage only strengthened her determination to change Mr. Rendel's mind. She would never be safe until she was married. Somehow she must make him understand that he was the only man she could trust.

"Each of my cousins is accounted a good shot on the hunting field," she began. "And wearing boy's clothing will not protect me for long."

"You must have a number of suitors," Mr. Rendel responded immediately, correctly anticipating her next argument, "any one of whom will doubtless make you a better husband than I would." Moving a step away from her, he pulled a pistol out from under his shirt and tossed it down on the table. Then he bent and took a wicked-looking knife from his boot.

He held the weapon in his hands, toying with it, then laid it down on the table, all the time watching her. With a flash of insight, she realized he was again trying to make her afraid of him so that she would give up her efforts to persuade him to marry her.

But *her* weapons, while of a different kind, were just as potent. Crossing to where he stood, she looked up at him. "Not many hours ago you told me I would be foolish to leap blindly into marriage with a stranger who might turn out to be a villain," she said.

He looked away, and for a moment she understood how a woman could die of a broken heart, but then he turned back, and she saw that he was not unaffected, no matter how cold and disaffected he tried to appear.

"Let us be married today," she whispered, knowing in

her soul that he did not have the power to resist her for long—not when he could no longer hide his feelings from her.

But he surprised her once again. His eyes became hooded, as if he had drawn shutters across his soul, and she was almost convinced that she had failed at the most important task in her life. What more could she do? There must be something else she could try. There had to be.

Walking a few steps away from her, he stared down into the fire. Finally he spoke. "It will not be that easy."

With those simple words she realized he had tacitly consented to do things her way, and her heart began to sing a happy little song.

"Of course it will be easy," she said. "We can run away to Gretna Green, or perhaps you know of someplace closer where we can be married without banns or license."

"And will your aunt give her permission?" he said, turning to look directly at her.

Bethia could not understand his objection. "I have always heard it said that English law recognizes any marriage contracted in Scotland," she said faintly, taking a step toward him, "even if the bride is underage in England."

"And do you wish to put it to the test?" he snapped back at her. "Suppose your cousins have me thrown into prison for the heinous crime of seducing an heiress and luring her away from her lawfully appointed guardian?"

"I d-do not think anyone would believe that you had taken unfair advantage of me," Bethia said, unable to keep the doubt out of her voice.

"Or believe that you were of unsound mind when you married me, a base-born smuggler? Do you not realize your cousins will seize upon any excuse to rush to the courts and demand legal redress?—to demand that the marriage be declared null and void?—to insist that you be locked up in Bedlam for your own protection?"

"We could tell the truth—"

"That two men were hired to kill you? And when asked to produce those same two men, what will you say? That you have no idea who they were? Do you wish to explain how they were killed and why their bodies were cast into the sea? All you have to do is tell nothing but the truth, and with every word you utter you will be condemning yourself as a madwoman, driven out of her wits by her fevered imagination."

"Then there is nothing we can do," Bethia cried out, fighting back her tears. "If what you say is true—and I cannot doubt your analysis of my cousins' probable actions—then all is lost."

Mr. Rendel looked at her in obvious amazement. "Don't be daft," he said. "Of course we shall marry, but not in some havey-cavey manner. For the marriage to help you, everything must be done in an absolutely correct way."

Taking the handkerchief he offered, Bethia wiped her eyes and blew her nose. "But for that we need my aunt's permission, which will be impossible to obtain."

Raising his eyebrows, Mr. Rendel regarded her with some amusement. "Do you wish to make a small wager that I shall have her permission to marry you before the week is out?"

"You do not know my aunt," Bethia replied. "Of all the high sticklers in London, she holds herself to be the highest. Half the people who are given vouchers for Almack's would not be permitted through her door."

"Do you wish to make a wager?" he repeated.

Nettled by his high-handed manner and his refusal to accept that she knew what she was talking about, she did not hesitate to nod her head.

"Then I shall set the stakes, and you have the right to accept them or not." He appeared to be thinking, but Bethia suspected he already knew what he was going to ask for.

"If you lose, then after we are married, you must, without protesting or trying to make me change my mind, grant me one request," he said.

"And if my aunt withholds her consent," Bethia countered boldly, "then you must, without any further argument, go with me to the Continent, where I am sure we can elude my cousins for the necessary months."

"Without marrying you?" he asked.

Looking him in the eye, she replied quite brazenly, "With or without benefit of clergy, the choice is yours."

"You are too innocent to know what you are proposing," he said with a superior smile. "But fortunately for you, I choose marriage—a legally sanctioned marriage accepted by one and all."

"Do you accept my terms?" she asked.

"If you will accept mine," he replied.

"I will," she said without a moment's hesitation.

"Then I do also," he said.

"Either way I shall win," she could not resist pointing out with a smile.

But his answering smile made her begin to wonder what it was he would ask of her after they were married. What could she have to give him? Her grandfather's money would be his once the marriage documents were signed.

And her very life already belonged to him, for every breath she took, every minute she lived, she owed to him.

"While we are waiting for the others to report back, we may as well start packing," Mr. Rendel said.

"I have nothing to pack in," Bethia said, "but that matters little, since I have nothing to pack except for one rag, which used to be a charming day dress, and a linsey-woolsey gown, which does not belong to me, and which the rightful owner doubtless would prefer to have returned."

"The dress is yours. It belonged to my aunt, and since she is now resting beneath the sod in the churchyard, she will make no protest if you carry it off to London. There is a trunk full of her belongings over there by the window, and you are welcome to sort through them and pick out whatever might be useful. I realize the garments are not à la mode, but that is for the better since you will attract less attention along the way if you appear to be from the merchant class, rather than a member of the *haut ton*."

Without further discussion he went into the bedroom to pack his own clothes.

Bethia crossed to the window and lifted the lid of the little chest, but she made no effort to sort through its contents. Since she was about the same size as Mr. Rendel's late aunt, and since it mattered not whether the garments were flattering, there was little point in trying any of them on.

While she was thankful once again to have a change of

clothing, she was beginning to understand how difficult it was to accept charity.

Right now she was—and indeed always would be—greatly in debt to Mr. Rendel, to whom she owed her very life. But doubtless after they were married, he would feel as if he were in debt to her, because she would be bringing with her a truly magnificent dowry.

Men—at least men who had a modicum of pride—were funny about accepting presents from women, and she suspected Mr. Rendel was a man who was more accustomed to giving help than to accepting favors.

Jem was thoroughly discouraged by the time he entered the Double Anchor. So far no one in the parish or any of the surrounding parishes remembered seeing three strangers, only two of whom Jem could describe.

But to his surprise, the landlord, who introduced himself as Tom Cardin, recognized the men when Jem described them. "The two of them spent the whole day and half the night sitting at that table over there, drinking and muttering to each other. Made no effort to be sociable."

"Just two of them? There wasn't a third?" Jem asked, his hopes dashed as quickly as they had been raised.

"Not at the same table, no," Cardin said. "But my wife is a clever one. She spotted something wrong about a sailor sitting over there in t'other corner—had hands as soft and white as any lady, the man did. And all he did was sit and stare at the other two. Not hard to figure they was all three up to no good."

"Aye," Jem agreed, "murderers is what they were." Then he realized he was talking too much about things that were best kept secret, and he left off further explaining. "What else can you tell me about the third man?"

"Didn't ever see him up close," the landlord said, "but my wife might know more."

He called her over, and after thinking a moment, she said, "He was scruffy looking—hadn't shaved in several days, I'd say. Had a knit cap pulled down low over his forehead, but I could see a bit of his red hair sticking out from under it."

The rest of her description could have fit any man in Cornwall who went to sea for a living, but the red hair was indeed a stroke of luck. Now all Jem had to do was spread the word to the others, and with luck, they would catch the murdering villain before he managed to leave Cornwall.

In the middle of the afternoon Harry and Big Davey stopped by briefly to report that their mission was accomplished. They looked at Bethia out of the corners of their eyes and carefully spoke in a most roundabout way, but even so she had to swallow the bile that rose up in her throat when she thought about the two bodies sinking down to the cold, cold bottom of the sea.

She knew from her own experience with the kidnappers that they had not been good men. Not merely depraved, they had, in fact, been downright wicked, and the violence of their deaths only matched the violence of their lives. And yet, the very suddenness and unexpectedness of their passing still had the power to shock Bethia.

Could anyone know the number of days he had remaining on this earth? Those men had thought they would live, and she had thought she would die; yet here she was and there they were. And she could not even discuss such subjects with Mr. Rendel because now that he had agreed to marry her, she did not want to do anything or say anything that might cause him to change his mind.

For even though he had agreed, she knew he still did not think himself the proper man to be her husband.

Jem showed up late in the afternoon just as Mr. Rendel was dishing up a tasty mutton stew. Accepting an invitation to join them for supper, Jem pulled up a chair and began a terse recital of where he had gone and whom he had spoken with.

"Could be he's halfway back to London," Jem said when he'd finished both the account of his activities and his bowl of stew. "And could be he's hiding somewhere in the neighborhood," he added, taking a wicked-looking knife from his belt and using it to cut himself a thick slice of rye bread. "You've got problems either way," he concluded.

"Miss Pepperell and I have decided it will be best if we

marry as quickly as possible," Mr. Rendel said quite formally.

"Thought you might," Jem said. "Couldn't believe a man with your book learning would miss the obvious."

From his cocky grin Bethia thought there was a lot he left unsaid, and she rather suspected his restraint was due to her presence.

"To be of benefit to Miss Pepperell," Mr. Rendel continued seriously, "the marriage must be completely legal beyond a shadow of a doubt, which means we cannot elope. Since we must obtain her aunt's permission for the marriage to take place, we need to go to London with all possible speed."

"You can borrow my yacht if you wish," Jem said. "Sailing to London will be easier than trying to make speed on the wretched roads between here and there, and I will be happy to crew for you."

Bethia did not utter a word of protest. She could not. Her mind was filled with such horror—such dread. She could not even bear to think about hearing again those eternal waves, feeling again the constant motion of the boat, losing her way forever in another cold fog.

"Thank you, but I think it will be best if we travel by coach," Mr. Rendel said, and Bethia found she could breathe again.

"In that case, you'd best take Big Davey with you," Jem said, "for he's a much better hand with the horses than I am."

According to the coachman, another half hour would see them across the Tamar River, and Mr. Harcourt knew that once he was in Devon, he would be able to breathe a bit easier.

Of course no one searching for him would ever suspect that the clergyman in the threadbare frockcoat who was occupying the middle seat of the London stagecoach and the redheaded seaman who had spent the entire previous day sitting in the shadows at the Double Anchor were one and the same person.

It was amazing the transformation one could achieve

with a wig and an unshaven chin. And he was reasonably sure that none of the men who had ambushed Fane and Williams at the cove had gotten close enough to see his face. His mind, therefore, should be at ease.

But several things troubled him about the unfortunate events that had occurred that morning. The most important was the identity of the men who had been hiding behind the rocks. Nothing about their appearance suggested that they were excise men or soldiers.

Knowing the amount of French brandy that entered England without the benefit of a tax stamp, the obvious answer was that they had been smugglers who had mistakenly thought his two hirelings were themselves government agents.

But Harcourt had seen no sign of any kegs—only Bethia's body lying at the water's edge.

Surely the men on the beach could not have missed seeing it also. And having discovered it, would they not, in the normal course of things, have carried it back to the village or to the nearest magistrate?

Had there been something about the body that had aroused their suspicions? Had Fane or Williams disobeyed his orders and tied the girl's hands before they drowned her? Well, if they had, they'd paid with their lives.

One thing was certain—that had been his cousin's body lying there on the sand, half in and half out of the water. He had recognized her dress. There was no doubt in his mind that she had drowned.

Which meant that the most crucial part of his plan had succeeded. And now that she was dead, he stood to inherit one third of her grandfather's fortune. There remained only the minor problem of identifying her body, which he could no longer do in person.

He pondered his options while the coach lurched along, taking him farther and farther away from the scene of the crime and from his pursuers, if indeed there were any.

By the time the coach reached the Tamar, he realized that rumors might very well do the trick. Gossip, whispered in the right ears and then carefully nurtured, would eventually force Lady Clovyle to admit that his poor cousin Bethia was missing.

After which an anonymous letter could be sent to the *Gazette*, informing the world that Miss Bethia Pepperell had drowned herself in a fit of despondency. Once that was made public, the proper authorities would be dispatched to Cornwall, where they would soon identify the missing girl.

Having thought of such a clever way to come about and salvage his perfect scheme, which had unaccountably suffered a few unfortunate setbacks, Mr. Harcourt settled down to sleep away the tedious hours it would take for him to reach London.

The coach lurched sideways into a deep rut, and for a moment Bethia thought they were stuck again. Twice today she had climbed out of the carriage and waited on the verge while the three men put their shoulders to the wheels, but this time with Big Davey cracking his whip and Little Davey calling out encouragement, the horses managed to pull the coach free.

"We will be stopping for the night soon," Mr. Rendel said once they were again moving at a less than brisk pace down the lane.

Pulling her cloak more tightly around her, Bethia leaned her head against his shoulder, too tired to offer comment. It was not merely their journey that had exhausted her. The previous night—her second in the little cottage—had not been a repeat of the first.

Every time she had dozed off, the nightmares had come—weird, distorted dreams of boats and bodies, of foul-tasting wine filling her mouth and choking her, of dark water closing over her head.

Shortly before dawn she had awakened from a particularly horrible nightmare to hear men's voices from the other room, and she had been thankful that the long night was over. Dressing herself as quickly as possible, she had lost no time in joining the others, who were already half through with their breakfast.

Big Davey had borrowed a coach and hired a team, Mr. Rendel informed her, and Little Davey had decided to go with them also. No one explained Little Davey's reason for coming along, but from the guns he had brought with him, it was obvious he was to serve as their guard.

Despite their early start, they did not, however, proceed to London with all possible speed. With the sun now beginning to set behind them, Bethia asked, "Are you sure we have not just been going around in circles? I vow, we have been down this selfsame lane at least three times already today."

"And I have been down this road a dozen times before," Mr. Rendel said, "and I can assure you that we are making better progress than I had thought we would. In fact, we are less than a mile from where we will spend the night."

Ten minutes later the coach slowed its already snail-like pace, then turned sharply to the left and stopped.

Peering out the window of the coach at the hedgerow tavern, Bethia could not keep the horror out of her voice. "Surely you cannot mean for us to spend the night here?"

Perhaps in the bright light of midday the inn might not look so villainous, but in the dusk the Spotted Boar definitely had a malevolent air about it. Damp sheets would be the least of her worries if she were forced to spend the night in such a place.

"There's less chance of your being recognized here than if we stayed at a fancy inn on one of the main post roads," Mr. Rendel said, reaching past her to open the door.

"And more chance of us being murdered in our sleep for the few shillings we might have on our persons," she retorted, shrinking back in her seat. "Given the choice, I prefer to risk my reputation and save my skin."

Ignoring her objections, Mr. Rendel climbed out of the coach, then held out his hand to assist her.

Frantically, Bethia sought for some argument, some means of persuading him that this was all a very bad mistake.

"I am well known here," he said quietly, "and no one will harm you so long as you are with me."

Still she could not bring herself to quit the coach in which they had been riding all day. As tired of being jounced around as she had become—and the coach was not at all well-sprung—at this moment its worn velvet squabs represented all the security she had.

"I am sure I could not sleep a wink in such a place. Why, they are bound to have . . . to have damp sheets!"

"And more than likely bedbugs," Mr. Rendel said quite cavalierly, as if such matters were of no particular importance. "But the choice is yours, and if you prefer, I shall have your dinner carried out here." Then to her horror, he turned away from her and began walking toward the Spotted Boar.

In an instant she was out of the coach and after him. Safety, she discovered, had nothing to do with coaches. Security meant staying as close as possible to Mr. Rendel.

"Changed your mind?" he asked when she caught hold of his arm.

"That was a thoroughly unscrupulous, unprincipled, *dastardly* way to win an argument," she said, "and I want you to know I absolutely loathe and detest being coerced into doing something I do not wish to do."

Pulling the hood of her cloak up so that it concealed her face, he said with a smile in his voice, "If I had intended to coerce you, I would have pulled you bodily out of the coach. As it was, I feel I acted with great tolerance by allowing you to choose where you would spend the night."

Bethia tipped her head back far enough that she could see his face. He was smiling, blast him! But by the light spilling out the window—the grime-covered window—of the tavern, she could see that his eyes were dead serious.

"When you are with me, you will always be free to choose," he said simply. "I only advise, I do not command."

Leading two of the unharnessed horses past her, Little Davey said, "But you'll find things go better if you do what Mr. Rendel 'suggests.' He's dragged us out of many a tight spot with our skin intact."

"And was he also perhaps the one who led you into those selfsame tight spots?" Bethia snapped back, still feeling a bit aggravated by Mr. Rendel's smug air of superiority.

"In the general course of things, I'd have to say that was the case," Big Davey said, leading the second pair of horses past them. "But we try not to hold it against him, for he does keep life from becoming too tame," he added with a deep chuckle.

"Come now," Mr. Rendel said, putting his arm around her shoulders. "With three such stalwart protectors, do you really think anyone in this place will attempt to molest you?"

Although she was loathe to admit it, Bethia rather thought that it would take at least a half dozen men to go up against Mr. Rendel, even if he were alone.

Placing his hands on her neck and using his thumbs to tilt her chin up, Mr. Rendel smiled down at her and said, "Do you really think I am such a fool that I would deliberately lead you into danger?"

Bethia looked deep into his eyes and admitted to herself that she would follow this man wherever he led her. But the last remnants of her pride did not allow her to tell him that. "I shall endeavor in the future to follow your advice," was all she said.

He held her gaze, and for a long moment she thought he was going to kiss her, but then he removed his hands, readjusted her hood, and taking her by the arm, escorted her into the Spotted Boar.

The air inside was redolent of gin, and the pipe smoke made Bethia's eyes water. The coarse voices around her gradually stilled as the clientele of this wicked place became aware of her presence.

She did not need any advice from Mr. Rendel about keeping her face covered; no power on earth could have forced her to lift her eyes from the straw-strewn plank floor to stare back at the men she knew must now be staring at her.

"Ah, Mr. Rendel, we have not had the pleasure of your company in over a year now," the landlord said. "And what can we do for you this fine evening?"

"I require stabling for my horses, two rooms for me and my men, and supper for four," Mr. Rendel said, his hand on her back pushing her toward the stairs she could see a few feet in front of them.

"And who's with you tonight?" the host inquired in a genial way, which nevertheless rang false to Bethia's ears.

"Big Davey and Little Davey," Mr. Rendel replied, his tone of voice cutting off any further questioning.

"You can have both rooms on the left," the landlord called after them when they were already halfway up the stairs.

Behind them the sound of men's voices rose again, louder even than before, only now it was interspersed with raucous laughter. Bethia had no doubt that she was the main topic of conversation.

The first room on the left already contained someone else's portmanteau, but Mr. Rendel simply pitched it out into the hallway, then shut and bolted the door behind them.

To Bethia's surprise the room appeared to be remarkably clean, and a comforting fire was crackling in the fireplace. Sinking down onto the bed, she found it soft and inviting. The bedbugs had apparently been her companion's idea of a joke.

"I shall have to spend the night in this room with you," Mr. Rendel said, taking off his jacket and hanging it on a hook by the door. At the sight of him in his shirtsleeves, Bethia again felt every muscle in her body tense up.

"It is not what I would wish," he continued, "but I fear in this case I must protect my own reputation."

Sitting down in a chair by the fire, he began to pull off one of his boots. Wide-eyed, she stared at him, too astonished to speak.

"If I sleep in your room tonight, everyone below will assume you are my doxy, and therefore no one will question your presence here." He pulled off the second boot and set it beside the first. "But if you sleep alone, there will be talk from here to the coast, with everyone speculating as to who you might be and why you are traveling with me."

In his stockinged feet he came toward her as silently as a cat. Pulling her unresisting to her feet, he untied her cloak and lifted its heavy weight off her shoulders.

When he hung it on a second hook by the door, she found herself watching with delight the way his muscles rippled beneath the thin fabric of his shirt.

So this is seduction, she thought. This is what poets write

about—this feeling of fires igniting in every vein when he looks at me—this desperate longing to have him touch me—this aching need to feel his arms around me.

But Mr. Rendel showed no sign of wanting to hold her. "I shall, of course, sleep in the chair," he said, moving past her to resume his place by the fire.

He did not meet her eyes—deliberately?—and she could not tell if he felt any of the pain she was now feeling. Seduction and abandonment—she had experienced both in the space of a few minutes. It had all the makings of a farce and would doubtless be a great hit on the London stage.

Unfortunately, she did not feel like laughing, and when the landlord fetched them their supper, she managed to choke down very little of it.

"This is the world I come from," Mr. Rendel said when she shoved her plate away. "You would do well to think a second time before you decide to marry me."

"So this has all been a test?" she asked, her nerves too much on edge for her to control her temper. "You deliberately brought me to this thieves' den in order to dissuade me from marrying you?"

"Lower your voice," he said curtly, and in direct contradiction to his earlier denial, it sounded very much like a command.

Embarrassed by her emotional outburst, she bit her lip and turned to stare mutely into the fire.

"Despite what you have obviously been imagining, the men below are nothing but honest farm laborers, relaxing after a day of toil in the fields."

Bethia blinked rapidly, trying desperately to hold back the tears that were filling her eyes.

"And it is likewise only in your imagination that I am a gentleman," he added. "No matter how you try to pretend otherwise, I do not belong in your world."

Bethia's jaw quivered despite her best efforts to control it, and she said, "My world contains someone who is trying his best to kill me. How long do you think I shall stay alive in my world if you refuse to join me there?"

Chapter Six

Digory looked at the resolutely squared shoulders and stiff back that were turned to him, and he cursed himself for being a fool. "I apologize, my dear," he said.

"For what?" Miss Pepperell asked with a watery sniffle.

Giving her his handkerchief, he said, "For every one of my numerous and assorted shortcomings."

She managed to wipe away all trace of tears before she turned back to face him. "I do not think that you belong in this world of simple fishermen who turn out to be smugglers and of thieves who turn out to be honest farm hands any more than I do."

"Why do you say that?" he asked, surprised that she had seen the truth after such a brief acquaintance.

"The other smugglers call one another by their given names," she said, "but you they call Mr. Rendel."

"Such is the fate of most gently born bastards," he said, pushing back his chair and striding over to the window. Peering out into the darkness, he explained, "We discover quite early in life that we are neither fish nor fowl. We are too well born to be part of the peasantry, yet the stigma of our birth keeps us from entering the world of our fathers."

"Who is your father?" she asked, coming up behind him and leaning against him as if needing the comfort he could not give her. "Or is it a secret?" she asked when he did not immediately reply.

"In London, perhaps, but not in Cornwall. I bear too marked a resemblance to my father, the Earl of Blackstone." He turned to face her, and she backed a few steps away.

"But I have seen him in London," she said. "Surely he is much too young to be your father."

"My father, the fifth earl, died eight years ago, so it is unlikely that you ever met him. The man you saw was doubtless my half brother, Geoffrey, who was the second son but the first legitimate child born to my father, and who therefore became the sixth earl."

"My aunt warned me about Lord Blackstone. In fact, she ordered me to have nothing to do with him. The one time I saw him, though, he did not look particularly depraved, and I made sure my aunt was only being her usual snobbish self."

"So much innocence is dangerous," Digory said, feeling much older than his years. "My brother's nickname was Lord Blackheart. Did you never hear him called that?"

Eyeing him warily, Miss Pepperell admitted that she had. "But they call David Lord Helston 'Devil Helston,' and he is not at all wicked," she added.

"Be that as it may, Lord Blackstone's heart was indeed blackened by sin," Digory said. "You must take my word for it that no matter how appalling the stories were that you may have heard, he was in truth much more wicked, more evil, than even your aunt would have believed it possible for a man to be."

"Why do you keep saying he *was*? Is he also deceased?"

How had they gotten on this subject? Digory wondered. And how could he answer the question she had asked in all innocence? What could he say?

He could hardly tell her the truth—that he had paid men to abduct his own half brother. Nor could he admit that on the way to Morocco, where the ship's captain had orders to sell the wicked earl into slavery, My Lord Blackheart had escaped his captors by jumping overboard.

"They say my brother fled to the Continent to avoid his debtors," Digory said finally. "In truth, I have no idea whether he lives or not."

It was amazing how one could, without actually lying, bend the truth so that it became unrecognizable. The gossips in London did in fact say that the earl had fled to the Continent. And without seeing the body, Digory could not absolutely swear that his half brother was dead. But there was no doubt in Digory's mind that the sixth Earl of Blackstone had drowned when he chose to take his chances with the sea.

Moving closer, Miss Pepperell laid her hands on his chest. "Does no one then call you by your given name?"

Digory looked down into brown eyes that were soft with concern. "My aunt did before she died, and my half sister, Lady Cassie, does, but she is married now and lives on an estate near Wimbledon."

"Speaking of marriage," Miss Pepperell said, a faint blush creeping up her cheeks, "since you and I are going to be married, might I not have leave to use your Christian name?"

He had to clear his throat before he could answer her. "I was baptized Digory."

"Digory," she said, and his name had never sounded so sweet to his ears. "An uncommon name for an uncommon man."

"Actually it is quite common in Cornwall, and not altogether uncommon in Devon."

"Digory," she repeated, reaching up to run her fingers lightly along his jaw. "I rather like it."

And he rather liked what she was doing to him. He had spent many an evening with accomplished courtesans, but none of his companions of the night had been as seductive as this inexperienced young lady.

He knew full well that it was up to him to control the explosive situation they were in. Miss Pepperell was too innocent to know what she was doing—to have any idea how her touch was affecting him. It was clearly his responsibility to end this dangerous game she was playing all unawares, and he resolved to do just that quite soon . . . in another minute or two . . .

"I give you leave to use my Christian name also."

"After we are married will be soon enough for that," he said, catching both her wandering hands in his and holding them still against his chest.

"I do not wish to wait," she said, and the bold look in her

eyes dared him to admit that what they were talking about had nothing whatever to do with given names.

For a moment he was tempted to forgo the role of gentleman and take what she was so freely offering, but then her gaze faltered, and he knew she was only bluffing—that she had no real idea what stakes she was playing for.

"It is time for you to go to bed, Bethia," he said, turning down the invitation in her eyes even while he gave in to her request that he use her Christian name. "We must make an early start in the morning."

It was as gentle a rebuff as he could manage, but the flash of pain in her eyes told him he had not been gentle enough. All he could do was curse the black-hearted villain who had torn her out of her safe world and thrust her into the world of assassins . . . and base-born smugglers.

As tired as she was, Bethia found she could not fall asleep. Every voice she heard rumbling below sounded like Jacky-boy, every thump and thud sounded like a fist striking bone, and despite the fire in the fireplace, the darkness seemed to ooze through the room like fog, making it difficult for her to breathe.

When she shut her eyes, it was even worse, for the events that filled her mind were more real than what she could see with her eyes open. All she could think about were men's hands forcing her head back, pouring wine down her throat—wine that choked her and gagged her. She could not forget the futility of her desperate efforts to persuade the two men not to kill her, nor the overwhelming realization that she was totally helpless. And then the feel of the water closing over her head, and her desperate need to breathe.

And always and again the memory of the villains' bodies sprawled on the beach as motionless as dummies stuffed with straw, their life's blood staining the sand red before the waves washed it clean again.

As if that were not bad enough, the bed she was lying on was scarcely more satisfactory than were her thoughts, and no matter how she tossed and turned, she could not find a comfortable position.

It was totally incomprehensible to her that despite the fact a chair must by its very nature make a most disagreeable bed, her companion was sleeping soundly by the fire.

Or was he sleeping? Perhaps he, too, was finding it difficult to forget the events of the last three days.

"Digory," she whispered softly, and before she could say more, he was on his feet. In the faint light provided by the fire, she could see the glint of steel in his hand.

It was not at all the response she had expected.

"What's wrong?" His low voice was harsh and demanding, and she felt like a total fool.

"I cannot sleep."

"You woke me up to tell me that?" he asked, and the knife disappeared from his hand.

"I did not mean to wake you," she said apologetically. "I only meant to determine if you were sleeping or not."

"Well, I am awake now, so what do you want?"

"I told you, I cannot sleep."

With a yawn that was halfway to being a moan, he dragged his chair across the room and settled himself near her bed. "So what do you want me to do?" he asked with a second mighty yawn.

"Perhaps you could fetch me a glass of warm milk?"

"I doubt the menu in the Spotted Boar runs to such tame fare," he replied with a smile in his voice. "And since we already know you have no head for brandy, I shall not venture below to inquire further."

Nor did she want him to leave her, not even for a few minutes. Reaching out, she touched his arm and felt immensely comforted. "It is the nightmares," she confessed. "Every time I close my eyes, it all comes back to me."

The darkness made it much easier for her to confess her fears, which seemed childishly silly by daylight. "When those men had me in that rowboat, I was so sure that I was going to die—that I had but a few minutes left to live. And doubtless for that very reason life seems more precious to me now than ever before."

"I know." Digory reached over and took her hand in both of his.

"How can you know?" she said, shivering despite the

warm quilts tucked around her. "How can anyone know who has not been in my position—who has not looked his own death in the face?"

There was a pause, and then he said, "I have also seen his face. Three times in my life I have known that my own death was inevitable and mere seconds away. Yet here I am, still among the living."

"Will you tell me about . . . about . . ." She found she could not utter the words. That he might have died before he met her was too horrible to contemplate.

"I have never talked of such things with anyone before," he said, "but yes, some day I will relate to you all my daring exploits."

"Why not tonight?"

"Because my adventures are not the stuff of which bedtime stories are made," he replied.

"Did you have nightmares afterward? After you were quite safe?"

"They grew less frequent with time."

"How much time?" she asked, her voice rising. "How many sleepless nights must pass before I can forget? Is there nothing that will help?"

"Whenever I am unable to sleep, I find it effective to think back to the days of my childhood and to recall as many pleasant memories as I can." Her companion's voice was quiet and calm, and his words had a soothing effect on her nerves.

Taking deep breaths, Bethia tried to focus her thoughts on another time, to remember the happy years she had spent growing up in her grandfather's house, but it was as if her past had been erased. "My childhood is not real to me now. The events of the last few days keep crowding all other memories out of my head."

Digory could not only hear the despair and incipient hysteria in Bethia's voice, but he could also feel her hand trembling with remembered fear.

"Then I will share my memories with you," he said calmly, beginning to rub his thumbs on the back of her hand. "The first thing I remember—and I have no idea how old I was—I was sitting in our apple tree, throwing green apples at another little boy, whose identity is likewise lost in the mists of time."

"Undoubtedly not an incident he recalls with any degree of fondness," she said, and he could feel the tension begin to leave her hand.

"My best memories are connected with sailing," Digory said, and he felt her hand twitch spasmodically in his. He knew full well that he was venturing into a dangerous area. Whatever her feelings had been previously, over the last few days Miss Pepperell had developed a strong aversion to the sea. But perhaps if she borrowed some of his happy memories of sailing, her own terrifying memories would fade all the more quickly?

"I can still recall the first time Jem's father took us out fishing with him. I am sure we were more hindrance than help pulling the nets in, but we felt such pride, such delight, when the catch spilled like quicksilver into the bottom of the boat."

He continued to talk quietly about people and events he had not thought of in a quarter of a century, and whether it was the sound of his voice or the feel of his hand holding hers that finally put her to sleep, he could not say.

Nor did it matter, not even when he awoke stiff and sore after a third night spent sleeping in a chair.

"You look absolutely miserable," she whispered, but she herself looked more bright-eyed and cheerful than he'd yet seen her. "At least after we are married, you will be able to sleep in bed with me."

He did not bother to correct her.

They made better progress the second day of their journey since Digory deemed it unnecessary to continue using the back roads, and when they stopped at dusk—this time at a more respectable inn—he offered no excuse for sharing her room. But Bethia did not question his right to do so, for fear he might change his mind and decide it would be better to hire two rooms.

He left her alone while she changed into her nightgown, and when he came back, she was sitting up in bed, the covers pulled around her.

"We could have easily made it to London yet tonight," he said, shutting and bolting the door behind him.

Staring at him across the few feet of room that separated them, Bethia felt her heart begin to speed up. Why had they stopped here then? Could it be that he wanted to take what she had offered earlier? After three nights spent sleeping in a chair, did he mean to share her bed tonight?

She could not say him nay, no more than she could prevent the color from rising to her face at the thought of his arms around her—of his mouth pressed against hers—of his heat burning through her.

"But we need to arrive in London at a time when it is least likely that anyone who knows you will be out and about, which means in the morning hours when the *ton* is still abed. I have given instructions to Big Davey to harness the horses before daybreak." Without meeting her eyes, Digory walked across the room and stared out the window.

Disappointment pierced Bethia's heart like a cold piece of steel, and at first she could not trust her voice enough to speak. Finally, she said, "Will you come sit by me again?"

"And tell you tales to keep the nightmares away?"

No, she wanted to say, it has nothing to do with nightmares. After two days of sitting next to you in the coach—of being alone with you in our own private world—I cannot bear for there to be any distance between us. I need . . . I want . . .

But she could not put into words the aching need she now felt, and yet her torment was so great, she could not keep from climbing out of bed and walking over to him and laying her hand on his back.

Instead of taking her in his arms, however, Digory turned away and walked the few feet to the chair already positioned by the fire. Settling down in it and stretching out his legs, he stared at the flames licking at the logs. "Once when I was about ten, Jem and I decided we were big enough to take the boat out alone."

His low voice rumbled on, but Bethia heard not a word he said. She did not want to hear his stories; she wanted to feel safe and secure, and for that she needed to be as close to him as possible.

And he wanted to be with her also. Despite his deliberate rejection of her, she knew it had cost him dearly to walk away from her. She marveled at his will power, even while wondering just how much control he actually had.

What would he do if she sat down on his lap? Would he wrap his arms around her and hold her tight? Or would he unceremoniously dump her on the floor? It would be worth the risk of a few bruises to find out.

But no matter how much she wanted to discover how he would react, she found she could not be so brazen. On the other hand, there were two chairs by the fire . . .

Before she could have second thoughts, she walked over to the empty chair and sat down mere inches away from him. Emulating his posture, she slid down in her seat and stretched out her legs so that her bare toes—her already almost frozen bare toes—could be warmed by the fire.

Fearful of another rejection, she did not look at him when she held out her hand in invitation. He did not take it at once, but at least he paused in his recital of childhood mischief. She could almost hear him mentally weighing the risks involved in touching her, but finally, to her great relief, he took her hand in his and began again to speak.

It was not as much as she wanted, but it was better than nothing—far, far better. The warmth now flowing through her veins came from his touch rather than from the fire in front of her. Staring into the flames, she relaxed, relinquishing her thoughts and giving herself over to her dreams.

By the time the coach carrying Mr. Harcourt rumbled through the poorly lit London streets, he had not only realized it was vital not to let anyone know he had been out of London for the past several days, but he had also come up with a simple way to guarantee that if questions were asked, various of his minor acquaintances—not his best friends, of course—would provide him an alibi.

To begin with, he would not hire a hackney to convey him from the coaching inn to his rooms. No, he would simply melt away into the crowd. That way no one would have any reason to link him to the vicar who had just returned from Cornwall.

The second thing he needed to do was create confusion in people's minds as to which of the Harcourt brothers had spent the last week in London and which had not.

To accomplish that, he would ask a chance-met acquaintance if he had seen his brother. If the man replied that he had seen the older of the two, then he himself would pretend that he had spent the last several days looking for the younger.

If, on the other hand, the acquaintance said he had seen the younger of them, then he himself would pretend that he had been searching London for days, trying to run to ground the older of the two.

Before the night was over, enough confusion would thus be created, and in addition the idea would be firmly fixed in assorted minds that he himself had been in London the entire time.

It was bound to work, especially if he sought out men whose minds were already befuddled by strong drink.

It was still dark when Bethia woke from a deep, dreamless sleep, and she was surprised to discover herself tucked snugly into bed. Bethia knew at once that the shadow crossing soundlessly in front of the window was Digory. Already he was so much a part of her that she thought she would have known he was near even if she were blindfolded.

A few minutes later the light from the single candle chased the darkness back into the corners of the room.

"I am awake," she whispered. "Is it time to get up?"

"Yes," he replied, coming to stand by the bed.

His face was so familiar and so dear to her. Reaching out, she ran her fingers gently over his features, skimming over his forehead, stroking down his cheek now rough with whiskers, lingering on his lips, which were softer than she had expected.

He shut his eyes momentarily, as if in pain, then he stepped back just enough to be out of reach of her hand. "I will go make sure Big Davey and Little Davey are awake. Please be dressed and ready to go by the time I get back." His voice was again harsh and colder than the air in the room, and in a moment he was gone.

He had left the candle behind so Bethia did not have to dress in the dark. And he also had given her the knowledge that he was not immune to her touch. Once they were wed . . .

Oh, please, dear God, let my aunt be agreeable to this marriage, and let the wedding be soon, ran like a litany through her head all the time she was packing her things for the last leg of their journey.

Bethia peered out the window of the coach and wondered if London seemed different only because it was early morning and the streets were filled with heavily loaded carts and peddlers hawking their wares and servants hurrying along on errands.

Did the familiar streets and squares seem so strange only because the members of *haut ton* were not to be seen strolling and riding and driving about? Or was it because she herself was not the same person she had been when she had been abducted less than a sennight ago?

Had London changed? Or had she changed?

She rather suspected the latter.

The coach stopped in front of a strange house, and Digory said, "Make sure your hood is pulled down far enough that no one can see your face." Then he adjusted her cloak himself, as if not trusting her to do a proper job of it.

"Where are we?" she asked, stepping down to the pavement.

"At Lady Letitia's house," Digory replied, grasping her elbow and hurrying her across the sidewalk and up the steps to the door.

Although Bethia was not personally acquainted with Lady Letitia, she knew the elderly lady was the most infamous matchmaker in London, and her exalted status impressed even Bethia's aunt, who counted herself fortunate to be on a nodding acquaintance with Lady Letitia.

Which did nothing to explain what they were doing on Lady Letitia's doorstep at such an uncivil time of day.

Digory's forceful knock quickly brought a servant to open the door, and despite orders to keep her face well hidden, Bethia raised the edge of her hood just enough that she could see who it was—the butler himself, apparently, to judge by his age and his clothing, and a very stiff-rumped one at that.

To her surprise he ushered them in without demanding to know their names or their business, and as soon as the door was shut behind them, he even unbent enough to smile. "Lady Letitia has not yet come down, and since you did not let us know you were coming, I am afraid your room is not ready. I shall give orders to have a fire lit there immediately, but you will have to wait in the breakfast room for a bit."

"Do not scold me, Owens," Digory said. "I would have sent word I was coming if there had been time."

Without waiting for the servant to show them the way, Digory grasped her elbow again and headed for the back of the house, going straight to a pretty, sunlit room that obviously served as the breakfast room.

"I believe you have been lying to me," Bethia said, throwing back her hood.

"How so?" he asked, untying her cloak and lifting it off her shoulders.

Too angry at his deception to look at him, she stalked over to the French doors and stared out into a tiny, well-tended garden. "You have claimed that you do not belong in my world, and yet you run tame in Lady Letitia's household." Turning to glare at him, she continued, "My aunt's fondest dream is to be taken up by Lady Letitia for a turn around the park in her carriage, and you appear to have your own room in her house. Indeed, it makes me wonder if anything you have been telling me is the truth."

Digory chuckled, which made Bethia want to hit him. Then he crossed to stand in front of her, and his smile made her want to kiss him. Really, the man was totally impossible.

"I have never lived in Lady Letitia's world—" he began, but Bethia interrupted.

"Then how do you explain our presence here?"

"Lady Letitia has, on occasion, seen fit to enter *my* world."

Bethia found his statement harder to believe than everything he had told her previously, but looking up into his eyes, she was forced to conclude that he was telling her nothing but the simple truth.

"Why is it," she asked ruefully, "that every question I manage to persuade you to answer only creates more questions in my mind?"

Before he could reply—if indeed he even intended to answer—the door was opened, and an old lady entered the room with a vitality and energy that belied her years.

"Digory, my dear boy, I am truly delighted to see you." Instead of giving him her hand, Lady Letitia threw her arms around his neck, then pulled his head down and kissed him on the cheek, quite as if he were her favorite grandson.

Then turning to Bethia, the old lady inspected her from head to toe. "And you have brought along Miss Pepperell."

Bethia was astonished that her hostess knew her name, but then it was commonly understood in London that Lady Letitia knew everything about everybody.

With what could only be termed a mischievous smile, the elderly lady said, "I can only suppose you have come to embroil me in another adventure, and I must say, I shall be glad of it. London is decidedly flat after Marseilles."

"As much as I hate to disappoint you, I sincerely hope that this adventure is all but over," Digory said, pulling out a chair for his hostess. Then seating Bethia on her right, he took his own place on Lady Letitia's left. "But I am afraid at this point we do still need your help."

"You know you may depend on me for anything," she said.

Digory was silent for a moment, then he said, "Miss Pepperell and I need to be married as quickly as possible, and the marriage must be above question. For that reason, we must secure her aunt's permission rather than simply eloping."

Lady Letitia turned to Bethia and said, "If any other man had said 'need to,' I would have assumed that the bride-to-be had been compromised—even seduced. But I know Digory too well to believe he would take advantage of a young lady. So perhaps you would be kind enough to tell me what adventures you have been having that have brought you to me under these circumstances."

Before Bethia could reply—and she was not at all sure she could relate the story to a total stranger—the butler entered, accompanied by three footmen, each carrying loaded trays that gave off tantalizing aromas, reminding Bethia that they had left the inn without breaking their fast.

The dishes were lined up on the sideboard, except for one plate, which was almost entirely covered by an exceedingly large beefsteak. It was placed in front of Digory.

Owens then filled a second plate with more normal breakfast fare and set it in front of Lady Letitia.

"And what would the young lady prefer?"

"Just toast and hot chocolate," Bethia said, still feeling quite intimidated by her surroundings. "I am not really hungry."

"Nonsense, child," Lady Letitia said. "In my experience, when one goes adventuring, one builds up a remarkable appetite."

Bethia's stomach chose that moment to growl, making it a bit difficult to continue claiming lack of hunger.

At a nod from her hostess, the butler filled a third plate with assorted viands and placed it in front of Bethia. Then he and the footmen withdrew, closing the door behind them.

The food was excellently prepared, and eating it gave Bethia an excuse not to talk, but dawdle though she might, eventually she reached the point that she could not swallow another morsel. Raising her eyes from her plate, she saw that Lady Letitia was again looking at her expectantly.

"I am sure Mr. Rendel can explain what has happened better than I can," Bethia said, casting him a look of entreaty.

But he did not come to her rescue. Instead he said, "On the contrary, all I can tell would be hearsay. No, you had best tell her yourself."

Anger, Bethia discovered, was a great loosener of tongues. Thoroughly aggravated with Digory, she turned to her hostess and began her story. "It all started with my grandfather's will."

Lady Letitia was a good listener, but the more Bethia talked, the more powerful her memories became, and she was shaking with emotion by the time she reached the part of the story where the villains had thrown her overboard.

This time Digory responded to her silent plea for help, and he continued the story from there, describing their failed attempt to capture one of the kidnappers alive.

"Well," Lady Letitia said once the story was told, "I must say I envy you."

"Envy me? But I was nearly drowned," Bethia said.

"And you are probably thinking I belong in Bedlam," the old lady said with a smile. "But although I have never come that close to dying, I have been bored nearly to death for more years than I care to remember. And having gone adventuring with Digory, I have discovered physical danger gives one a new zest for life. If you will pardon the cliché, all's well that ends well. You have survived, and with time, I am sure you will likewise come to see that even if you could go back and change things, you would not have had events happen any other way."

If she could change things? Bethia had spent so many months wishing her grandfather had written his will differently, and yet . . .

Looking across the table at Digory, she had to admit that no, she would not have had anything happen differently if it meant that she would never have met him.

Chapter Seven

Having faced down the dragon—Lady Letitia as it were—and come through unscathed, Bethia still found herself quite dismayed at the prospect of explaining things to her aunt. And as the coach rumbled through the streets, bringing her closer and closer to the actual confrontation, Bethia realized that she had not the faintest idea what to say. The more she thought back over her recent adventures, the more she realized that not a one of them was fit for her aunt's ears.

Her niece had been rescued from certain death by a smuggler? Utterly preposterous! She had slept in the same cottage with him without a chaperone? Too shocking for words! She had traveled alone in a closed carriage with him? Quite scandalous! She had twice shared a room at an inn with him? Beyond belief!

No, if Bethia even mentioned the half of what she had gone through, her aunt would be so horrified at the gross impropriety of it all that she would never consent to the marriage.

As if he could read her thoughts, Digory turned to her when the coach pulled to a stop and said, "If you prefer, I will do the explaining when we see your aunt."

"I shall be more than happy to leave everything to you," Bethia said, feeling nothing but relief that he would be taking the burden off her shoulders.

"Which leaves us with the problem of smuggling you into the house. It might be best if you waited in the carriage until I signal you that it is safe to enter."

"Do you really think the servants will be fooled? By now they must all know that I am not really sick in my room, and when I miraculously return on the same day and at the same hour when you also first appear on the scene, then it will not be difficult for them to conclude that my return is somehow connected with you."

"But on the other hand," Digory pointed out, "if they do not actually see the two of us together, it will be easier for them to pretend that you have not been in my company."

And to that she had no reply, because she recognized the truth in what he said.

Knowing that surprise alone was often sufficient to carry the day, Digory did not wait for the footman who opened the door to ask his name and business. "I wish to speak to Lady Clovyle," he said, his tone unbearably supercilious.

Then before the man could make the usual polite excuses and shut the door in his face, Digory pushed past him and entered the house without being given leave to do so.

The servant opened his mouth to protest, but Digory forestalled him by handing over his top hat. "My business is most urgent," he said when the man started to stammer something. "Please inform your mistress at once that I am here."

When the man still hesitated, Digory glared at him, and his expression was ferocious enough that the poor man visibly quailed in his shoes, and with a last few incoherent stammers, he edged his way around Digory and vanished in the direction of the back stairs.

As soon as the footman was out of sight, Digory opened the front door and signaled to Bethia, who hurried to join him, her hooded cloak once more pulled low over her face.

She caught his arm, but before she could speak, they heard sounds of someone approaching.

"Wait in here," he whispered, shoving her bodily into a small room at the front of the house. He pulled the door almost shut, leaving it open a mere crack so that Bethia would be able to hear what transpired.

The footman had not sought out his mistress, but had provided himself instead with the assistance of the butler, whose stately bearing made it obvious that Digory was about to be cast out into the cold . . . or so the two men thought.

"Might I inquire what business you have with Lady Clovyle?" the butler said pompously.

"My business is of a private nature," Digory said, his tone quite bland.

"Lady Clovyle is not receiving guests at this time. I suggest you return at a later hour, Mister . . . Mister . . . ?"

Digory did not give his name, nor did he take back his top hat, which the footman was smugly holding out to him. Instead he went to the door of the room in which Bethia was hiding. "I shall wait in here while you inform Lady Clovyle that I wish to speak with her."

Pulling the door shut behind him, he pressed his ear to the panel and could hear low voices on the other side. But no one attempted to enter the room, and after a while he heard footsteps going up the stairs, from which he surmised that his efforts to intimidate the servants had been adequate.

"You had best conceal yourself," he said, and Bethia looked around, then ducked behind the drapes.

Lady Clovyle sat propped up against her pillows, sipping a cup of hot chocolate. Already her head was aching, and she was tempted to remain in bed all day. Really, it was vastly inconsiderate of her niece to disappear the way she had. There was something so common—so *vulgar*—about being put in a position where she had to fob people off with lies about Bethia's having a slight fever.

Sooner or later someone was bound to suspect—there was always some busybody who positively *delighted* in ferreting out such scandals—and the strain of waiting in hourly expectation of exposure was becoming unbearable. How could her niece, who despite her stubborn streak had never been in any way inconsiderate, have done something so thoughtless as to vanish?

There was a light scratching at the door, and then a maid poked her mobcapped head in and said, "My lady?"

"Yes, yes, do come in," Lady Clovyle said crossly. "What is it?"

"Begging your pardon, my lady, but there is a man below."

Instantly, the nagging headache was replaced by a sick feeling in Lady Clovyle's middle. The time of reckoning was apparently at hand. "A man?"

"A *strange* man," the maid repeated, her eyes wide. "Mr. Uppleby says as how the man says as how he's got urgent business with you. Mr. Uppleby says as how if you want, he will get Charlie and Joe and John Coachman to throw the man out."

For a moment Lady Clovyle was tempted to claim that she was too ill to see anyone, but in the end she was compelled to discover the worst. "No, no, I shall come down. Send Agnes to help me dress."

By the time Lady Clovyle descended to the ground floor, her headache had returned, but the pain in her stomach vied with it in intensity.

Her niece's butler was waiting in the entry hall, and two of the footmen were hovering anxiously behind him. "He is in here," Uppleby said, indicating the door. "Although he is dressed as a gentleman, there is something about him I cannot trust, and I have been watching to make sure that having gained admittance to the house, he does not attempt to sneak away while our backs are turned, taking with him any of the silver or other valuables."

It was not a thief that Lady Clovyle feared to find in her anteroom, but the bringer of scandal, because she knew in her bones that whatever urgent business this stranger had with her, in some manner it concerned her wayward niece.

"If you want, I could go in with you and provide some degree of protection," Uppleby said.

But Lady Clovyle had no desire for the servants to know any more than was absolutely necessary about this whole sordid affair. Waving him back, she entered the room alone, then closed the door firmly behind her. Doubtless the butler and footmen would immediately press their ears against the door panels, but that could not be helped.

The visitor—and he was indeed a complete stranger to her—was standing in front of the window. With the light behind him it was difficult to see his face, but his size alone made her thankful that the three servants were right outside the door and almost made her wish she had accepted Uppleby's offer of protection.

"You wished to speak with me?" she said in the same voice she used to depress the pretensions of encroaching mushrooms. This time it failed to produce any noticeable effect.

"My name is Rendel," he said, moving away from the window. "Digory Rendel at your service."

Now that she could see her visitor better, she inspected him from head to toe. To be sure, he was indeed dressed like a gentleman, but Uppleby had been right: There was something about the man that made him look out of place in a lady's drawing room.

He was not handsome. Although his features were regular, they were a bit too strongly drawn, and as a result, he exuded a bit of something that . . . that . . . well whatever it was, it did not matter. She would soon be rid of him.

"My butler informs me that you have urgent business with me. I cannot believe that such is the case, Mr. Rendel, so I suggest you quit these premises at once before I have you forcibly removed."

As if he had not heard a word she said, he wandered over to the fireplace and pretended great interest in the painting hanging above it. It was a portrait of her niece, taken when Bethia was but six years of age.

"I am here on behalf of Miss Pepperell," the man said, turning to face her.

Despite her resolve to handle this affair with the proper decorum, Lady Clovyle's knees weakened, and she was forced to sink down upon the chair closest to hand. "What about my niece?" she asked, her voice a hoarse whisper. "What have you to do with her?"

"She was abducted from this house exactly one week ago today," he said.

"You lie," she croaked out, but he went on, each word more astounding than the last.

"She was kidnapped by two men who were hired to kill her. They are now both dead."

It was such an obvious fib that lady Clovyle sat up

straighter and said quite forcefully, "Preposterous! Such things do not happen in polite circles. You must think me quite green if you expect me to believe such a tale."

The man shrugged his shoulders. "Very well, what actually happened is that your niece eloped with me. We had intended to go to Gretna Green, but after a sennight together, she finds she has quite changed mind."

"No, no, Bethia would never do a thing like that—she could not be so lost to propriety," Lady Clovyle said, feeling faint at the very thought of the scandal that would result if her niece had succumbed to the temptations of the flesh.

That this man could appeal to the baser instincts of a woman was quite obvious. She knew now what it was about his eyes that frightened her—he looked like a man who would be much more at home in a lady's boudoir than in her drawing room.

While she was staring at him, he suddenly strode over to where she was sitting, and she could not keep from shrinking away from him. He was too forceful, too strong, too . . . too masculine.

Looming over her, he said, "You refuse to credit the truth, and you do not choose to accept a perfectly plausible Banbury tale, so there is nothing left for you to believe but your own falsehood."

Cowering back in her chair, Lady Clovyle said weakly, "My niece is upstairs in her own room, laid low with a slight fever."

"Just so," the stranger said. "If you wish to have further discourse with me, I am staying with Lady Letitia." His smile was mocking and his bow was insolent, and before Lady Clovyle could stop him, he turned and walked out of the room.

"But . . . but . . ." With unaccustomed alacrity she sprang from her chair and hurried after him. "But where is my niece?" she cried out. Her only answer was the front door closing in her face. Turning to the servants, who were attempting to disguise their eagerness to know what had transpired, she pulled herself together and attempted to salvage what she could from this whole sordid mess.

"The man was here by mistake," she said firmly. "He

was seeking another—a *different* Lady Clovyle." Her lie sounded implausible even to her own ears.

"Then if he returns, we are not to admit him?" Uppleby asked, his tone decidedly lacking the proper respect.

Dangerous strangers she might not know how to deal with, but Lady Clovyle was quite adept at handling insolent servants. Her tone frosty, she said, "If Mr. Rendel should return, you will of course inform me of that fact, and *I* shall decide if I shall see him again. Is that clear?"

"Quite clear, m'lady," Uppleby said.

"Then you are dismissed."

In but a few seconds Lady Clovyle was alone, and she had not the slightest idea how to proceed. "Oh, that wretched girl, wherever can she be? What have I done to deserve such cavalier treatment?"

She stood there in the hallway, wringing her hands, unsure what her next move should be, and knowing no one she could turn to for advice and assistance, when a voice spoke behind her.

"If you care to join me in here, Aunt Euphemia, I believe we have things to discuss."

"Bethia!" Lady Clovyle said, hastening back into the room where she had so recently spoken with the enigmatic Mr. Rendel. "Thank the dear Lord you are safe."

But as soon as she shut the door and turned to face Bethia, her eyes widened in horror. "Dearest child, whatever can you be thinking of? That gown is quite outmoded and a most unbecoming color. I can only hope that no one has seen you dressed in such a . . . a . . ." The look of scorn on her niece's face made the words of reproach die in her throat.

Feeling the tiniest bit guilty—although in truth it was not at all her fault that her niece had chosen to disappear without a word to anyone—Lady Clovyle pulled together the shreds of her composure and said, "You have a lot of explaining to do, young lady."

Her voice was not so firm as she might have wished, but that was not to be wondered at. Her niece could not possibly understand how she had suffered, being left behind to try to stave off the gossips.

Feeling much put out, she continued, "While you have been out jaunting around the countryside doing heaven knows what, I have been in a veritable agony of nerves not knowing what to tell people. And here you return with that *dreadful* man, who told me such ridiculous stories, I cannot know what to believe. Never would I have suspected you had it in you to be that inconsiderate of me. Already I can feel palpitations coming on. Have you had no thought for the worries you have been causing me?" She tottered over to a chair and sank down in it.

Looking not the least bit repentant, Bethia said, "In the last few days I have been bound and gagged and lowered out my window on the end of a rope. I have had drugged wine poured down my throat, and then been cast into the sea to drown. I have also watched while the two men who were paid to kill me were themselves killed. Rather than to have wasted your time worrying about my reputation, you would have done better to have hired a Bow Street runner to try to find me. As it is, Mr. Rendel saved my life, and if he had not been there, you would never have seen me alive again."

"I cannot believe," Lady Clovyle said, her head now splitting from the pain, "that you—"

"I care not what you believe," her niece said, looking mulishly stubborn. "Whether you wish to acknowledge it or not, one of my mother's cousins is trying to kill me!" As if that statement were not preposterous enough, she added, "And whether he meets with your approval or not, Mr. Rendel is the man I am going to marry." And with those astounding words, Bethia virtually ran out of the room.

Lady Clovyle sat where she was, too flabbergasted to move. Whatever had happened to her niece in the last week, it had wrought an unfortunate change in her personality. Not that she herself believed for a moment that Bethia had been kidnapped. Why, in all her years she had never even *heard* of a properly brought-up young lady being abducted, at least not against her will.

There was, unfortunately, no such problem with believing that Bethia had indeed eloped with the thoroughly unsuitable Mr. Rendel. Flighty young girls had been doing that for time out of mind. Fortunately, so long as she was safely home again, and provided no one had actually *seen* the two of them together, it would be possible to work around that problem.

An ill-advised marriage with a stranger was not, however, the desired solution, and so Lady Clovyle intended to inform Bethia—just as soon as the poor child recovered from her ordeal, of course. There was no point, after all, in trying to reason with someone whose nerves were clearly overset and whose wits were patently disordered.

Her headache quite diminished, Lady Clovyle rang for Uppleby and instructed him to have hot tea sent up to her niece. Then she mounted the stairs to her own room, where she instructed the maid to close the curtains. Then reclining on her chaise longue, she contemplated the immediate future.

In one respect Bethia was right—it was indeed high time she was married. And once she was in a calmer frame of mind, the two of them could sit down and decide which of her suitors—her *acceptable* suitors—it would be best to encourage.

It was indeed unfortunate that Bethia could not be brought to favor one of her cousins, but then young girls could often not see the advantages of taking a much older husband. She herself had married a man forty years older than she was, and consequently she had only had to endure seven years of marriage before she became a widow, which was without question the most desirable state a female could aspire to.

But as was so often the case, the younger generation did not wish to learn from the wisdom of their elders.

Bethia knew she should be overjoyed to be home again, safe in her own room, wearing her own clothes, and waited on by Mrs. Drake, the dresser whom Aunt Euphemia had insisted upon hiring for her.

But she had never felt so out of place in her life.

"If you have no objections, I shall have this . . . this *garment* burned." Using two fingers, Mrs. Drake held up the dress Bethia had been wearing when she had arrived home.

Bethia had always felt quite intimidated by Mrs. Drake. Only a few years older than Bethia, the dresser had lost her father at Trafalgar and her husband at the Battle of Corunna. Lacking any other close male relatives, she had been forced to go into service to support herself. More gently born than the other servants, she was treated with awe by the servants, and she was absolutely inflexible when it came to matters of style.

"I wish to keep it," Bethia said flatly, amazed at her own temerity. "See that it is cleaned and then hang it in my wardrobe."

Mrs. Drake looked at her for a long moment, and by screwing up all her courage, Bethia managed to meet her gaze squarely and without flinching. Finally, the dresser asked, "Do you intend to wear it again? For if you do, I shall be forced to seek employment elsewhere, else my reputation will be ruined."

Although her mouth did not actually turn up at the corners, there was a smile in her voice and her eyes sparkled, and all at once Bethia felt the tension drain out of her. With a smile she said, "On the other hand, your consequence is so great, according to my aunt, we might instead set a new style. We could call it neoprovincial dowdy."

This suggestion was too outrageous even for Mrs. Drake, and she could no longer keep a straight face.

"Tell Cook that I shall have supper on a tray in my room," Bethia said.

Still chuckling, the no-longer-formidable dresser departed with the offending garment, and Bethia began to wander aimlessly around the room, which was large enough to contain Digory's entire cottage—much too large, in fact, for one single, solitary, and incredibly lonely young lady.

All her anxieties about the future returned, and she found herself also biting her lip to keep from crying. She had never known it was possible to miss someone as much as she missed Digory—never known it would be this painful to be separated from him.

She wanted to crawl into bed and pull the covers up around her chin. But what good would that do when there was no one to sit by her bed and hold her hand and tell her stories?

Alone . . . alone . . . alone . . . she could not get past that thought. How would she ever survive without him? Thank goodness they would soon be married. That is, assuming she could obtain her aunt's permission.

And if she could not?

Fear knotted her stomach and made her tremble all over. What would she do if Aunt Euphemia could not be talked around?

For a moment Bethia felt the same panic she had felt when the water had closed over her head, but then she remembered the wager: If her aunt did not agree to the marriage within one week, Digory had promised he would elope with her to the Continent.

One week, and then one way or another, the two of them would be man and wife—only one week, a mere seven days . . . and seven nights. . . .

Looking at the clock on the mantel, Bethia saw that barely an hour had passed since Digory had walked out the front door and vanished into the London crowds.

A most horrifying thought struck her. Suppose he never returned? Suppose he had never intended to marry her? Perhaps he had felt obligated to see her safely home, but then nothing more. How could she ever find him in London?

Then she remembered Lady Letitia, but just as Bethia was taking a breath of relief, she realized she was clutching at straws. Lady Letitia was Digory's friend, not hers. If he asked her to, she would doubtless lie through her teeth to protect him—to hide him.

The simple truth was that she had no way of finding Digory if he chose to hide himself from her. She had no idea where—other than somewhere in Cornwall—he lived. His cottage was close to the sea, but then her grandfather had once told her there was no place in Cornwall that was more than fifteen miles from the sea.

She did not even know which town or city he lived near, because they had wandered around on back lanes until they were well into Devon.

Had they really kept off the major post roads to avoid detection by her cousin? Or had Digory wanted her to be confused, unable under any circumstances to find her way back to that little cottage?

"You are being irrational," she scolded herself.

But reason told her it was illogical to expect any man to agree on such a slight acquaintance to marry a woman he barely knew. The more she thought about it, the more convinced she became that she would never see him again.

Her aunt, of course, probably thought that Digory was a fortune hunter, out to marry an heiress. But Bethia could only wish such were the case. Then, at least, she would be assured that he would not jilt her.

A light tap came at the door, and Aunt Euphemia entered, a smile on her face. "Oh, good, you are looking quite pale and wan. How clever of you to manage it, my dear. Anyone seeing you like this will be quite willing to believe that you have spent the last week in bed."

The mention of bed was unfortunate, since it brought to Bethia's mind memories of Digory—memories that might be all she would ever have of him.

"I have been thinking about it, dearest Bethia, and I have decided that the best thing is for you to be seen in public again, but not doing anything so strenuous as shopping or being fitted for a new dress, although Madame Arnault did send word yesterday—or was it the day before yesterday?—well, it doesn't matter precisely when—although now that I think about it, it must have been Friday, because Saturday all I got was a letter from my goddaughter—"

Bethia interrupted her aunt, who could prose on for hours. "I am not going out this afternoon or this evening. In fact, I intend to stay in this room until after I have married Mr. Rendel."

Her aunt's right eye twitched, but other than that, she gave no indication that she had heard a word Bethia said. "I think the card party at the Craigmont's would be best for our purposes. Lady Craigmont has assured me that it will be quite an intimate gathering. You will not find any other young people there, which is a pity, because all those delightful young men you have cast your spell over will be much distressed that they cannot dance with you again, but I should not want you to overdo and have a relapse. And there is no point in rushing things. Tomorrow's ball at the Feathergills' will be soon enough. Although if your temperature becomes elevated by this evening's entertainment, perhaps it would be best to postpone dancing until Wednesday evening at Almack's, which is not to say that you would have to forgo the Feathergill's ball entirely, just that you might wish to sit out the dancing."

Aunt Euphemia was apparently determined to erase from her memory—and from Bethia's memory—all the events that did not conform to her rules of proper behavior.

"No," Bethia said tiredly. "No, I am not going to the card party. No, I am not going to the dance at the Feathergills' house. No, I am not going to Almack's."

Her aunt opened her mouth to say something more, but Bethia forestalled her. "No, no, no, no, no, no, no! Have I made myself perfectly clear? No, no, no! I can repeat it if you did not understand it. No, no, no, no—"

"That is quite enough," Aunt Euphemia said, looking vexed. "One would think you did not even know the word 'yes.'"

"Ask me if I intend to marry Mr. Rendel, and you will hear that word."

"If you mention that man's name again, I shall send for the doctor, for the only explanation that I can think of for such obstinate behavior is that you are suffering from a brain fever."

"And if the doctor agrees with you, then I am sure he will insist that I stay in my room," Bethia said with a smile.

Her aunt attempted to scowl back at her, but finally she too could not refrain from smiling. "Well, if you are absolutely positive that you wish to remain at home, then I shall send a note to Madame Arnault, and she can do your fittings here."

"That is a splendid idea," Bethia said. "I believe with very few alterations, my new pale gold walking dress will be eminently suitable for a wedding dress."

Before her aunt could reply—and from the expression on her face, it was obvious that she intended to protest vigorously—there was loud knocking at the door—not a scratching or a light tapping, but a pounding that made the door positively shake.

Hurrying across the room, Bethia opened the door and found herself face-to-face with Uppleby. Crowding close behind her butler was Little Davey, who smiled and winked at her.

Bethia's relief was overwhelming. All the time she had been arguing with her aunt, a niggling little voice in the back of her mind had kept repeating, "How will you ever find Digory if he chooses not to be found?"

But surely Little Davey would not be here if Digory intended to vanish out of her life. So long as this overly large, genial young smuggler was here, Bethia could put aside her fears that she would never see her very own dearly beloved smuggler again.

Her butler, however, was looking neither relieved nor happy nor reassured. Instead he seemed to be quite offended. "I regret the need to bother you, miss, but this man barged right in without waiting for me to consult you. He is making some ridiculous claim that he has been instructed to change all the locks in the house—"

"Nay, I never said that," Little Davey protested. "It is Mr. Donovan here who is the locksmith."

A tiny man wearing eyeglasses poked his head around Little Davey and politely tipped his hat.

"As a matter of fact," Little Davey said, clapping the butler on the shoulder, "I am here because I have always wanted to be a footman."

Neither Uppleby nor her aunt, who appeared to be shocked into silence, seemed to find his statement amusing, but it was all Bethia could do not to laugh out loud. "I am not sure we have any livery large enough to fit you," she said.

Hearing a moan behind her, Bethia turned to see that her aunt was now a sickly shade of green.

"Surely, my dearest Bethia, you do not seriously intend to employ this . . . this *person* as a footman in this house?"

"Of course not, Aunt Euphemia. He was only joking."

"Well, someone should tell him that his attempt at levity is sorely misplaced."

"Shall I summon the watch to have him removed?" Uppleby said, his face all pinched up with distaste for the intruder.

"That will not be necessary," Bethia said. "You see, I have hired this gentleman to be my personal bodyguard."

Now it was the butler who turned green.

Chapter Eight

Matthew, Viscount Edington, had already removed his jacket, and his valet was in the process of untying his neckcloth, when there was a light tapping at the door, followed after only a perfunctory pause by the butler, who entered the room rather nervously.

"Yes, what is it?" Matthew said crossly. The hour was far too advanced for him to wish to deal with any petty household affair. Moreover, on the way home from the opera, his wife had volunteered to rub his bad leg. Not only was her touch capable of soothing the pain of his old wounds, but more important, whenever she massaged his leg, it invariably led to other, even more enjoyable activities in bed.

"Beg pardon, m'lord, but there is a man below who wishes to speak with you."

"At this hour? Why are you even bothering me with this? Tell him to come back in the morning—and not before eleven o'clock, either, if you please."

"I suggested as much, m'lord, but—"

"But what?"

"He said he prefers to discuss his business—though he declined to state what that business might be—during the dark hours of the night, which sounds rather havey-cavey if you ask me." The butler cleared his throat and glanced sideways, apparently realizing too late that Matthew had *not* asked for his opinion.

His tone once more properly deferential, the servant continued, "He instructed me to tell you his name is Rendel— Digory Rendel—and he insisted that you would see him no matter what the hour."

"Good Lord, of course I'll see him." Matthew started toward the door, inadvertently dragging along the valet, who seemed in some way to be attached to his neckcloth. Impatiently shaking himself free, Matthew strode down the corridor. "Where have you put Mr. Rendel?"

"He is w-waiting outside the t-tradesmen's entrance," the butler said, and he got a black scowl for having failed to anticipate his master's wishes better.

"Bring Mr. Rendel to my study at once, and then fetch us some brandy and glasses. And send up one of the footmen to build up the fire, and have Mrs. Wake fix a cold collation in case Mr. Rendel is hungry."

Although six years had passed since Digory had seen the viscount, Lord Edington looked a good ten years younger than the last time they had been together. To be sure, on that occasion it had still been a toss-up as to whether or not the viscount would survive his wounds.

"Ah, my good friend Digory Rendel, smuggler of first-rate brandy and rescuer of second-rate spies." With a smile, Lord Edington offered him his hand.

Digory shook the viscount's hand, but did not return the other man's smile. What he was doing now, he was forced to do for Miss Pepperell's sake, but that did not make his task any easier.

"I have come to ask . . ." Taking a deep breath, he forced the words out. "To ask a favor. But be assured that if it is inconvenient or against your principles for you to comply, you need only say the word, and I shall think none the less of you."

The other man smiled engagingly. "Beholden as I am to you for my life, which for some obscure reason I value more highly than any of my worldly possessions, I can only say that anything I own is yours, you have but to name it— money, land, even my horses—ask for what you wish and it is yours, and I will still consider myself in your debt."

"Nothing like that," Digory said quickly. "All I ask is that—if it does not go against your conscience, of course— that you do not reveal to anyone that you know who I am and what I have done for a living."

"Now you begin to make me suspicious," Lord Edington said, seating himself in a leather-upholstered chair and indicating with a wave of his hand that Digory should be seated in its twin. The glint of mischief in his eye made Digory regret more than ever that he had come on this errand.

"In the normal course of events," his lordship said, "I do not go out of my way to mention any of the activities I engaged in during our recent altercation with Napoleon, nor have I ever yet had reason to mention your name or the names of any of the others who shared my clandestine life. Which means there must be some pressing reason for you to appear on my doorstep in the middle of the night, only to ask me to refrain from doing something you should have had no reason to expect me to do in the first place."

He eyed Digory thoughtfully. "It is a good thing that nothing you could do nor anything I could ever hear about you would be sufficient cause for me to think you capable of treason. So that means . . ." All at once his expression brightened. "That there is a woman involved in this somehow."

Digory forced a smile onto his face, although he was not the least bit amused by this turn of events. "Your powers of deduction astound me." And dismay me, he might truthfully have added.

"They should not," Lord Edington said with a laugh that held much bitterness. "After you deposited my half-dead carcass on their doorstep, so to speak, the War Office informed me that while it greatly appreciated my earlier efforts, they had no further use for a spy who now had only one sound leg. So I spent the remainder of the war sitting in a windowless office here in London, analyzing reports other men had gathered. And what my superiors required of me was that I deduce everything from virtually nothing."

"You sound a dangerous man to know. I had hoped I would not need to tell you everything that is going on, for as you well know, the more people who hear a secret, the more likely it becomes that the secret will be compromised. But since it appears likely that you will guess the half of it, I might as well tell you the whole."

Digory quickly and efficiently related the essential de-

tails of Miss Pepperell's predicament. "So she has persuaded herself—and I have reluctantly agreed—that the
only viable solution to her problems is to marry, thus making it impossible, under the terms of her grandfather's will,
for any of her three cousins to inherit.

"And she has decided you are the man she wishes to
marry? I admire her taste, and I will be happy to welcome
you to the ranks of the leg-shackled. The married state is
really not so bad as it is reputed to be. In fact, you will find
that the side benefits that accrue once you step into par-
son's mousetrap are more to be desired than any financial
gain."

"Miss Pepperell is determined to marry me, but—"

"But you have objections? Is she an antidote?"

She is the most beautiful woman in the world, Digory
wanted to say, but he contented himself with saying, "Not
at all. But I question her motive for wishing to marry me. I
fear that the real reason she has chosen me over her other
suitors is merely gratitude that I saved her life. Added to
that is fear that one or the other of her suitors may be in
league with her villainous cousin. And to my way of thinking, gratitude and fear are not a sound basis on which to
build a happy marriage."

"But you are going through with it?"

"I have agreed to the marriage, but I have no intention of
sharing her bed. I fully intend to have the marriage annulled once she is safely past her twenty-first birthday."

"I had never thought you a dunderhead, yet hearing you
utter such rubbish makes me begin to doubt your intelligence. What is the help you wish from me? Do you perhaps
need me to speak up for you at the hearing on your sanity?"

"This is no laughing matter," Digory said sharply. "Miss
Pepperell must be married as quickly as possible, and there
must be nothing havey-cavey about the marriage, or else
her cousins will be quick to appeal to the courts to have it
set aside. And since she is a minor, that means we must
have her aunt's permission. And to gain her aunt's approval
and written consent, I must pass myself off as a gentleman,
not only until we are safely married, but also until Miss
Pepperell is of age, lest her cousins become suspicious."

"Ah, the last piece of the puzzle falls into place," Lord Edington said. "And the aunt—Lady Clovyle did you say?—would never, of course, give permission for her niece to marry a smuggler."

"Ex-smuggler," Digory said absently. "But more to the point, she would not wish her niece to marry the unacknowledged by-blow of a singularly unadmirable peer of the realm."

His friend raised an eyebrow, and Digory reluctantly said, "My father was the Earl of Blackstone."

Lord Edington gave a low whistle. "Which would make Lord Blackheart, as he is called, your brother."

"Half brother."

"I have always considered him living proof that a title and a country estate and the proper schooling cannot make a gentleman out of a scoundrel. In fact"—he paused, scrutinizing Digory carefully, then continued—"I would say that with the help of a good valet, we can turn you into a much more credible gentleman than he could ever hope to be."

Lord Edington was quite serious, but he failed to grasp the most essential fact. "I cannot *become* a gentleman," Digory pointed out. "I can merely pass myself off as a gentleman. Which is why I have come to ask your help," he added, lest his companion had forgotten the original purpose of the visit.

"And all you wish me to do is pretend I have never met you?" Lord Edington shook his head. "It will never do. What you need is someone to vouch for your credentials, as it were. People are suspicious of anyone they know nothing about. To begin with, I shall propose your name at White's, after which we must see about getting you into Almack's, for if you make no attempt to be accepted everywhere—and I mean without exception—then people will begin to whisper. 'Why do you suppose he does not go riding in the park at five?' they will ask. 'If he is who he claims to be, why is he not a member of such-and-such club?' 'What is his shortcoming, that he was not invited to Lord What's-his-name's ball?'"

"With every word you speak, you make the task seem

more impossible," Digory said. "Perhaps Miss Pepperell is right. Maybe we should elope to the Continent."

"Nonsense," Lord Edington said. "You must trust me on this. While I bow to your superior knowledge of the winds and the tides, and I readily admit that your mastery of the French tongue far exceeds mine, in matters of society I am the expert. And in my opinion, you will take the *ton* by storm if you are once properly introduced. I can see it all now," he mused. "If we play our cards properly, the hostesses will be falling all over themselves to secure your attendance at a dinner party or ball, and you could easily become the latest fashion."

"Do not forget that notoriety could be as dangerous for me as for any spy," Digory pointed out.

"Except, of course, that if this charade comes unraveled, you will not pay with your life," Lord Edington said. "Now then, we must consider who else we can enlist in this project, because the more people who claim you as friend, the less speculation there will be about your origins. And we must also do something about your wardrobe."

"And I suppose I must again bow to your superior knowledge of fashion," Digory said, unable to keep a trace of sarcasm from his voice.

"Actually I don't pay a bit of attention to what I put on," Lord Edington said. "I am not a dandy, after all, so I find it easier to leave everything up to my valet. *He* knows precisely which way the winds of fashion are blowing. But I am not willing to give him up, not even to you, so that means—"

"No," Digory said flatly. "I am only too aware of the way servants gossip about their masters, and I want no strangers in my house. Almost all of Miss Pepperell's servants have been with the family since she was small, and I am reasonably sure they can be trusted. Moreover Big Davey has agreed to act as my coachman, and Little Davey will be my groom, although in actuality they will be protecting Miss Pepperell."

"But you must have a valet who is *au courant*," Lord Edington protested.

"I have managed to dress myself for many years now,

and as I am not yet in my dotage, I believe I can continue a bit longer."

"You cannot refuse to have a valet," Lord Edington said. "Every *gentleman,* no matter how flat his pocketbook, *has a valet.* Period. No exceptions."

Digory opened his mouth, but Lord Edington forestalled him. "Did you or did you not come to me for advice as to how to be a gentleman?"

As much as Digory wanted to quibble—for in the beginning he had only intended to ask Lord Edington not to betray him—he knew it was pointless. As much as Digory hated to admit it, he did need a valet. Not having one would only cause tongues to wag in the servants' hall.

Apparently taking Digory's silence for tacit consent, Lord Edington said, "And I know precisely who we shall get; we shall steal Lord Vernon's valet."

"Wonderful," Digory muttered, "and now I am to have as my personal servant a man whose loyalty can be bought."

Lord Edington began to curse with astounding fluency. Finally, he took a deep breath and said, "There are times when I don't know whether I should laugh or draw your cork, and right now is one of them. Did you ever meet Joe Youngblood?"

Digory thought for a minute. "Wickham's batman?"

"More than just a batman—could pass for brothers if they were dressed alike. Wickham made full use of that. Used to dress Youngblood up as a gentleman and use him as a decoy. Not even the War Office knew anything about it. Anyway, he's a good man—knows how to keep his mouth shut—and he's a superior valet now. Since Wickham was killed at Quatra Bras, Youngblood has been working for Lord Vernon, but he'll come to us once I explain why we need him. I will *not* have to buy his loyalty. Since he was privy to all of Wickham's secrets, he doubtless knows what you did during the war, and that being the case, you will be hard put to get him to accept a salary. Buy his loyalty—bah!"

Digory began to wonder how many other servants in London might be former government men—men who would recognize him—but he kept his worries to himself. Now was not the proper time to trouble Lord Edington with additional worries—not when the viscount was rubbing his bad leg.

Despite her red hair, Adeline Lady Edington was by nature a patient, easy-going woman. Nonetheless, when she had sufficient cause, her temper could be awesome. In this case a full half hour of waiting in bed for her husband was ample time for her to lose all interest in massaging Matthew's leg and to begin instead to consider which vase she should break over his head.

What could he possibly be doing at this hour of the night that was more important than being with her? Leaning back against her pillows and watching even more minutes tick away on the mantel clock, she pondered that question.

Rather belatedly the obvious explanation occurred to her: While she had been sitting up waiting for him, he had undoubtedly fallen asleep in his own room.

Muttering several very unladylike oaths under her breath, she threw back the covers, climbed out of bed, found her robe and pulled it on, then jerked open the connecting door.

Her husband, however, was not in his bed. To her astonishment, the only occupant of the room was her husband's valet, who was dozing on a straight-backed chair.

"Abbott, what have you done with my husband?"

Startled, the valet leaped to his feet and stared goggle-eyed at her.

"Where is my husband?" she repeated, her voice rising with her temper.

"Well, I was merely undoing his cravat, just as I do every night"—he held up a man's neckcloth—"and then Mr. Briston came in and said that a man had come round to speak with his lordship."

"At this hour of the night?" Adeline's mood did not improve. So her husband had left her waiting while he attended to some kind of business? The nerve of him! Well, when Matthew deigned to notice her again, he would find himself on the wrong side of a locked door.

Wilting under her gaze, the valet stammered out further

explanations, even while he edged his way toward the door leading out to the corridor. "The visitor—I believe Mr. Briston said his name was Digory Rendel—insisted that his business could not be conducted during daylight hours, but what the man's business is and why it can only be conducted in the wee hours of the morning, I am sure I cannot tell you." With that he opened the door and eased himself out into the corridor.

Abandoned a second time, Adeline paced the room, planning several different kinds of mayhem to enact on her husband's person, but then she stopped stock-still in the middle of the room. Something was bothering her. . . .

Rendel . . . Digory Rendel . . . the name sounded familiar. Yes, now that she thought about it, she had definitely heard that name before. But where?

It took her only a moment of concentration to remember where she had heard it. Rendel—that was the name of the man who had rescued her husband in France and brought him back to her more dead than alive. And she had never even had a chance to thank him.

But why had he come back without warning after all these years? Surely he did not want to—

Oh, dear God, no!

She would not—could not!—let Mr. Rendel once again embroil her husband in some kind of clandestine operation. Whatever he wanted her husband for—or whatever the War Office wanted him for—Mr. Rendel would have to find someone else. Never would she allow her husband to risk his life like that again, never!

More angry than she had ever been before, she hurried from the room. One way or another she would stop Mr. Rendel from dragging her husband back into a world where lies and deceptions and intrigue—and near fatal wounds!—were the order of the day.

Matthew had just finished outlining the strategy he thought would best serve their purpose when the door was thrust open so forcefully that it crashed against the wall.

Adeline entered the room, her glorious hair streaming loose about her shoulders and a look of fury on her face, and Matthew realized he had committed a major error in judgment by not speaking with her before he came downstairs. "I can explain, my dear," he said, but she ignored him completely.

"Get out of my house!" His normally soft-spoken spouse screeched at his visitor like a fishwife and then attacked him with her fists. "How dare you come here—how dare you! You are not welcome in this house! Get out, get out, and never come back!"

Mr. Rendel made no effort to defend himself for the few minutes it took Matthew to catch his wife from behind and pull her away from his visitor. Then he said, "I apologize for coming here. Upon thinking it over, I believe that it would be better if I made plans for an immediate trip to the Continent." He had to raise his voice slightly to be heard above Adeline's shrieks.

His arms tightly wrapped around his wife, who was now attempting to strike him, Matthew felt greater shame than he had ever thought it possible to feel. That his wife could treat a guest in their house so shabbily was beyond belief. And not just a guest, but the very man without whose courage and ingenuity Matthew would have died in France years ago. He had never thought she was particularly high in the instep, and to the best of his knowledge, she had never been rude to anyone, so her behavior was totally inexplicable.

"You promised, you promised," she wailed.

Promised? What had he promised? "Don't leave!" he said. "Please," he added when he realized he had barked out an order quite as if Rendel were one of his servants. "I am sure this is all a misunderstanding."

Digory was not so sure. Not only did Lady Edington seem to know who he was—apparently Lord Edington did not keep secrets from his wife—but her outrage at finding someone so far outside her own class being entertained in her house was but a foretaste of how others of the *ton* would react if he tried to insinuate himself into their society.

He would have preferred to have simply left the house quickly and quietly, but Lord Edington had a look of such desperate entreaty on his face that Digory decided to stay a bit longer. Although since he was the cause of the present contretemps, it was hard to see what he could do to help.

On the other hand, his lordship seemed to be fighting a losing battle, so it would hardly be fair to desert him.

"What did I promise?" Lord Edington finally managed to ask.

"You promised never to go off spying again!" his wife replied, continuing to beat on him with her fists.

At her words Lord Edington began to laugh, and even Digory was forced to smile.

The laughter worked where attempts at physical restraint had not. Lady Edington ceased struggling and stood quietly in her husband's arms, her eyes still flashing with temper, but otherwise remarkably calm.

"You have it backward, my love," Lord Edington said. "Mr. Rendel has not come here to entice me into performing foolhardy acts of misplaced bravery."

"He has not?" she asked in a very tiny voice.

"He is here only because he wishes an entree into society."

"Oh."

Digory watched the color rise in Lady Edington's face.

"Oh, dear." She grabbed onto her husband's shirt front and tried to hide her face from view. Then she mumbled something Digory could not hear.

"My wife wishes to apologize for her outburst," Lord Edington said with a chuckle. He bent his head and listened for a minute, then added, "She says to tell you that it is mostly your fault anyway, because if only you had come at a more normal time of day, she would not have jumped to such unwarranted conclusions about you."

"I accept full blame," Digory said.

Lady Edington turned toward him and said in a much calmer voice, "You are too much the gentleman, and you must be thinking I am not at all a lady. Please believe me when I say that my husband and I will do whatever we can to help you in any way. Although it must seem that I am a veritable ingrate, I am fully conscious of what I owe to you."

Better the whole truth now, rather than later, when his deception could only bring disgust. "But you see, I am not, in fact, a gentleman," Digory said quietly.

Lady Edington looked puzzled.

"He is a smuggler, my dear," her husband explained. "Or I should say, he *was* a smuggler. During the war with France, he carried not only kegs of brandy, but also spies and couriers back and forth across the Channel."

Lady Edington's eyes lit up again, this time with interest rather than anger. "How delightful. I have always wished to meet a smuggler. You must have many stories to tell about the stratagems you employed to outwit the excise men. I would dearly love to hear them all."

Digory bowed. "Perhaps another time. Right now I am sure you would much rather I took my leave so that—"

"Nonsense," Lady Edington interrupted him. "I have no intention of going meekly off to bed until I have heard the full story of why you wish to become a gentleman."

"But my dear," her husband said, "the story is quite long, and the hour is rather advanced, and—"

"I know exactly how long the story is," she said, seating herself on the chair recently vacated by her husband. "In case it has slipped your mind, I was waiting for you the entire time Mr. Rendel was telling *you* the story. It is hardly fair that I should now be deprived of hearing it just because you were so inconsiderate, so thoughtless, so—"

"I quite understand," Lord Edington said, sending a mute appeal to Digory. "Perhaps now would be the best time to discuss things after all?"

This visit was not going at all the way Digory had planned, and the knowledge that he was no longer in complete control of events was making him more than a trifle nervous.

But pressed as he was by his host and hostess to stay, there was little he could do except sit down beside Lady Edington. She smiled at him while pointedly ignoring her husband, who pulled up another chair.

"Although I have had no formal training as a spy, nor any practical experience with espionage, you will soon learn that I have a natural talent for intrigue," she said.

"Not even Matthew knows the half of what I have been up to since we were married."

Lord Edington did not rise to the bait, which only confirmed for Digory his opinion that the viscount was a man of superior intelligence.

By the time the dairymaids were calling out their wares and the housemaids were beginning to scurry about their business of cleaning out grates and laying fresh fires, Bethia was totally exhausted.

The noises of the city had never bothered her before, but this past night, the slightest sound had jerked her awake, her heart pounding in her chest, her ears straining to hear footsteps, her eyes searching the darkness for the shadowy form of another kidnapper.

If she had slept an hour all told, it would be a wonder. Each time she had started to doze off, a board had creaked or the wind had rattled a pane of glass, or someone had driven by in a carriage or cart.

It was not the peacefulness of the countryside that she missed. What she missed—and needed—was Digory's reassuring presence beside her while she slept. Without him, the night was unbearably long and every familiar object in her room became strange and menacing.

Even knowing Little Davey was close at hand was not sufficient.

In truth, if the wedding ceremony was long delayed, her wicked cousin—whichever one he was—would not have to lift a finger to dispose of her. She would doubtless expire from exhaustion and lack of sleep.

Chapter Nine

A fter spending only one morning in her room, Bethia decided she was being excessively cautious. Remaining inside her house was merely common sense; restricting herself to her own bedroom was bordering on the irrational. In truth, she was beginning to suspect that if she were to stare for an entire week at the same four walls, no matter how pretty the green silk they were covered with, she would go stark raving mad.

She therefore decided to lunch with her aunt in the breakfast room, rather than having her meal brought up to her room on a tray.

It was too much to expect that she might actually enjoy dining with her aunt.

"Really, Bethia, I cannot understand how you came to hire such a person as footman," Aunt Euphemia whispered, glancing over her shoulder to where Little Davey stood waiting patiently by the sideboard.

"He is not a footman; he is my bodyguard," Bethia replied calmly, taking another bite of steak and kidney pie.

"Please do not ever again use that word in my presence," her aunt said crossly. "It is enough to make me lose my appetite completely. I declare, I do not know if I am coming or going." She shuddered. "I do wish we could simply forget all these . . . these . . ."

Bethia wondered if her aunt was at long last ready to admit that wicked things had been happening—that in fact one of her Harcourt cousins was conspiring to have her murdered.

". . . these flights of fancy you have been having. Really, my dear, the more I consider it, the more I think it would be wise to send for Doctor Abernathy. He is bound to have some powder that will make you feel more the thing."

Bethia rolled her eyes, but Lady Clovyle continued to prattle on in much the same vein while she ate, and despite her claim, Bethia did not notice any diminishing in her aunt's usually healthy appetite.

Since reasoning with her had failed, Bethia gave up all attempt to persuade her aunt to accept the truth. Instead she thought about Digory, wondering where he was and what he was doing. Was he even now lunching with Lady Letitia?

As if her thoughts had conjured up the spirit of that infamous matchmaker, Uppleby entered the room, bearing a note on a silver salver. Bowing, he presented it to Bethia's aunt, who quickly broke the seal and unfolded it.

"Oh, my. Oh, my! Oh, *my*!" she said. "Oh, I cannot believe it. Oh, you will never imagine what has happened! I never thought this day would come, and yet here it is!"

Smiling radiantly, Aunt Euphemia held out the invitation, but before Bethia could take it, her aunt clutched it to her bosom.

"I am sure I cannot hazard a guess," Bethia said.

"Lady Letitia"—there was reverence in Aunt Euphemia's voice when she uttered that name—"Lady Letitia has invited me to tea. Think on it, dearest niece, she has *invited* me. Me! It is beyond my wildest dreams that she has singled me out for such attention."

A rapturous look in her eyes, she stood up and drifted to the door, still clutching the invitation.

It was easy to tell that she had not yet put two and two together and come up with the conclusion that Digory was behind this invitation, Bethia realized. And when Aunt Euphemia discovered that pertinent fact, she would probably come down to earth with a thud.

Fortunately, that was Lady Letitia's problem.

With great consternation Lady Clovyle watched Lady Letitia bid a fond farewell to That Wretched Man, even going so far as to turn her cheek up for him to kiss. There had to be some explanation, but it defied Lady Clovyle to find it.

"Just who is Mr. Rendel?" she asked after he had left the room. "I must confess that I am not acquainted with his family."

She was amazed at her own temerity, because one did not, as a general rule, question, contradict, or gainsay Lady Letitia, unless, of course, one had no desire to come within a hundred miles of London for the next twenty odd years or so.

Fortunately, Lady Letitia did not take offense, but instead immediately launched herself into a recital of Mr. Rendel's ancestry.

Lady Clovyle did her best to follow the convoluted lineage, although not a single name was familiar to her. Then Lady Letitia said, "And he, as I am sure you know, was killed in the Battle of Hastings—"

Lady Clovyle's blood ran cold. She was no historian, but even she knew that the Norman invasion of England had occurred in 1066. Surely her hostess did not intend to recite 750 years of begats?

Apparently she did.

"—and his son Robert married Maria, daughter to Sir Geoffrey Tylle, who was married to Margaret, daughter to Roland of Sanslevieux. Sir Geoffrey's mother, of course, was Anne, sister of Sir Ethelred Arnold the Younger, and not his daughter as some people have claimed. Sir Ethelred did have a daughter Anne, but she is the Anne who married Guy de Fontainelle, and she unfortunately died in childbirth and the child with her. Anne's mother—that is, of course, the Anne we are interested in, who was the mother of Sir Geoffrey—"

If the truth were told, Lady Clovyle was not interested in that Anne or any other Anne, and she sorely regretted having asked Lady Letitia about Mr. Rendel's family.

"—was Gertrude of Saxony, and her father's name is uncertain, although I am inclined to think that she was descended from the lesser branch of that family, not the major one. That would explain why her shield is quartered with three lions gules rather than two griffins verts."

Lady Clovyle's mind began to wander, and at some point when she was not paying strict attention, Lady Letitia slid over from Norman nobility into a long recital of Welsh kings. Lady Clovyle was not sure just how they were connected to Gertrude of Saxony—in fact, she had long since given up trying to sort everyone out.

"—Madog ap Gruffydd Maelor ap Madog ap Gryffudd ap Maredudd ap Bleddyn ap Cynfyn ap Gwerstan ap Gwaethfoed ap Gwrhydr ap Bleddyn ap Caradawg ap Lles Law Deawg ap Ednyfed ap Gwynnau ap Gwynnawg Farfsych ap—" Lady Letitia's voice droned on and on.

Lady Letitia reached over and removed the teacup from her guest's slack hand. Then she smiled in satisfaction. One could always count on dear Lady Clovyle's dropping off to sleep in her box at the theater or during the Sunday services at St. George's in Hanover Square.

Rising silently from her chair, Lady Letitia tiptoed across the room and rang for Owens, who had provided her with the book from which she had obtained the long and monotonous Welsh genealogies. He had also coached her on the proper pronunciation of the Welsh names, although it is doubtful that Lady Clovyle would have noticed anything amiss even if Lady Letitia had invented some wholly fictitious names.

In any event, it was now time for the second act to commence.

Startled out of her sleep, Lady Clovyle sat up and gazed around her in bewilderment that rapidly turned to horror. She had dozed off while Lady Letitia was speaking—her life was ruined, absolutely ruined! She would never again be able to show her face in London!

But Lady Letitia did not appear to have noticed the social solecism her guest had committed.

"And that is his father's side, so I am sure you will understand why I call him cousin. Now on his mother's side—"

Lady Clovyle gave a mental groan. Surely she had been tortured enough? Why had no one ever warned her not to bring up the subject of ancestors and lineages when Lady Letitia was present?

The door opened, and Lady Letitia paused in her recital. "Yes, Owens, what is it?"

Her butler replied, "Lady Edington has come to call. Do you wish to see her or shall I deny her?"

Lady Letitia frowned. "Dear me, this is unfortunate. I have not seen her for an age, but on the other hand, Lady Clovyle and I have been having such a pleasant coze." Turning to Lady Clovyle she said, "Would you mind dreadfully if I postponed telling you about my cousin's mother's family until another time?"

"No, no, not at all," Lady Clovyle hastened to assure her.

"You must be sure and remind me the next time we are together," Lady Letitia said.

When pigs fly, Lady Clovyle said to herself. Then she was shocked at the vulgarity of her own thoughts.

"Lady Letitia, the most delicious bit of gossip—I had to be the first to tell you." Acting as if she did not even notice that Lady Letitia had another guest, Adeline crossed to where her coconspirator was sitting and kissed her on the cheek. Then she sat down in her appointed chair, which had been cleverly placed so that she had her back to Lady Clovyle.

I should have been born to the stage, she thought to herself. This is vastly entertaining, and I am clearly blessed with hitherto unsuspected thespian talent.

Without giving her hostess or their audience of one enough time to speak, she launched herself into her monologue, which Lady Letitia had written and which she herself had finished memorizing a bare half hour ago.

"You will not credit it when you hear who I saw climbing into a coach at the Red Stag in Staines. Surely, I thought when I saw him, that cannot be Lady Letitia's cousin, Mr. Rendel, but I could not doubt the evidence of my eyes, for I find him quite the handsomest of men. It was indeed he, and you must have a word with him. He is being quite a naughty boy, you know, because his fair companion was no cyprian. Imagine my surprise when I beheld her to be none other than the rich Miss Pepperell. Really, as well heeled as he is, I would not have thought he would need to seduce an heiress."

There was a gasp behind her, and Adeline turned, as if only then becoming aware of the third person in the room.

"I am not sure you two have met," Lady Letitia said. "My dear Lady Clovyle, may I present Lady Edington?"

"Not the aunt?" Adeline said, clasping her hands to her cheeks in a bit of impromptu acting that was so overdone, she was surprised that Lady Clovyle did not immediately tumble to the truth.

Lady Letitia nodded. "Just so."

Affecting a look of deep chagrin, Adeline said, "Oh, dear, I do believe I have put my foot in it now."

Conflicting emotions ran across Lady Clovyle's face, and Adeline felt the urge to prompt the older lady, who seemed to have forgotten her lines.

"You have completely misunderstood the matter," Lady Clovyle finally said. "Mr. Rendel and my niece have long been betrothed, only . . . only . . ."

"Only they did not wish to make it public because of a recent death in my dear cousin's family," Lady Letitia said smoothly. "They are being married here at my house tomorrow, and I must ask you not to tell a soul, for we wish to keep the ceremony private, since dear Digory is technically still in mourning."

Enjoyable as it might be to playact, Adeline had to admit that Lady Letitia's skill as an actress far surpassed hers. Listening to her talk, Adeline almost felt that they should be speaking in hushed voices out of respect for the dear departed.

"I shall not say a word to anyone," Adeline promised. "But only on the condition that we are invited to the ceremony. Matthew would be devastated if he were not able to stand witness to Mr. Rendel, who is one of his oldest and dearest friends." Turning to face Lady Clovyle, she begged, "Do say we may join you tomorrow in celebrating this happy occasion."

Still looking a little pale, Lady Clovyle hastened to say, "Of course you and your husband are welcome to come."

Adeline smiled. Lady Letitia smiled. Lady Clovyle, on

the other hand, looked as if she had been handed an invitation to her own execution.

Bethia was sitting by her window, watching the sky change from blue to purple and wondering, as she had been doing the entire day, where Digory was and what he was doing. Her musings were interrupted by a light tap on the door.

"Come in," she called out, although in truth she was not in the mood for company.

Aunt Euphemia entered, looking girlishly coy. "There is a gentleman come to see you," she said.

"Tell him I am not at home," Bethia said, turning to stare once more at the darkening sky.

"It is your Mr. Rendel who is below in the library," her aunt continued as if Bethia had not spoken, "and he has asked for and I have given him my permission to address you."

Bethia could not believe what she was hearing—indeed, it was too wonderful to be true. How could Digory, in only a day and a half, have effected such a change in her aunt's attitude toward him?

But the evidence was right before her eyes. Aunt Euphemia was smiling and looking as pleased as if she herself had arranged the match.

"You will, of course, not wish to keep him waiting, but I do think he will not mind if you delay long enough to change your gown. Perhaps your new pomona green morning dress might be appropriate. Or do you prefer the jonquil silk with the gold embroidery?"

But Bethia was already hurrying out of the room and down the stairs. Digory had come back—he was here!

She paused in the doorway of the library, feeling unaccountably shy, but then he turned toward her and smiled, and she ran forward and threw herself into his arms.

"Oh, you cannot know how much I have missed you," she said, hugging him as tightly as she could and laughing out of sheer joy.

Holding her in his arms, feeling her warmth through the

thin layers of clothing that separated them, Digory had a grim foretaste of the hell he was letting himself in for.

How had he ever thought that he could marry her and then not be a proper husband to her? Her curves fit against him as if God himself had created the two of them specifically for each other.

Before he could set her aside—and his arms blatantly disobeyed his command to release her—she pulled his head down and kissed him full on his lips.

This is not supposed to be happening, he thought before all logic fled his brain, to be replaced by passion.

"I love you," she murmured finally, giving a contented little sigh. "Indeed, I feel as if I have loved you forever, and I know I shall love you with all my heart for the rest of my life."

Her words were like a cold bucket of water thrown into his face, bringing him back to the reality he could not ignore, no matter how desperately he might wish to do so. But even knowing their embrace could not—must not—continue, he did not find within himself the resolution needed to release her.

"However did you manage to persuade my aunt to agree to this marriage?" Bethia asked, leaning back in his arms only enough that she could look into his eyes. "No, do not tell me. It is enough that you have achieved this miracle. Oh, I cannot believe that we will be married a week from now."

Her eyes were filled with delight and trust and innocence, but his own heart was heavy with guilt. "Tomorrow," he finally managed to say.

"Tomorrow?"

"Your aunt has agreed that we shall be married tomorrow at Lady Letitia's house," he said.

"Can it really be? Do I have to suffer through only one more night alone before we are together?" Even while she was smiling up at him, her eyes filled with tears. "Do you know," she said, her lower lip quivering, "you have given me so much more than I could ever have hoped for, and yet I am still not satisfied. I wish we could be married this evening, this hour, this very minute."

What had he ever done in his life that was wicked enough to deserve such punishment? Digory wondered. The fires of hell would seem a relief compared to the torture he was now enduring.

"Yoo-hoo," a voice called out. Looking up, Digory saw Lady Clovyle standing in the doorway, smiling coyly at him. "It would appear your suit has prospered, Mr. Rendel. I vow, I have never seen my niece looking quite so happy."

"Oh, Aunt Euphemia," Bethia said, running to throw her arms around her aunt's neck. "Oh, thank you, thank you, thank you. You have made me the happiest person in London."

"No, no, my dear, it is quite clear to all but the blindest eye that it is Mr. Rendel who has made you this happy. I am only thankful that I was able to do my small part in helping Cupid aim his little arrows."

Lady Clovyle smiled at Digory as if he were the catch of the Season, and he could but marvel at her talent for self-deception.

"If you will excuse me, I must see about making arrangements for tomorrow's ceremony," he said. Only by avoiding looking into Bethia's eyes was he able to take his leave.

Late that night, Lord Edington hosted a bachelor party for Digory, although a stranger entering the library would have deemed it a very odd sort of affair. For one thing, although the butler had produced a truly mellow port, no one was imbibing deeply.

The four men Edington had invited had been espionage agents, and during the war with France their lives had depended upon being able to think more clearly than their opponents. Even though the hostilities were over, they had not yet entirely cast off their habits of caution and moderation.

But it was not so much the lack of drunken revelry that made this evening unique, Digory realized, rather it was the lack of ribald banter and raillery that set this gathering apart from the usual such parties. Instead of needling him about the pleasures of the bachelor life he was about to give up, Digory's companions were discussing how best to bamboozle the *haut ton* into thinking he was and always had been one of their own.

"It is obvious that Rendel cannot have spent his entire life in England without anyone becoming acquainted with him except the five of us," Roger Nyesmith said. His voice was mild, but he was peeling an apple with a knife that had never been designed for kitchen use.

"But then we must perforce have met him abroad, and the problem with that is we cannot claim to have encountered him in India or Macao or Russia if we have never been to any of those places ourselves," Edward Townsley said, wandering around the room as if possessed of too much energy to sit down. "I cannot speak for the rest of you, but the only time I have traveled outside of England was when I went to France, and that is not common knowledge, nor would the War Office be at all happy if it were to become widely known. So if I were to claim I had met Rendel on the Continent, it would raise more questions about my past than it would answer about his."

"Such a homebody you are," Roger Nyesmith said. "I, on the other hand, have traveled extensively in Canada and the United States. Went over in the spring of '04 and didn't come home until the fall of '06. We could say we met . . . where?"

"Never having been to America," Digory answered, "I would be undone the first time anyone asked me the simplest question about that country."

"That is the other side of the problem," Patrick Fitzhugh said. "To avoid exposing our little sham, we must limit ourselves to where Rendel himself has actually been."

The others all looked at Digory expectantly. "I have been to the Low Countries, and France, Portugal, and Spain, and to most of the countries around the Mediterranean," he admitted. "But I have always stayed close to the coastline and never ventured far inland."

"More than likely I have been to all the Mediterranean and Channel ports that you have visited," Oliver Lord Cavenaugh said, idly swinging his quizzing glass back and forth. "Yet I must decline to tell anyone that I made your acquaintance in Cairo or Barcelona or even in Naples."

Lord Edington immediately took umbrage. "If you do not wish to play the game," he said, anger sharpening his voice, "then you are free to ignore us all. But you betray Rendel at your own peril." Lame he might now be, but the reputation Edington had acquired while spying on the French was sufficient to make the others eye him with apprehension.

Only Cavenaugh appeared not the least bit dismayed. Raising his quizzing glass, he stared at Edington while the murmurs of the others died down and the room became quiet enough that the ticking of the mantel clock could be heard.

How much they knew about Cavenaugh, Digory could not say. But what he himself knew made him sure that Cavenaugh was in truth the most dangerous and most ruthless man in the room. He was likewise the only one whose thoughts had ever been one step ahead of Digory's.

Slender of build and not above average height, Cavenaugh was decked out tonight like the veriest coxcomb. But his present appearance to the contrary, he had for years successfully played the role of wharf rat, ready to do any job, no matter how loathsome, for the price of a bottle of gin or a flagon of brandy.

Speaking an almost incomprehensible mixture of gutter Arabic, the most vulgar Italian, and French patois, he had slunk into and out of French, Italian, and Spanish ports with the greatest of ease, and without anyone ever suspecting that he was English, much less that he was a spy. The information he had obtained had been invaluable, his methods never fully disclosed.

But it would seem that Cavenaugh's conscience, which had been most accommodatingly flexible during wartime, would not allow him to participate in any peacetime deception.

"I cannot fault you for not wanting to have any part of this," Digory said, but Cavenaugh paid him no attention.

"You know I must always be more than happy to meet you at dawn with a sword or pistol in my hand, Matthew," he said, "but before you arrange for your seconds, permit me to say that I have nothing against fooling the *ton*. Why,

I would even be willing to persuade half of London that Rendel here is the long lost Dauphin if such were his wish. But what you have overlooked in your childish plotting is that Englishmen, when they are away from these hallowed shores, cling to one another in veritable clumps, as it were, and they will only wonder that Rendel was conspicuously absent from their fellowship."

"Then what you are saying, in essence," Fitzhugh said, "is that we have set ourselves an impossible task."

"Not at all," Cavenaugh said, a bit of a smile creeping into his voice. "But you are all approaching this problem from the wrong direction. You think we must come up with answers to every possible question we might be asked, but the fact of the matter is, for every question we answer, we will surely be asked a dozen more."

"So what would you have us do?" Nyesmith asked. "Are you suggesting that we admit defeat before we have even begun?"

"Au contraire, mon ami," Cavenaugh said smoothly, flicking an invisible bit of lint off his sleeve. "We have only to act the way we would naturally act if someone were to begin quizzing us about our personal affairs, namely we shall become highly indignant. For if I call a man friend, then who has a right to question where I have met him or how long I have known him? Observe the only proper response to an impertinent question." He raised his quizzing glass and regarded Nyesmith with a look of frosty disdain that would have chilled the Beau himself.

Townsley was the first to laugh, and even Edington began to smile.

"Since it appears we have nothing more to do here except to wish Rendel a long and happy married life," Fitzhugh said, "I suggest we take our leave."

"There is one more item on the agenda," Edington said, and he glanced over to Cavenaugh, who nodded his head as if he already knew what the viscount was going to say. "There remains the matter of the wicked cousin. I cannot feel easy so long as we remain in ignorance of his identity."

There were murmurs of agreement from the other men, and Digory swore to himself, then spoke up quickly, in hopes that he might yet divert them all from this line of reasoning. "I have no desire for revenge. Being deprived of the fortune he sought to inherit will be punishment enough for Miss Pepperell's cousin."

Five pairs of eyes looked at him impassively. Although they were experienced at hiding their thoughts, in this case their very silence revealed clearly what they were thinking: Miss Pepperell had nearly been drowned. The three men who had attempted to kill her had acted deliberately and with malice aforethought. One of them had died accidentally while engaged in that wicked piece of work. The second was dead at the hands of the third. It followed therefore that the third man—the one who had instigated the plot— likewise deserved to die.

"You are good-hearted, Rendel, and I applaud your Christian sentiments," Nyesmith said, "but in my opinion, you are making an error by discounting the danger inherent in this situation. Ignorance may be bliss, but it is never my choice when it comes to survival."

"It is not as if we would have to hire a Bow Street Runner," Townsley explained, beginning once more to ramble restlessly about the room. "We have sufficient expertise to ferret out the truth, and even you must agree that it will be safer to know which cousin is the viper and which two are merely harmless garden snakes."

"Has it occurred to any of you," Digory said, "that if you expose the villain, you will at the same time destroy Miss Pepperell's reputation?" He looked from one to the other, but none of them would meet his eye. "Since I am the one who is most deeply involved in this affair, I believe it is, in the end, my decision. And I have decided that nothing will be gained by any attempt to unmask the murderer."

Chapter Ten

Valid though it was, Digory's objection did not end the discussion. "If you do not wish to have the wicked cousin brought before the courts," Fitzhugh said, "and I am inclined to think you are right regarding public knowledge of these things—then there are still innumerable ways that the offensive gentleman can be permanently . . . removed, shall we say?"

The others agreed, and with growing enthusiasm and truly fiendish ingenuity they began discussing the possible ways to eliminate the wicked cousin. That everything must be done in total secrecy was quite to their liking, and that they were proposing to take justice into their own hands troubled them not at all.

And indeed, what else could Digory have expected? These five men were not soldiers who had been trained to carry out commands.

To succeed as a spy—and often success was measured simply by whether or not one lived to see the next sunrise—one had to be able to decide for oneself the proper action to take. An English spy could not have survived in Napoleon's France if he had attempted to follow precise instructions from the War Department in London, no more than Wellington could have won the Battle of Waterloo if he had allowed Parliament to decide where he should make a stand against the French forces and how he should deploy his troops.

Moreover, a good spy needed to be willing to do whatever had to be done to reach his goals. And he had to be able to keep dangerous, even deadly secrets.

In short, a successful espionage agent was not particularly good at listening to whoever was in charge, which in this case was Digory. He, on the other hand, was quite accustomed to having his every order obeyed instantly by his crew.

His patience at an end, he interrupted the others, saying firmly, "I repeat, I do not wish anything to be done about exposing Miss Pepperell's cousin—or disposing of him, as the case may be."

As if Digory had not spoken, Townsley asked, "Is anyone here acquainted with the Harcourt brothers? For if I have ever been introduced to them, I disremember it."

Digory felt a mounting frustration—quite like Pandora must have felt after she opened her box. It had been his decision to ask Lord Edington for his help, and Edington in turn had seen fit to involve the other four men. Now there did not seem to be any way to set limits on their actions.

"If I am not mistaken, they manage to cling precariously to the fringes of Prinny's crowd," Nyesmith said.

"Then that narrows our search to the more disreputable gambling hells, wouldn't you say?" Fitzhugh said with a mocking grin. "And here I had thought the hunting season over. Do you come with us, Cavenaugh? There is bound to be great sport in it."

Fitzhugh's tone might be light, but there was a gleam in his eye that made it abundantly clear to Digory exactly why he had no control over these men. Despite appearances, they were not coming to his assistance because of any deep and abiding friendship for him or any true concern for Miss Pepperell's well-being.

The war with France had brought together people of diverse station—people who would normally never have met. Extraordinary times had indeed called for extraordinary measures.

But Digory was a realist. The war was over, and he strongly doubted that even one of these men had spared a thought for him during the several months of peace following Waterloo.

On the other hand, just as he had been bored in his retirement, it was quite clear that the others had likewise been finding life in peacetime England a trifle flat. Lord Edington had summoned them for this meeting, and he had dangled the lure of excitement and adventure before them, and now it was clearly impossible to deflect them from their self-appointed task.

"I am afraid I must decline," Cavenaugh said with a smile. "I am engaged for the opera tomorrow, and my valet will be most put out with me if I show myself in public with bags under my eyes. I shall just stay a moment or two with Matthew and then toddle along home to bed."

"But if you have good hunting," Edington said, "send me a note detailing what you have discovered. Since we do not normally frequent the same circles, we cannot afford to be seen together too often, else people will begin to gossip."

The three younger men promised to keep him informed, and after a few minutes they departed, leaving only Digory, Cavenaugh, and their host, whose face was now deeply lined with the pain he had done his best to conceal while the others were there.

Wordlessly, Digory filled a glass with port and passed it over to him, but Edington pushed it aside. "I would be a drunkard by now, were I to allow myself to seek respite from pain at the bottom of a bottle."

"Then we shall not take advantage of your hospitality any longer, Matthew, but be on our way," Cavenaugh said smoothly, "and leave you to the tender ministrations of your good wife, who doubtless has better means of taking your mind off your bad leg."

Edington's protests were a mere formality, and he made no real attempt to detain them, so it was not long before Digory found himself walking down the street with Cavenaugh. The moon had already set, and Mayfair was shadowed and silent. Only a few carriages still rumbled by, carrying the last of the *ton* home from their revels.

Despite the dozens of times Lord Cavenaugh had been on Digory's yacht, where he had joked and acted as if he were part of the crew, here in London Digory did not feel at ease with him. Digory was, in fact, amazed that he'd had the temerity to ask a peer of the realm to help him deceive other lords and ladies.

But Cavenaugh did not appear to feel the slightest bit of

self-consciousness or constraint. Falling into step beside Digory, he began to speak as if they were equals, which they were not and never could be.

"How much do you know about the Harcourt brothers?" Cavenaugh asked bluntly.

"Nothing that will help us discover which one is the villain," Digory said. "Miss Pepperell knows her cousins far better than I, and even she has no way of knowing which one has been trying to kill her."

"But what is this, Rendel? Have your wits gone begging? We may not know much about two of the brothers, but we can certainly deduce from his actions a great deal about the particular Harcourt whom we seek."

As much as Cavenaugh's words rankled, Digory could not deny the truth in what he said. "You are right. To begin with, we know the murderer is completely ruthless."

"In addition, he is reasonably clever, else he would not have been able to react so quickly when his plans went awry," Cavenaugh pointed out. "We must therefore assume that he has covered his tracks well."

Three men were coming toward them, obviously foxed from the way they were staggering and holding onto each other. Cavenaugh waited until they were past and out of earshot before he continued.

"Our best chance to identify the villain would be if he were to try again to murder Miss Pepperell. But as you say, he is not lacking in wits. Once his initial rage is over, he will realize that such a deed would avail him naught."

"Which is precisely the point I was trying to make," Digory retorted. "We need no longer concern ourselves with him after the wedding. And until the ceremony, which is but a few short hours away, Miss Pepperell is being quite safely looked after by Big Davey and Little Davey Veryan."

"A truly formidable pair if I remember correctly," Cavenaugh said. "But just what is to prevent Mr. Harcourt from thinking a bit more? What makes you sure he will ignore what must be obvious?"

"Obvious?"

"But of course. Once Miss Pepperell is married, then his

only remaining chance to get his hands on her grandfather's money is to have her marriage declared invalid."

Digory started out to explain the steps he had undertaken to ensure that the marriage would be legally binding, but then he cursed under his breath. Whether the marriage was legal or not was immaterial. Even though any effort to have the marriage set aside would ultimately fail, the attempt itself would be sufficient to expose his true identity.

And her villainous cousin, having shown himself capable of cold-blooded murder, would not hesitate to crucify Bethia in the court of public opinion. Indeed, merely the whiff of a scandal would be enough to make the *ton* ostracize Bethia.

"In other words, I need not fear accidentally encountering someone who might recognize me, because the Harcourt brothers will spare no expense to discover precisely who I am and where I came from," Digory said.

"Unfortunately," his lordship continued, "we cannot simply assume that whichever cousin protests your marriage is the villain, because all three will have ample reason to rant and rave and cry foul. And since the murderer was resourceful enough to find and hire two assassins—and I must point out that such scoundrels do not normally advertise their services with the employment agencies—we can therefore assume that he will also be resourceful enough to hire someone to go to Cornwall and investigate your background. And that means we have very little time to act."

"Act? Have you thought of some way to prevent this? A practical plan, not another flight of imagination like the ones Fitzhugh and his cohorts were offering? For I must admit I can see no solution to the problem of keeping my identity secret."

"The simplest thing is usually also the best," Cavenaugh said mildly. "Which in this case means we need merely eliminate all three of the cousins. From what little gossip I have heard about the Harcourt men, I doubt any of them are of particular value to society."

With effort Digory managed to keep his tone civil. "There is another alternative that you have apparently not considered."

"Something that I, in my infinite wisdom, have over-looked? How extraordinary."

"We would have no problems with any of the cousins if you were the one to marry Miss Pepperell tomorrow."

Cavenaugh stopped dead in his tracks and regarded Digory with open amazement, then he burst out laughing. "I would be on the next boat to Calais if I thought you were serious. No, no, you are the one the fates have chosen to be the sacrificial lamb—the one who must give up his freedom in this noble cause."

Digory was not amused. How could he joke about receiving Miss Pepperell's hand in marriage when he knew himself to be unworthy of receiving even one of her smiles?

Shortly thereafter he parted company with Cavenaugh and continued on alone the short distance to Lady Letitia's house. He assumed his elderly friend would have long since gone to bed, but instead he found her still awake and comfortably ensconced in front of the fire in the drawing room, a glass of sherry in her hand.

Sitting down beside her, Digory briefly related the high points of the meeting with the former spies, concluding with his fears that the situation was getting desperately out of hand.

"But my dear boy," she said with a wicked smile, "what makes you think you have ever been in control of anything? You should know by now that I am the master puppeteer in London. Mine is the hand that jerks the strings and makes the marionettes perform on cue."

"Then discover a way I can prevent my eager companions from destroying Miss Pepperell's reputation by unmasking the villain, or what is worse, killing two innocent men just to eliminate one murderer."

"Certainly," she said. "I shall be happy to oblige, just as soon as you convince me that the villainous cousin is no longer dangerous. If I remember correctly, that was one of the first rules you taught me in Marseilles, namely never to turn my back on a known enemy. And that is precisely what you are now intending to do, figuratively speaking."

Her voice was light, and a smile lurked around her eyes,

but Digory was not deceived into thinking she was joking. And if she was likewise determined to unmask the murderer, then he might as well stop struggling against the inevitable. Instead he should do his best to minimize the damage to Miss Pepperell's reputation.

Unfortunately, his own past was more dangerous than anything the other agents might contrive. All it would take to undo everything they had accomplished so far was for one person to point a finger at him and say, "That man is no gentleman; that man is the bastard son of the Earl of Blackstone and a notorious smuggler to boot."

Staring into the fire, Digory could see no possible way to prevent such an eventuality, and he wondered how he could ever have been so naive as to think their only problem was simply the matter of gaining Lady Clovyle's permission to marry.

"Come, come, my dear boy," Lady Letitia interrupted his thoughts. "You must not look so glum the night before you are to be married, else someone might think you were not happy to be acquiring a beautiful, intelligent—to say nothing of rich—wife."

It was not the port he had drunk that made him answer her more frankly than was his wont. In the past, no matter how unsure of himself he had been, he had carefully hidden his doubts and anxieties from everyone else. And by careful observation coupled with a logical mind, he had always managed to figure out the best thing to do.

But now, for the first time in his life, he feared he might find himself unequal to the task he had undertaken, and he wanted the advice of someone older and more experienced than he was.

"Ours will not be a real marriage," he said. "Once Bethia is of age, I will arrange for an annulment."

"What is this—am I becoming senile in my old age? I cannot believe that I was so totally mistaken about the child. However could I have missed seeing that she is self-centered, greedy, grasping, thoughtless, and unkind?" Lady Letitia said, her indignation fierce and immediate. "My dear boy, if I had but known that she was planning to use you and then discard you, I would never have assisted her in deceiving her aunt."

She paused, as if she had just realized something, then said in a much calmer voice, "And I cannot believe that she duped you also, so you will please explain why you have agreed to play a leading role in such a foolish venture."

"You mistake the matter entirely," Digory said softly. "Miss Pepperell knows nothing of any annulment. She is exactly as sweet and kind and good-hearted as you thought her to be when you met her, although I cannot claim that she is always even-tempered and obedient. In truth, I foresee a rather vigorous campaign on her part to dissuade me from this course."

There was no immediate answer from his companion. Turning his head, he looked in her eyes and saw pain there equal to his own.

Lady Letitia was wise enough not to badger him with questions, nor did she instantly inundate him with well-meant but ill-thought-out advice. "Surely you cannot doubt but that Bethia loves you—it positively radiates from her eyes," was all she said in the end.

"My mother loved my father desperately, and yet by his selfish actions, he destroyed her life," Digory replied. "If I consider nothing but my own desires, then I am as loathsome as he was. While it was doubtless amusing to invent a preposterous pedigree for me, I have learned by experience just how small-minded people can be. How can I pretend that Bethia will not suffer because I was born out of wedlock? And suppose we were to have a child? There is no way I could prevent the other children from teasing my son or daughter unmercifully for having a father who is a bastard."

"Your sister is married to Richard Hawke, a most estimable man, but one who does not even know who his parents were, much less whether or not they were married. And yet she is the happiest of women."

At the mention of Cassie, Digory attempted to smile, but his voice was bitter when he spoke. "Richard Hawke has no cause to fear his past. He was but a young lad when he left England, and he was gone so many years that no one, no matter how diligently he might search, would ever be able to connect the child he was with the man he has become. And in a way Richard is doubly lucky, for he did not have to watch his mother suffer—to see her die a little more every day, all the while knowing there was nothing he could do to alleviate her pain."

"You were but a child. No one can blame you for what you were too young to prevent."

"You miss the point. I do not blame myself; I blame my father. And that is precisely why I cannot allow myself to follow in his footsteps. No matter how many excuses and rationalizations I come up with, I cannot ignore the truth: If I consummate this marriage with Bethia, then I am no better than my father, for in the end I will surely destroy the happiness of the woman I love."

There, he had finally admitted the truth he had been trying not to face. However impossible, however hopeless, however futile it might be, he loved Bethia more than he had thought it possible for a man to love a woman. But confession, while it might be good for the soul, did not bring him any measure of relief; it merely served to focus his grief.

Up until the moment that Digory said he loved his betrothed, Lady Letitia had been considering whether or not she should explain to him that contrary to popular opinion, not consummating a marriage was insufficient grounds for an annulment. But Lady Letitia was too much a matchmaker to interfere once Digory admitted his feelings for the woman he had rescued from the sea for if he knew the truth, he would no doubt attempt to cry off.

Moreover, the chance of his discovering that she had withheld the pertinent information about annulments was slim.

He was in all ways too much a man to remain celibate for months with such a lovely—and even more important, such a loving—wife as Miss Pepperell. Days, perhaps, and possibly even a week or two. But over four months? It would never happen.

The night had been unbearably long, but Bethia could not blame her sleeplessness on any nightmares. Rather it was anticipation of her coming wedding that had kept her from finding release in the arms of Morpheus.

At the first hint of morning—the first subtle lightening of the sky—she climbed out of bed and pulled on her robe, then went to the window and sank down on the window seat.

Only a single star was still visible, and even while she watched, it slowly faded away. By the time its light could again be seen, she would be a married woman, and she would never again have to face the darkness without Digory there beside her—truly beside her in the bed, not sleeping uncomfortably on a chair positioned close by.

Watching the sky change from deepest blue to palest rose, she could not keep from smiling and hugging herself. She had always thought marriage was a serious, even solemn occasion—a step into the unknown, from which there was no retreat. Each time she had watched other girls go to the altar, she had wondered how they could be certain they were doing the right thing.

To give a man total control over your life, your fortune, your heart—how was it possible to be sure?

But today was her wedding day, and she was not marrying some virtual stranger—someone she had danced with a few times at Almack's, someone who had paid a dozen proper morning calls, someone who had taken her up on occasion for a turn around the park.

She was marrying Digory Rendel, an uncommon man with an uncommon background. He was nothing like the many men who had courted her—men whose faces she could no longer remember in any detail—men whose effusive compliments and practiced smiles and fatuous remarks all blurred together in her mind.

"Digory Rendel." Just whispering his name to herself made her heart sing, and she could not keep her thoughts from flitting off in first one direction and then another.

How strong he was to have pulled her from the sea. Yet how gentle he had been, brushing the tangles from her hair.

How near he was tonight, just a few streets away. Yet how agonizingly distant he seemed—beyond the reach of her hand, beyond the sound of her voice.

How short a time yet to be gotten through—how unbearably long the hours until she would see him again—be with him again, forever.

It was unfortunate that her aunt was the one to find her sound asleep on the window seat with the curtains drawn. Shaking Bethia awake she fussed, "Anyone passing by— the butcher's brat or a chimney sweep—might have looked up and seen you sleeping here like a . . . a . . ." Words failed her at that point, or at least words that were proper for a lady to say.

Much invigorated by her short nap, Bethia smiled, yawned, stood up, stretched, and then began to dance around the room, humming softly to herself.

Her aunt made a noise remarkably like a snort—only ladies, of course, never snort. "I cannot think what is keeping that wretched Mrs. Drake," she muttered, or it would have been a mutter, if 'twere not for the fact that ladies always enunciate clearly whatever it is they wish to say.

Crossing to the bellpull, she jerked on it several times, so vigorously that Bethia would not have been surprised if the whole thing had come off in her aunt's hand.

"Stop that infernal spinning around! You are giving me the headache," Aunt Euphemia said crossly—except that a true lady never, ever is moody or crotchety or displays anything but an unflagging, unfailing, unwavering evenness of disposition. "There is so much to be done, and we will never be ready in time for the wedding if we do not make a start at once. You must have your bath, then Mrs. Drake must do your hair and help you dress."

It was a measure of how deeply distressed Aunt Euphemia was that she actually said the word *bath,* since she did not normally deem it a proper word for a lady to say. *Morning ablutions* was her preferred expression.

"That is really very little to accomplish, considering that we have a full four hours," Bethia said, dancing over to give her aunt a kiss on the cheek, which only halfway mollified her. "I am sure we will have ample time. Although actually it will not even matter if my hair is not properly curled or my dress ironed to perfection. After all, Mr. Rendel has seen me looking quite like a drowned duck."

Her aant puckered up immediately, of course, but before she could begin a lecture on the proper behavior for a young lady of quality who has just been dragged from the sea, there was a light tapping on the door, and Mrs. Drake entered, carrying the pale gold walking dress, which Madame Arnault had altered beautifully.

"The maid will be along directly with some hot chocolate, and I have instructed the footmen to bring the hot water up in half an hour. The day looks to be quite pleasant, and Mr. Rendel has sent round a posy for you to carry."

Which left Bethia's aunt with really nothing more to worry about.

So why was she still looking so agitated? Why had she now begun to pace back and forth, even going so far as to wring her hands, which was not at all her usual manner.

Stopping abruptly a few feet away from Bethia, Lady Clovyle blurted out, "Have you been properly instructed as to a wife's duty to her husband?"

"To be sure, Aunt Euphemia. You yourself have given me a most thorough education in the proper way to direct servants and manage a household."

"No, no," her aunt said impatiently, waving her hands in dismissal, then again clasping them together so tightly the knuckles were white. "What I mean is, has anyone ever told you precisely what is involved when a man and a woman . . . when a husband and wife . . . that is to say when they . . ."

Her aunt abruptly resumed her pacing, then stopped again and asked, "Have you ever been on a farm and observed—but no, you have not, I know that. Heaven knows, I have always done my best to persuade your grandfather that London was not a proper place to raise a child, especially a female with tender sensibilities, but he was the most stubborn and aggravating man it has ever been my misfortune to meet—quite unable to consider anyone's wishes except his own."

Thoroughly intrigued, Bethia said, "Are you perhaps

asking me if I know what happens when a man shares a woman's bed—"

"When a *husband* exercises his marital rights," her aunt corrected. "Yes, precisely that." Looking at Bethia out of the corner of her eye, she said, "Did perhaps your governess . . . ?"

Feeling a bit embarrassed herself, Bethia shook her head.

"It is indeed most unfortunate that your mother died when you were so young," Aunt Euphemia said with a heartfelt sigh.

Bethia nodded her head.

"Well." Her aunt clasped her hands tightly together, looked directly into Bethia's eyes, did her best to smile, and finally said firmly, "The most important thing you must know is that whatever your husband wishes to do in your bed, no matter how peculiar it may seem to you, no matter how . . . how . . ."

She faltered and her smile tightened into a grimace, but then she straightened her shoulders and tried a second time. This time her gaze fixed itself on the door, as if she were already eyeing her escape route, and her voice came out in a high squeak, the words tumbling out one on top of the other in an almost incoherent jumble.

"If you will only keep reminding yourself that what he is doing will not last terribly long, and that every woman since Eve has had to endure what you are enduring—if you will remember that no matter how unpleasant it may be, it is your duty as his wife to allow him to do anything he wants to do, then I am sure you will not find it totally unbearable."

Taking a handkerchief from her sleeve, Aunt Euphemia mopped her forehead. "There, I have done my duty and explained it all to you."

"But I do not understand precisely what you mean," Bethia said.

"Well, I am sure that if you have any questions, Mrs. Drake can answer them as well as I can." And with those words, Lady Clovyle fled the room without a backward glance.

There was a peculiar sound behind her, and Bethia

turned to see that Mrs. Drake was no longer behaving like a properly trained servant.

She was, in fact, grinning from ear to ear, and despite her efforts to control her mirth, she was soon chuckling, and that in turn started Bethia laughing.

"Oh, dear, I should not carry on so," Mrs. Drake said finally. "It is only that I can picture your aunt so clearly in bed—" Her smile faded, but her eyes still twinkled. "But I can see that you have no idea what Lady Clovyle was trying to explain." She hesitated, as if debating within herself, then obviously making up her mind, said, "If you wish me to, I shall be happy to answer any questions you might have, and if you do not feel comfortable discussing such private matters with me, then I will keep my own counsel."

Bethia said, "I am afraid my ignorance is so extensive that I do not even know what questions I should ask, but I would be most grateful if you would enlighten me as to what will be expected of me in the marital bed."

After they settled themselves comfortably side-by-side on the window seat, Mrs. Drake explained simply but precisely how men differed from women, and exactly what happened when a man "slept" with a woman. She did not mince words, nor indulge in any roundaboutation, and the longer she talked, the more heated Bethia's cheeks became.

"It is small wonder my aunt could not bring herself to explain any of this properly," she said when Mrs. Drake was done talking, "and I must thank you for telling me everything, so that I will not be totally ignorant of my duties."

"But I have not yet told you the most important thing. While there are some ladies, such as your aunt, who simply endure what they must to satisfy their husbands, there are many others who find lovemaking quite . . . pleasurable. After the first time, of course." From the blush now tinting Mrs. Drake's cheeks a most becoming pink, it was not hard for Bethia to deduce which category of women her dresser belonged to.

Chapter Eleven

It would have been much easier to get through the ceremony if Mrs. Drake had not been so frank. Bethia's mind was so filled with anxiety and anticipation of what was to come that she was able to keep from blushing only by staring at the Reverend Mr. Gorham's Adam's apple, which was remarkable both for its prominence and for its agility.

Unfortunately, the vicar spoke in a relentless monotone, which made it difficult for her to concentrate on what he was saying . . . and for her to disregard the warmth of Digory's hand holding hers.

Repeating the vows that would bind the two of them together for all eternity, Bethia was filled with such joy that she did not believe it possible to be any happier than she was at this moment.

"You may now kiss the bride," the vicar said, closing his book.

Without releasing her hand, Digory gently raised her chin with his other hand and looked into her eyes. The moment seemed to stretch on forever, but then he bent his head and brushed his lips against hers.

From a great distance someone coughed, and there was the sound of shuffling feet. Then Digory lifted his head, and the spell was broken.

The guests began to congratulate her husband and offer her their best wishes for the future, but as far as Bethia was concerned, being married to Digory was everything she had dreamed about and more.

Digory would have given anything if this were in truth his wedding day—that is to say, if this marriage he had en-

tered into was real and not a sham. Climbing into Lady
Letitia's town coach and taking the seat beside his wife, he
was as close to losing control of himself as he had ever
been.

Everything about her was enticing—every glance beck-
oned him, every touch tantalized. The memory of her lips,
so soft and cool under his, made him want to show her how
a man's touch could ignite a woman's passion.

She leaned her head on his shoulder, and he could smell
the clean scent of her hair. He would have cursed the fate
that had so thoroughly entangled them in this impossible
situation, but he had learned at an early age the futility of
wishing for what could never be.

"Before we go back to your house—"

"Our home," she corrected him.

"—we must speak with your solicitor about the trust."

She looked up at him, her eyes reflecting remembered
pain and fear. "Do you know, at this moment I would rather
be ten miles out to sea without a boat if it meant I never had
to think about my villainous cousin again." Her voice was
quite fierce, and Digory bent his head and deposited a
quick kiss on her mouth.

At least he intended it to be quick. Somehow it lasted all
the way to the City, and by the time they stopped, Bethia
was sitting on his lap.

Sticking to his resolution was going to be even more difficult than he had imagined.

"So, Miss Pepperell," Mr. Kidby said after a clerk ushered them into his office, "you are contemplating marriage
with Mr. Rendel here, and you wish to begin discussing the
settlements."

"You misunderstand; I am already Mrs. Rendel. My husband and I were married an hour ago." Bethia held up her
left hand and showed him the emerald ring on her finger.

"Indeed?" the solicitor said, adjusting his spectacles and
staring first at the ring and then at Digory. "Well, in that
case, you will want to take care of ending the trust your
grandfather arranged." Swiveling his chair around, he

reached up and tugged on a cord. Somewhere in the outer office a bell jangled.

Bother the trust, Bethia thought, and curses on my cousins, one and all! Here she was, married at last, and forced to sit in a musty old office, discussing legal affairs with her grandfather's solicitor.

She turned and looked into Digory's eyes and saw a gleam of amusement, as if he knew precisely what she was thinking, and she could not hold back an answering smile.

It took a full hour before they were finally done—before the last document was signed and witnessed. With the ordeal at an end, Bethia was able to smile at Mr. Kidby. "You cannot begin to understand what a relief it is to know that my cousins will never be able to touch a penny of my grandfather's estate."

The solicitor frowned. "As much as it pains me to contradict you, I would be failing in my duty as your solicitor were I not to inform you that such is not the case."

Surprised by his remark and dismayed by the thought of additional complications, Bethia said, "But I have met the only provision required by my grandfather's will. I am married, and you saw that my aunt gave her written permission, so the marriage is valid."

"But if you wish to disinherit your cousins, you must have a will of your own," Mr. Kidby said.

"As things now stand," Digory explained, "if you die first, then I will inherit everything you own and possess at the time of your death. On the other hand, if I were to die before you, then your legal heirs would be your closest relatives."

If he were to die? All at once Bethia understood what he had not said. By marrying him, she had put him in danger—had made him a target for murder. Thoroughly aghast, she could only stare at her husband.

"But that is only if you die intestate," Mr. Kidby said in his impartial lawyer's voice. "By writing a will, you can devise your property to whomever you wish."

Clenching her hands to stop them from trembling, Bethia said, "I wish to leave everything to my husband." Taking a deep breath, she continued. "And if he should die before

me''—she had to blink back her tears—"then I leave everything to my aunt, Lady Clovyle."

As soon as she said the words, Bethia realized that such a
provision would only endanger her aunt's life.

Feeling as if she were trapped in a waking dream that
was worse than her nightmares, Bethia tried desperately to
think of a way to stop forever her cousins' claims to her
grandfather's money.

Finally, she knew what had to be done. "I have changed
my mind. I do not wish my aunt to be my heir. In the event
that my husband predeceases me, then I wish my entire estate to be used to establish a home for foundlings in Cornwall."

"You might wish to consider setting up a trust, the income from which would be more than adequate to support
a foundling home," Mr. Kidby said, "but that will take
time, so for now, if you want to be sure that your cousins
do not inherit anything, we can draw up a simple will that
will be adequate for that purpose."

A simple will, Bethia discovered, took only an hour and
a half to write and proof and sign and witness.

"Before you go, I have one more suggestion," Mr. Kidby
said. "I shall, of course, notify your cousins that the trust
has been dissolved, but if you wish, I can also tell them the
terms of your will."

Her grandfather had always considered Mr. Kidby a
most astute man, and Bethia was inclined to think her
grandfather had not erred in his judgment. "Yes," she said,
feeling more than a little sad. "Please inform my cousins
exactly where my money will go if anything untoward happens to me or to my husband."

When they finally arrived home, Bethia discovered that
the normally well-run household was at sixes and sevens.

Not only was Aunt Euphemia supervising the packing of
her own trunk, bandboxes, and portmanteaus, but she had
also directed the servants to move Bethia's belongings into
the master suite, which consisted of two connecting bed-
rooms, each with its own sitting room and dressing room.

Maids were bustling back and forth along the corridor,

their arms filled with dresses and scarves and shoes, and a valet named Youngblood was busily unpacking her husband's clothes into what had once been her grandfather's wardrobe.

Watching the confusion, Bethia decided it would definitely be a wedding day to remember. To preserve her sanity, she kept reminding herself that night would come in its proper time. Candles would be lit, and the doors securely locked. Aunt Euphemia would retire to her room, then the servants would remove themselves one by one to their own rooms.

Even allowing for unforeseen delays, by eleven o'clock she would surely be alone with her husband. And they would, after all, have the rest of their lives to be together.

"You look a most becoming bride," Mrs. Drake said after she had assisted Bethia into a long-sleeved nightgown made of softest flannel and embroidered all over with pale yellow flowers.

"You needn't brush my hair," Bethia said. "I shall do it myself."

"Just as you wish," Mrs. Drake said, her manner once again that of a proper servant. Gathering up the clothes Bethia had worn that day, she left the room without a backward glance.

For a moment Bethia felt the urge to run after her, to tell her she was afraid—no, never afraid when it was Digory. She was just a bit nervous—she just needed a bit of reassurance that she would not displease him, that he would be happy with the marriage she had forced him into.

Picking up her brush, she began pulling it through her long hair, automatically counting the strokes. Before she reached forty, the connecting door opened, and her husband entered the room.

She watched him in the mirror, expecting him to take the brush from her hands, but instead he stopped a few feet away. Clasping his hands behind his back, he said, "I believe it is time for us to discuss the bet we made."

"Bet?" she asked, turning to face him.

"The wager we made—that in less than a week I could

persuade your aunt to give her permission for you to marry me."

"Ah, that bet." Bethia smiled up at him. "I admit you have won the wager fair and square. Ask anything of me that you wish, for I can deny you nothing."

He did not return her smile, and she felt a frisson of fear.

"I do not want to consummate this marriage."

The brush dropped from her suddenly nerveless hand. "You cannot mean that," she whispered. "You cannot ask that of me."

"After your birthday, we shall have the marriage annulled," he said, his voice devoid of emotion.

Her mind screamed denials, but all that came out was a breathless, "Please . . . "

He said nothing.

Standing up, she tried frantically to think of some way to persuade him not to do this—this terrible, awful, unbelievably cruel thing.

"That is two requests, and I need grant you only one," she said, feeling some of her energy return. She would never agree—never! The wager was ridiculous, unimportant, immaterial. They were joined together in the eyes of God and according to the laws of men.

"I am asking only for an annulment," he said, and she was close enough to see that the pain in his eyes matched her own. "But since we have taken such care to make the marriage valid, the only way we can legally dissolve it is if we do not consummate the marriage."

"We did not shake on the wager," she said, her entire body beginning to tremble.

"The wager is unimportant," he replied. "I have decided that we will have the marriage annulled as soon as you are one-and-twenty, at which time you will be free to marry the man of your choosing."

"And if I choose you?"

"I am not the proper husband for you."

Great wracking sobs burst unannounced from her throat, and immediately Digory took her in his arms and pressed her head against his chest.

"I cannot endure another night alone—I cannot," she heard herself begging. "Please, you must stay with me."

"Of course I shall stay with you," he replied, his voice once again warm and comforting. Then he picked her up in his arms and carried her to the bed. Laying her down, he tucked her in, then stood beside her looking helpless. "Don't cry, please stop crying."

Wordlessly, she held out her arms to him, and to her great relief, he hesitated only momentarily before climbing under the covers and taking her back into his arms.

Holding his sleeping wife, Digory reviewed the events of the last week and decided that he had done absolutely nothing right except to rescue Bethia from drowning.

Every action he had taken since that time, from allowing her to drink her fill of punch to agreeing to marry her, from neglecting to consider the possibility of a third man in Carwithian Cove to asking Lord Edington for help. Every decision, both major and minor, had been exactly wrong.

And now, the woman whose happiness he had wanted to ensure had cried herself to sleep in his arms.

He was at *point non plus*—damned if he did and damned if he didn't.

If he continued to refuse to consummate the marriage, then that meant months of misery for both of them. Yet if he yielded to her entreaties, their happiness would last only until he was discovered to be a counterfeit gentleman, after which the rest of their lives would be filled with misery.

And the sins of his father would be carried on to the next generation.

He spent the night praying as he had never prayed before, not even when he had lost a rudder during a storm at sea and it had seemed as if his yacht would surely founder.

Yet even that moment had not been as dark as this night.

"The servants will know that this marriage has not been consummated," Bethia said matter-of-factly. She was standing in front of the window, and the early morning light surrounded her with the aura of an angel. Turning her head, she gazed at him with eyes that had aged a dozen years in one night. "Do you imagine there will be no gossip?"

"No one will suspect," Digory said, taking a hat pin from one of her bonnets and pricking his finger. Squeezing out a few drops of blood, he smeared the sheets where his wife-in-name-only had been lying.

She moved so softly he did not hear her approach, and only knew she was beside him when she spoke.

"Does it not bother you that we shall be living a lie? That we are deceiving our friends?"

Even knowing that in the long run the truth would be best, he found it hard to utter the brutally honest words. "My whole life, starting from my conception, has been a matter of lies and deceit. As I have told you, I do not belong in your world, and you do not belong in mine."

"I would give up everything—" she started to say, but he quickly laid his hand on her mouth.

He could not allow her to demean herself by begging, and yet he could not give her what she wanted. "When we made the wager, you also promised that you would not argue about it."

The anger that flashed in her eyes was a vast improvement over the grief. "And what difference does it make what I promised? After all, you have just said you are quite accustomed to lying and deception."

"But in all the years of my life, I have never gone back on my word," Digory said.

Struggling to hold back tears, she said, "Some day you will suffer as I am suffering today, and then you will regret what you have done."

"I am already suffering, and I am already sorry, but there is nothing you or I can do to change the world."

"Now, then, be sure you do not live in your husband's pocket, for that is not at all *comme il faut*," Aunt Euphemia said. Her luggage and her maid were already loaded into her ancient traveling coach, but she herself kept remembering last minute instructions for Bethia. "And we do not want people to decide that marriage has made you fall into bourgeois habits."

"No, indeed," Bethia replied. "But perhaps it might be best if you did not delay any longer, else you will not reach Maidenhead before dusk."

"No, indeed, that would not do," her aunt replied, turning her cheek up for a kiss. "For no matter what people say, not even the turnpikes are really safe after dark." She allowed one of her grooms to assist her up the steps into the coach, and the door was shut behind her.

The groom climbed up beside the coachman, but instead of giving them the signal to start, Lady Clovyle poked her head out the window and continued with her instructions to Bethia. "Now you must be sure to write to me once a week and tell me how you are getting on. And if you can spare the time, you may visit me in September, or perhaps October would be better. Well, there is plenty of time to decide that."

Without waiting for Bethia to reply, she sat back in her seat, then rapped sharply on the roof of the coach with the handle of her parasol, and they set off on what would be, at the pace Lady Clovyle thought suitable for traveling, a four-day journey to Bath.

Bethia's emotions were too raw to allow her to face anyone, even Digory, who had disappeared into the study as soon as they were done breakfasting together.

So she returned to her room and wandered listlessly around, unable to come up with any solution to her problems.

Finally, resolving to think of something else, she unpacked the small trunk that had belonged to Digory's aunt, and examined its contents.

The clothing was still serviceable, and although too outmoded to be of any particular use in London, some of the items might be comfortable to wear when gardening in the country.

Then at the very bottom of the trunk, Bethia found a packet of papers tied up with a faded velvet ribbon. Laying the folded dresses back into the trunk, she rang for a footman and instructed him to carry it up to the attic.

Once she was alone again, she untied the knot and unfolded the topmost piece of paper, which turned out to be a love letter from the Earl of Blackstone to Mary Ann, whom Bethia assumed was Digory's mother.

The late earl had been quite eloquent, and it would have been most romantic reading, had not Bethia known that he was deliberately deceiving a chaste and honest woman.

She could not bring herself to do more than glance at the other love letters, but she did read the letter from a Mr. Jackson Thwaite, who informed Mrs. Rendel that she was not, in fact, the Countess of Blackstone, since she had been underage and had failed to obtain the necessary permission from her father for the marriage. Therefore the marriage was null and void, even if her father were now willing to consent.

At first Bethia thought that the solicitor had erred in referring to Digory's mother as Mrs., but the last document explained everything. It was the marriage certificate for Mrs. Mary Ann Rendel, widow, and Mr. William Blackleigh, Earl of Blackstone.

It was signed by the vicar, two witnesses, and both parties to the marriage. And it was a completely worthless piece of paper.

As much as Bethia hated her cousin—whichever one had conspired to have her killed—it was nothing compared to the hatred she now felt for the fifth Earl of Blackstone.

He had casually and wantonly destroyed innocent people. It staggered the imagination to think how different Digory's life would have been if he had been the heir instead of being the bastard. And how his mother must have suffered from shame! If the earl were not dead already, Bethia would not have hesitated to kill him herself.

She was still considering how satisfying that would have been, when her musings were interrupted by a tapping at the door. Quickly, she put the letters out of sight in the drawer of her writing table, then wiped the tears from her cheeks and called out, "Come in."

It was one of the maids, and she carried a note. "Beg pardon, Miss . . . I mean, *Mrs.* Rendel," the maid said with a blush for her slip of the tongue. "But this just come for you."

Thanking the girl, Bethia took the note and broke the

seal. It was from Lady Edington, who had been at the wedding along with her husband, and it was an invitation to go out for a drive.

The sun was high in the sky when Wilbur Harcourt ventured forth to begin his campaign to force Lady Clovyle to admit that her niece was missing. At the speed with which gossip spread, by tomorrow a hue and cry would be raised, and as a loving cousin, he would insist that a Bow Street runner be hired to find the poor child.

Since he would give the runner a few hints as to the most profitable area to commence his search, by the time the week was out, Wilbur would be rich.

He was sauntering down Bond Street looking for precisely the right ear to whisper into, when opportunity found him in the person of Lord Keppel.

"I say, Harcourt, is it not ghastly? Like to have turned my stomach when I read it in the *Morning Post*."

"Read what?" Wilbur said absently, his mind occupied with choosing the precise way to arouse the viscount's curiosity and suspicions.

"Why your cousin, of course—Miss Pepperell. Or I suppose now I must call her Mrs. Rendel, though I never heard of the gentleman before. Can't believe I was cut out by a total stranger. Don't mind telling you, I'd not have been surprised if she'd taken you or one of your brothers, but this fair leaves me speechless."

His tongue continued to flap, but Wilbur was too stunned to breathe. Just as Keppel was turning to continue on his way, Wilbur managed to grab his arm and croak out, "What do you mean, *Mrs. Rendel*?"

The viscount shook off Wilbur's hand. "Confound it all, now you've wrinkled my sleeve," he said with a scowl that quickly changed to a grin "You don't mean to tell me you didn't know?"

"Please . . . " Wilbur said, reaching out blindly.

Deftly fending off another attack upon his clothing, Lord Keppel said, "The chit was married yesterday at Lady Letitia's house. Which means I've got to screw up my courage and offer for Witchell's eldest. Got a squint, but eight thousand pounds a year does remarkable things for her looks."

"She can't be married," Wilbur said, too dazed to believe what he had just heard. "She's—" He almost blurted out that she was dead, but he caught himself in the nick of time. "She's not mentioned a word of it to me," was what he said instead.

"If I were you, I'd be off to the Continent before your creditors get the word," Lord Keppel said, clapping him on the back and then strolling off.

Wilbur remembered nothing of the retreat to his rooms, but when he unlocked the door and let himself in, he found a letter on the floor. Picking it up, he broke the seal and unfolded it.

It was from Mr. Kidby, his uncle's solicitor, and as he read it, Wilbur felt a white-hot rage burning inside him.

His mind now clear, he began to plan how he would make his recovery.

Digory was ostensibly looking through the papers the solicitor had sent over relating to the management of various estates formerly owned by his wife's grandfather.

At a casual glance, the accounting seemed to be in good order, which was fortunate, since he could not focus for long on the columns of numbers. Despite his most valiant effort, he repeatedly found himself thinking about his wife and the reproach in her eyes, rather than about rents and expenditures.

He had just thrown down his quill in disgust when the door to the study opened and his wife entered. She had her bonnet in her hand, and although her color was high, her voice was calm when she spoke to him.

"I am going out for a drive with Lady Edington," she said.

"Are you sure that is wise?" he asked, rising to his feet and approaching her near enough to see that her eyes were red from crying. He reached out his hand, but she shied away from his touch.

"I understood that my will and Kidby's letters to my

cousins have taken care of any danger, so I should have nothing left to fear."

"I was not worried that you might be in physical danger," he said. "I merely thought to save you from needless embarrassment."

"Embarrassment?"

"Lady Edington knows I am a bastard, which might make you feel uncomfortable around her. I suggest you decline the invitation."

To his complete amazement, instead of seeing the reasonableness of his request, his wife turned into a veritable virago. She seemed to swell up to twice her normal size, and so fierce was the expression on her face that he found himself taking an involuntary step backward.

"How dare you!" she said, making no effort to moderate her voice. "How dare you imply that I should be ashamed of you! I am not such a shallow creature that I let other people's prejudices and bigotry determine my own opinions, so do not try to make me cower like a craven in my room, for I shall not do it."

He was trying with little success to calm her when the knocker banged twice, and with one last fulminating glare, Bethia marched out of the study, slamming the door behind her.

A moment later he heard the front door slam, and crossing to the window, he watched Bethia climb into a high-perch phaeton pulled by a pair of high-spirited chestnuts.

Then with a curse for his own lack of foresight, he dashed after his wife.

Chapter Twelve

With a smile for Bethia, Lady Edington signaled her groom to release the horses' heads, but as soon as the man stepped aside, Digory took his place, preventing her from setting off.

"It is perfectly all right with me if you drive over him," Bethia muttered under her breath, not even trying to keep the bitterness out of her voice.

Lady Edington glanced at her with one eyebrow raised. "So the honeymoon is over already?"

"I would prefer it if you took Little Davey along when you go out," Digory said.

"We have no need of a groom," Lady Edington said. "I am quite a noted whip, and even dearest Matthew trusts me to drive him."

"Please," Digory said, looking right at Bethia.

"No," she said flatly, and after a brief hesitation, he stepped aside.

Lady Edington set her horses going at a pace that was a bit faster than Bethia preferred, but she neither asked her companion to slow down, nor did she turn around to see what her husband was doing. She stared resolutely ahead, and did not even comment when they entered Green Park.

"Since Hyde Park is the only proper place to be seen at this hour of the day," Lady Edington said, "with luck we will not be interrupted here."

Bethia did not immediately reply, but the viscountess was not the least bit discommoded. "Please call me Adeline, and if you have no objections, I shall call you Bethia."

Bethia nodded briefly, but she was still too angry to speak.

Patting her on the hand, Adeline said, "If you will think of me as an older sister, I am sure you will find it is not at all difficult to tell me what has gone wrong with your marriage. I am not a gossip, and whatever you tell me I promise I will never reveal to another soul, not even to my husband."

Her voice shaking with outrage, Bethia said, "Digory has decided that if I stay married to him beyond my birthday, my life will be ruined. He plans to obtain an annulment. Have you ever heard of anything so ridiculous?"

"Astonishing! Does he give any reason for this peculiar idea?"

"Merely the fact that he is base-born, and that people will shun me if they discover his low origins."

"*When* they find out, for they will find out, you know," Adeline said gently. "It is not the kind of secret that can stay hidden for long. And he is correct. Everyone who is anyone will avoid you as determinedly as if you had the black plague."

"But I do not *care* what other people say or do," Bethia said, feeling quite put upon. "Why can no one understand that?"

"Well, then, if that is the case, there is nothing more to be said, and so you should tell your husband."

"I did tell him. And yet he still refuses to consummate the marriage." Bethia felt herself blushing, but when she turned her head, her companion was smiling. "And I do not find it at all amusing," she added.

"But my dear Bethia, it is positively hilarious," Adeline said. "There is no way on earth that he will be able to resist your charms for long, for it is quite obvious that the poor man is totally besotted with you."

"He may be head over heels in love with me, but he is also impossibly stubborn. You would not believe how pigheaded he can be. Why he slept in a chair for two nights during our journey back from Cornwall, and the beds were quite wide enough for the both of us," Bethia said, feeling her spirits lift a tiny bit at the thought that her companion might possibly be right.

"You must trust me, for I am very knowledgeable about

men, having lived with one for over nine years," Adeline said, pulling the horses to a halt and then executing a very skillful turn around so that they were heading back out of the park. "The only way your husband would be able to suppress his own desires for the next several months is if he were locked up in a monastery, and fortunately King Henry the Eighth dissolved them. Furthermore, so that you will not have to languish about for too many weeks, waiting for your husband to come to his senses, I am going to introduce you to my modiste, who is able to concoct the most wicked nightgowns imaginable."

An hour later Bethia was put to a blush by the sheer silks and delicate laces being displayed for her approval. "I shall look like some rake's mistress," she murmured for her friend's ear alone.

"Precisely," Adeline replied. "These will leave nothing to your husband's imagination. Once he sees what he has forsworn, he will soon contrive to overcome his scruples about taking advantage of your innocence."

"I am not sure I will have the courage to wear them."

Adeline shrugged. "Even if you pay Madame extra to have them put before her other orders, she will not be able to finish them for several days. When they are delivered, if you still feel they are too daring, you may pass them on to me, and I will be happy to pay for them. Matthew has grown a bit too complacent lately, and it is time he was reminded that I am not yet in my dotage."

Under normal conditions, Gervase Harcourt would not even have bothered to open the note from his brother, but having read the letter from Mr. Kidby, he assumed that Wilbur was interested in securing a place for himself in Gervase's curricle, to spare himself the expense of a ticket to Dover.

The note was brief and demanded that Gervase present himself without delay in Wilbur's rooms in Castle Street. So rudely was it phrased, that it was only the desire to rub his elder brother's face in their mutual misfortune that kept Gervase from ignoring it all together.

The address of his brother's lodgings was not bad, but

the rooms were low-ceilinged and miserable. Directly under the roof, they were unbearably hot for half the year and bitterly cold the rest of the time. They had obviously been used as servants' quarters when the building had been a private house, and Gervase was puffing by the time he had climbed the four flights of stairs.

His younger brother was before him and was already banging on the door. "I cannot believe Wilbur is so pinch-penny as to live in such squalor," Inigo muttered. "I warned him when he moved in that it would be his neck if any of my friends discovered how low he has sunk. Not that it matters now," he concluded as the door was swung open.

"It's about time you got here," Wilbur said crossly.

Feeling wonderfully cheered up by his elder brother's ill humor, Gervase smiled and said mockingly, "I see you have already read the *Morning Post*. If you want me to give you a ride to Dover, I must tell you that the only time I'd ever help you on your way is if you were crossing the River Styx."

"Don't be an idiot," Wilbur said. "I am not about to flee to the Continent when all is not yet lost. Now then, the first thing we must do is pool our resources and discover what we can about this Rendel fellow."

"Why on earth would we want to waste our blunt on a fool's errand like that?" Inigo said, leaning negligently against the wall and surveying the crowded room with distaste.

"What for? Why, so we can have the marriage declared invalid."

"Don't be daft," Inigo said. "Even if you succeeded—and there is no reason to think you will—no one but a parcel of gullible tradesmen ever believed that one of us had half a chance to marry our dear cousin." He picked up a half-empty bottle of Scotch and took a swig, then pushed himself upright. "So if you've nothing else to say, I've unpleasant business of my own to handle."

"You must help me," Wilbur demanded, but Inigo ignored him and opened the door.

"Hold on," Gervase said. "I begin to smell a rat."

At his words Inigo turned back. Standing shoulder to

shoulder, the two of them stared at their older brother, who now seemed to have difficulty looking them in the eye.

"Do you know," Gervase said, "Keppel told me a very interesting story about how Cousin Bethia's cinch broke when they were riding together. He said that if he hadn't been close enough to catch her, she would have been badly injured . . . or even killed."

"Accidents happen," Wilbur said with a shrug.

Inigo picked up the bottle again, this time by the neck. "I begin to see what you mean, Gervase. I also recall once when my cinch broke—cut in two it was."

"Cousin Bethia's cinch was old and rotted through," Wilbur said, backing away and almost falling over a chair.

"Now how would you know that?" Gervase asked, his temper rising. "Can it be that you arranged for the accident? What do you think, Inigo? Why do you suppose our dear elder brother is acting so distraught?"

"I wouldn't be at all surprised to discover he has been trying to gain an inheritance by killing off our cousin," Inigo said with a smile that made other men hesitate to challenge him to a duel.

"Stand back," Wilbur said, raising his fists, "or I shall thrash you the way I used to do."

Gervase began to chuckle. "It seems you have forgotten that we are now as big as you are."

"And that there are two of us," Inigo said, taking a step forward.

"And that there is no mother to run to with lies about how *we* have been picking on *you*," Gervase added.

The beating he and Inigo proceeded to administer to Wilbur was not bound by any code of gentlemanly conduct, and was far more savage than bare-knuckle boxing. By the time they tired of the sport, Wilbur lay unconscious and bleeding on the floor.

It was only a small return, however, for the many torments they had suffered at their older brother's hand when they had been too young to protect themselves. In consequence, even though his left hand was undoubtedly broken, Gervase felt a warm glow of contentment when he and Inigo descended the stairs and emerged into the fresh air.

Feeling more in charity with his younger brother than ever before, Gervase clapped him on the back and said, "I shall be happy to take you up in my curricle if you wish to make the dash to the Continent, but I warn you, I intend to leave within the hour."

"No, I fear I cannot tear myself away from all the lovely ladies in London," Inigo replied.

"You're a fool if you think they will visit you in the Fleet," Gervase said.

"Not to worry. I have been anticipating this eventuality ever since the old man died, and I have made adequate preparation. It is not, of course, the best of all possible fates, but I believe I can manage."

"Now you have aroused my curiosity. Have you perchance discovered another beautiful heiress?"

"Ugly as sin," Inigo said quite cheerfully, "and has not two thoughts to rub together in her noggin. Her father is a mill owner in Manchester, and he is so desperate to provide himself with an heir that he is willing not only to pay for my bloodlines, but also to allow me a comfortably long leash. Even got it in writing—signed, sealed, and delivered—that I can have as many mistresses as I want."

"The devil you say!"

Inigo nodded. "Four thousand a year and I don't even have to live with the old girl, just bed her until she's in a family way. After that little chore is taken care of, I'm free as a bird until the brat's two years old. The old man's going to pay me a bonus of five thousand for the first grandson and two thousand more for each additional grandson. He would have paid seven if he could have found a willing baronet or ten for a baron, but his daughter is getting so long in the tooth that he was not loath to settle for the grandson of an earl."

"Still and all, can't say that I envy you, but then I've always had a queasy stomach," Gervase said, offering his hand. "Well, I suppose this is good-bye then. Send word to me through Kidby if you ever decide to come to the Continent, and I'll be happy to introduce you to the more interesting people."

*   *   *

"What do you mean, you couldn't find her?" Digory said, rising to his feet.

"Just that," Big Davey replied, entering the study with Little Davey right behind him. "We looked all over Hyde Park, but she and Lady Edington were nowhere to be seen."

"Nowhere? Did you check any of the other parks? Did you check at Lord Edington's house? Did you check all the shops?"

"No, we didn't. Nor did we think to check all of Dorset or Somerset or Northumberland or the West Riding," Little Davey said sarcastically.

As much as Digory wanted to deny it, Little Davey was right. Without having some general area to concentrate on, it would be impossible to conduct an effective search.

And whatever happened to his wife, he was the one who would be responsible. Why had he ever been so foolish as to have allowed Bethia go out alone? He should have followed the carriage himself, rather than wasting precious minutes finding the two smugglers.

"There is no reason to worry," Big Davey said. "She has only been gone an hour and a half."

His words were no consolation, and from the expression on his face, he did not even believe them himself.

"We must work out a plan," Digory said, but his mind was in too much of a turmoil to concentrate. All he could think about was that the villainous cousin might not yet have read the letter from Kidby—that he might see Bethia unprotected and injure her or kill her in the mistaken belief that he could gain thereby. Or he might have read the letter and still want revenge.

Digory's thoughts raced down dark paths, but before he could give voice to his fears, he heard the front door open and close. Hoping and despairing at the same time, he strode out into the hall.

Bethia stood there calmly removing her bonnet and handing it to Uppleby, who had materialized silently from the nether regions.

Quickly, Digory looked his wife over from top to bottom, and he was relieved to see that she did not seem to have suffered any injury. In fact, she was smiling at him.

His relief that she was safe was tempered by the feeling that there was something not quite right about her smile. It took him a moment to realize that she was looking quite pleased with herself.

No, it was more than that. Hers was the smugly superior smile of a woman who has seen a man make a fool of himself.

Surely she could not guess that he had been so worried that he'd sent Big Davey and Little Davey after her?

He almost made his position even worse by asking her where she had been, but he caught himself in time. "Did you have a nice visit with Lady Edington?" was all he asked.

"Oh, yes," his wife replied, pulling off her gloves. "Adeline and I got along famously. In fact, we have both decided to attend the Chesterfields' ball this evening. It is sure to be a sad crush, and we agreed that we would not miss it for the world. Matthew is picking us up at nine, although if you have nothing to wear except your smuggler's smock, you have my permission to stay at home." Her smile became even more saccharine if that were possible.

"I have suitable evening wear," Digory said, thankful that he had listened to Lady Letitia the previous year when she had insisted that he purchase a town wardrobe.

Bethia looked at him expectantly, as if waiting for him to try to dissuade her from going to the ball, but he merely smiled back at her.

Married only a single day, and already he was beginning to realize that there were more dangerous reefs and shoals in marriage than he had ever suspected during his years as a bachelor.

The room was cold and shadowed when Wilbur regained consciousness. He attempted to get up, but the effort only triggered waves of excruciating pain that made him scream before he passed out again.

There could be no doubt but that their marriage was a nine-day wonder, Bethia realized once the four of them had worked their way up the stairs and the butler had announced them in stentorian tones. An expectant hush fell over the ballroom, and then everyone who could possibly claim the slightest acquaintance either with Bethia or the Edingtons began as unobtrusively as possible to work their way over to the door.

Despite their scarcely disguised eagerness to know more about the mysterious bridegroom who had succeeded in snaring for himself the most eligible heiress of the Season, Lord Edington introduced Digory simply as Mr. Rendel and added not a word of explanation.

The situation was becoming a little tense, and it was soon obvious to Bethia that the other guests were prepared to wait right where they were until their curiosity was satisfied.

But then a young man shouldered his way through the crowd, clapped Digory on the back, and said, "Rendel, by Jove, when did you get to London? And why did you not let me know you were in town? M'mother is still mad as hops that you did not visit us at Christmas as you promised to do. Now that you are married, she will be even less willing to accept any excuse, no matter how reasonable. You had best write her at once and say you will come in August, or she will make my life miserable."

The crowd began to whisper, but with three men to forge a path through the curious, Adeline and Bethia were soon comfortably seated in chairs set a bit apart from the chaperones and their young charges.

"My dear," Digory said, keeping his voice low, "permit me to introduce Edward Townsley, whose mother has doubtless never even heard my name mentioned."

"You wrong me," the young man said with a grin. "She not only knows who you are, but she has considered you only slightly below the angels ever since you brought her precious little boy back to her with his skin intact. I've written her, by the way, and coached her in what to say if any of the old biddies write for more information, so you need have no worries on that score."

Bethia decided that Townsley was the very person to ask about her husband's various adventures as a smuggler of brandy and men—he would doubtless be more forthcoming than Digory. But before the conversation could continue, the orchestra started playing a waltz, and Townsley led out Adeline.

"Well?" she asked.

"Well, what?" Digory replied.

"Are you going to invite me to dance?"

"I could tell you that I do not know how to waltz."

"Indeed you could. And then I would feel obliged to point out to you that there are at least a dozen of my former suitors in attendance tonight, all of whom waltz beautifully."

Without further demur, Digory led her out onto the floor and began to whirl her around the room with an expertise far beyond that of any mortal man.

The noise of the crowd faded, and all Bethia could see was her husband's eyes—all she could feel was his hand on her waist—all she could hear was her heart pounding in her ears.

It seemed a lifetime—an eternity—and yet the music stopped all too soon, and they returned perforce to where Lord Edington was sitting.

For the next dance she was partnered by Mr. Townsley while Adeline danced with Digory. When the music stopped the second time, other men approached to sign their names on her card. Some were turned away with a single look from Digory, but others were allowed to scrawl their names for the country dances.

Bethia did not question her husband as to why some were acceptable and others were not. She assumed that the men who were allowed to dance with her had been to a greater or lesser extent involved in espionage.

She also did not contest Digory's right to put his name down for all the waltzes. In fact, if it would not have been too scandalous for words, she would have preferred to dance with no one but her own husband.

In private he might not desire her as a husband is supposed to want his wife, but in public she could at least have his arms around her, and with that she must be content.

As soon as she was in her nightgown, Bethia dismissed Mrs. Drake and waited alone for her husband to join her.

But the minutes dragged past, one after the other, first a quarter hour, then a half hour. Despite the fire in the grate, a coldness began to spread, starting in her heart and chilling her to the marrow.

Finally, the need to be with him could not be denied, and she opened the connecting door. He was sitting staring at the fire, his legs stretched out in front of him. Without waiting for an invitation, she crossed the few feet separating them and laid her hand on his shoulder.

"Will you not come to bed now?" she asked softly.

"I think it will be better if we each sleep in our own beds from now on," Digory said, unable to meet her eyes lest he succumb to temptation. "So long as we muss both sides of your bed, the servants will not suspect anything."

His wife jerked her hand away as if she had suddenly been burned, and looking up, he saw such pain in her eyes that he knew himself to be lost. Fully aware that he was making a mistake, he stood up and put his arms around her. "I have changed my mind; we will sleep together if that is your wish."

"I am sorry," she said.

"It is not your fault. Come now, and I will tell you a story."

As soon as they were together in bed with his arm around her and her head on his shoulder, she said, "Tell me a story about when you were a smuggler."

"Those are not bedtime stories."

"You used that excuse before. But I need to know everything about you. Tell me how you saved Lord Edington's life."

She did not know what she was asking, but perhaps it would be best to tell her—perhaps if she knew more about the things he had done before he met her, then she would be more agreeable to having the marriage annulled.

So he told her, leaving nothing out and making no attempt to gloss over the ugliness—no attempt to alter the events so as to present his own deeds in the most heroic way possible—no attempt to make light of the danger he and Lord Edington had been in.

When he was done, she took a deep, shuddering breath,

and he thought she must be on the verge of tears. But when she spoke, her voice was calm.

"I feel as if I have been living in a fool's paradise," she said. "As if I have been little better than a songbird who is shut up in a cage, and who knows nothing of the great world beyond the window."

"The world is a dangerous place. Doubtless the bird is safer being cherished by its owner."

"Safer perhaps, but look what it has given up for that security—the sky, the sun, the wind, the rain. I was petted and cossetted by my grandfather, who could deny me nothing I wanted, and I thought I was more fortunate than the masses, who live in poverty and squalor."

"I am glad you recognize that."

"I am not so foolish as to think I would have preferred to live in Soho or in some peasant's hovel. But you have shown me just how restricted—just how superficial—my world actually has been."

She still had no idea how dangerous the world at large could be. As reluctant as he was to disillusion her, he had to do it for her own good. "Surviving by one's wits is not the same thing as uttering a witticism. Many of the spies who went to France did not come back."

"You need not worry that I am being romantic," she said, "for I know that war is not noble. But on the other hand, the tales you have told me have shown that there are things worth dying for, and that some men and women are willing to lay down their lives for others."

She was quiet for so long that Digory thought she was falling asleep, but then she spoke again.

"I think what I want is to find out what I am capable of doing. I want to decide for myself where I belong and how I want to spend the rest of my life. Do you understand?"

"Not really," he said.

There was another pause, and then she said, "Lady Letitia told me about going to Marseilles."

"I am not taking you to Marseilles," Digory said immediately.

"No, that is not my point. I just meant that I have never been allowed to think about what I want from life—I have never had the freedom to try something merely because it was what I wanted to do. Everything I have done, I have done because it was the proper thing to do. You may not have had a happy childhood, but you have taken the circumstances of your birth and made of yourself the man you wanted to be. I regret to admit that I have blindly accepted the life I was born into without even knowing that there could be more."

And then he understood, and he told her so.

Satisfied, she snuggled closer against him, and soon he could tell from her breathing that she was sleeping. Having her in his arms made desire turn into pain, and he was afraid that if he stayed where he was, he would forget all his resolutions and kiss her awake.

Before he could yield to temptation, he disentangled himself and slid out from under the covers. On tiptoe he returned to his own room and his empty bed, where after a long period of tossing and turning he likewise managed to drift off.

In his dreams he was a child again, listening to his mother crying in the night and wishing in vain that he could do something to comfort her. But gradually the dream faded, and he became aware that it was his wife who was crying in the other room.

He could not lie there and listen to Bethia weep, even if it was torture for him to share her bed.

"I dreamed I was drowning," she said when he slipped back under the covers and took her in his arms again. "The water was cold and dark, and I kept going down and down. And when I woke up, you were gone, and I was so afraid."

"You needn't fear your nightmares again," he said. "I promise I shall never again try to persuade you to sleep alone."

Chapter Thirteen

Oliver Lord Cavenaugh could not find fault with either the play or the performers, but he was well aware that the actors could have been speaking Russian and scarcely anyone would have noticed. The theater was packed, but virtually every eye was directed toward Lady Letitia's box, where that august personage was entertaining Lord and Lady Edington, and what was even more interesting, the former Miss Pepperell and her newly acquired husband.

During the first intermission the division had been sharply drawn between those fortunate enough to gain admission to Lady Letitia's box and those who knew all too well that they were in danger of receiving the cut direct should they seek to presume upon a mere acquaintanceship.

All in all, it was proving to be a vastly entertaining evening, and he was not at all sorry that he had invited several other aspiring dandies to join him in his box. Although none of them could properly be called friends of his, they resembled each other in their gullibility and penchant for gossip.

"I say there, Cavenaugh," someone behind him said.

Turning, Oliver saw it was Lord Herword who had screwed up his courage to ask the question Oliver knew they must all have been dying to ask.

"What can you tell us about this man Rendel? You seem to know him better than any of us."

With secret delight Oliver launched into the spiel that he had prepared for just this occasion. "Rendel? Indeed, it is impossible to explain. I cannot believe the scandal that will ensue if it becomes widely known."

"Scandal?" Bertram Brewster asked eagerly.

"Shocking, utterly shocking. That he would have dared—what gall he has displayed—what reckless disregard for the consequences."

He paused so long that Sir Edward Tyrwhitt blurted out, "Tell us more—we are all ears."

"All ears? No, no," Oliver corrected him, "one needs only eyes to see that abomination of a waistcoat he is wearing this evening. Ecod, did you not mark it? I vow, I was positively overcome with shame. Really, my dear Rendel, I told him, as delighted as I am to see you in London, you positively must allow me to introduce you to my tailor. Not that there is much chance, mind you, of making him into a pattern card of fashion, but there are limits, don't you know, and I cannot, I simply cannot have it bruited about that a friend of mine dresses with such total disregard for the sensitivities of his friends. I have my reputation to think of, I told him. Those were my exact words—I have my reputation to think of."

"Yes, but who is he?" Vivian Werge was foolish enough to ask.

Oliver raised his quizzing glass to his eye and inspected the corpulent young man from top to toe. Then his lip curled slightly. "He is my very dear friend. What else is there to know?"

Brewster snickered self-consciously and earned for himself a turn under the glass, so to speak.

After that everyone in the box displayed a passionate interest in what was transpiring on the stage, and nothing more was said about the mysterious Mr. Rendel.

In constant pain and too weak even to raise his head from the pillow, Wilbur Harcourt realized he was now in danger of starving to death. As near as he could estimate, considering that he had been drifting in and out of consciousness for the whole time, it had been at least two and a half days since his brothers had attacked him, and about a day and a half since he had managed to drag himself to his bed.

After calling for help until his throat was raw, he tried desperately to think of what he might be able to do to attract the attention of the tenants directly below him. He had still not come up with any plan when he heard someone unlocking his door. His life, he realized with relief, was going to be saved merely because he was in arrears with the rent.

"In here, Mrs. Fettes," he cried out weakly. "Help me, please, you must help me."

"It's six weeks you owe me for," she said from the doorway. "I'll be having what's due me, or I'll be turning you out on the street."

"Have mercy, my dear woman, for the love of God, have mercy. I am desperately ill, and I have had nothing to eat for days."

She crossed her arms above her ample bosom and said, "Ill, is it? With those black eyes it looks to me more like you ran afoul of some debauched female's cuckolded husband who gave you your just deserts."

"My dear woman, if you refuse to bring me food, I shall die in these rooms and then you shall have to testify at the inquest."

He could see from the expressions flitting across her face that she was weighing the advantages versus the disadvantages.

"And then you would never be paid for the amount I am in arrears," he added, hoping an appeal to her greed would tip the scales in his favor.

"Very well," she said, "I'll go to the market, but first show me the color of your money."

"My money?"

"You don't think that I am going to charge your food on my accounts, do you?" She let out a cackle and slapped her leg in mirth.

"Take one of my shirts—they each cost five guineas, so I am sure you can get enough by selling one to purchase a few days' supply of food for me." Actually, they had not cost him a farthing, because he had never settled up with his tailor.

She came into the room and began to paw through his shirts, which were folded neatly and stacked on the shelves he was forced to use as a makeshift chest of drawers. Then having apparently made up her mind, she scooped up two piles, one under each arm.

"Mrs. Fettes, I only want you to sell one shirt! All I need is some bread and cheese and a bottle or two of ale."

"I'll be having my rent first, my bully boy. And if these shirts don't bring enough, I'll be back, you can count on that. Once I have what's due me, then I may think about bringing you some food."

He started to protest, but she looked back at him and said, "That's presuming, of course, that you can keep a civil tongue in your head."

In the end it cost him not only a dozen shirts but also two embroidered waistcoats. He suspected she was cheating him, but at least she did not stint on the food or the ale when she finally brought them to him.

Indeed, she was quite pleasant when she assured him that she would also be willing to clean his rooms, which were disgustingly filthy, and do his laundry—all for a reasonable fee, of course.

By the time they returned from the opera, Bethia had the beginnings of a headache. She had never realized how exhausting it was to be on display—to smile and talk and never give any indication that she noticed all the eyes staring at her, all the fingers pointing in her direction. It was indeed a blessing that she had not been able to hear what the gossips were saying, for that she could not have borne.

But once she was safe in her own room, the tension slid away. Soon she would be in her husband's arms, and no one could hurt her there.

"A package came for you while you were out," Mrs. Drake said as she began to help Bethia out of her dress. "I put it on the bed."

"Thank you," Bethia said, wondering what it might be. She did not normally receive deliveries in the evening, and she knew of no reason why someone should have sent her a present.

But then she remembered the nightgowns she had ordered, and her face grew warm. Would this be the night when the argument about an annulment was settled once and for all?

It seemed as if everything her dresser did took twice as long as usual, but finally Mrs. Drake left the room.

Hurrying to the bed, Bethia picked up the parcel, which was much too lightweight to contain even a shawl.

Disappointed, she untied the string, unfolded the paper, and discovered she had erred. The package contained not one, but two gossamer creations. The first was palest ivory, as creamy as a baby's cheek, and the second was the yellow of a sunbeam and just as ethereal.

They were both the most exquisite examples of stitchery that Bethia had ever seen, as if fairies had done the embroidery. They were every bit as scandalously revealing as Adeline had promised.

With a sinking heart, Bethia realized that she could not wear any of these garments—not because they were too revealing, but because it would be nothing more nor less than the most dishonorable sort of knavery.

Perhaps knavery was not the right word to describe feminine wiles, but in any event, she knew she could not deliberately make it more difficult for her husband to spend the night in her bed.

For a moment she wavered, aware that she possessed the power to bind him to her forever, and yet knowing it was wrong to trick him into consummating a marriage he did not want.

On the other hand, there was no need to be precipitous about sending these garments to Adeline. As frustrating as her present situation was, things might change. There could come a day when she would be able to wear these lovely gowns with a clear conscience.

Carefully folding the nightgowns, she consigned them to the very back of the bottom drawer of her chiffonier, where neither her husband nor Mrs. Drake would be apt to discover them.

With one last sigh for what could not be, she climbed into bed and waited for Digory to join her.

The following morning Digory rose early. Leaving a note on his pillow so that his wife would not worry, he went for a ride in Hyde Park, where Cavenaugh and Edington had arranged to meet him.

Digory was a bit early, and he found the park deserted except for a few grooms exercising their master's horses. He had not long to wait, however, before Edington appeared with Cavenaugh beside him in his curricle.

They were laughing at something, and looked, in fact, as if this were nothing more than a game—a trifling amusement for whiling away a few idle hours.

"I was just telling Matthew here about my cousin's husband, the pompous Sir Percival Palk," Cavenaugh said when they were close enough for conversation. "He accosted me during the second intermission and said in his usually booming voice, 'My dear Oliver, pray tell me who this man Rendel is. Why, I have never even heard of him before this week, and one would presume that any friend of yours would be known to me.' So I replied in an equal bellow, 'Only if one were highly presumptuous.' He was quite put to the blush by the amusement of the crowd, and if I am extremely lucky, he may feel constrained to retire to his country estate for a long repairing lease."

Digory did not even smile. "I have been thinking of doing that myself."

"No!" both his friends cried in unison.

"Absolutely not," Edington said.

"The worst possible thing you could do," Cavenaugh said. "If you vanish from London as abruptly as you appeared, the *ton* will never stop talking about you."

"If you think to persuade me to stay here until the end of the Season, then I must warn you that nothing you say will change my mind. It is too hard on my wife to be the target of such gossip."

"You will cease to be of interest just as soon as someone else does something scandalous. In fact, you will slide down into anonymity so quickly, you will be lucky if anyone even remembers your name. And do not attempt to convince me that everyone will be on their best behavior for the rest of the Season, for that horse won't run."

"That is only half the problem," Digory said. "The other half, as you have so determinedly pointed out to me, is the matter of the wicked cousin. Or have you already determined his identity and neglected to inform me?"

"Actually Townsley, Nyesmith, and Fitzhugh have been busy little spies while we have been cavorting around town making merry," Cavenaugh said. "They have discovered that the youngest Harcourt brother—Inigo I believe his name is—was seen on the road to Manchester, and the middle brother was spotted in Dover."

"And the oldest brother?" Digory asked.

"No one has seen hide nor hair of him since the day before the wedding," Edington said, "but he has doubtless only been more successful at sneaking out of town than the other two. He cannot have stayed, because the tipstaves have been set on him by his creditors—he owes money to half the tradesmen in London if rumors are to be believed."

"Which means that as soon as some bored matron runs off with her groom, your problems will all be over," Cavenaugh said. "Perhaps you could persuade your wife to oblige us, Matthew. If none of your grooms are adequate to the task, I can loan you one of mine. He is a handsome brute, and would be positively irresistible to the ladies if he were decked out in evening wear."

With a laugh Edington cuffed him on the shoulder and threatened to make him walk home.

Digory did not laugh. Cavenaugh's words had come too near to the truth. What difference was there, after all, between a groom who aped his betters and a bastard ex-smuggler who passed himself off as a gentleman?

The answer was quite obvious: There was no difference.

"You are a fool, Digory," Lady Letitia said. They were sitting together at Almack's, watching Bethia, who was dancing with Roger Nyesmith. "Your wife has more courage than you give her credit for."

"My wife is afraid to be alone at night," Digory replied. "Without me beside her in bed, she cannot sleep."

"Did you hear what you just said?" Lady Letitia asked. "You have just admitted that your wife needs you, and yet you still insist that the marriage must be annulled. I repeat, you are a fool. And you are breaking her heart the same way your father broke your mother's heart."

"The situations are not the same," Digory said. "By her birthday, if not before, I am sure that Bethia will have found someone else to marry. Nyesmith, or perhaps Cavenaugh—she seems fond of them both. Even Townsley can give her a better life than I ever could."

"So you think her that fickle? That having given her heart to you, she should simply take it back and bestow it upon another man? There are women who can do that, but your wife is not one of them."

"She may think she loves me, but it is merely gratitude. She feels safe when she is with me; she has told me as much. Beyond that, I suppose she finds it intriguing that I am so different from the other men in her life."

"Bah," Lady Letitia said rudely. "I do not know why I bother with you. I had thought you had at least a modicum of intelligence, but now I begin to think you are as close-minded and stubborn as my first husband."

Before he could reply, he heard a commotion coming from the doorway. A crowd was gathering around a newcomer, and with a sinking heart Digory realized that the moment he had been dreading was at hand. The only thing to do was remove Bethia before the crowd became ugly.

He started to get up, but Lady Letitia caught his arm. "Stay right where you are," she said sternly.

He could have shaken her off without difficulty, but he did not find it easy to show disrespect for the old lady who had given him true friendship. On the other hand, his wife now had the right to his first loyalty.

"I am not going to sit here and allow Bethia to be pilloried for the crowd's amusement," he said. "The more she hears the offensive remarks people are bound to say, the harder it will be for her to forget."

Lady Letitia chuckled. "Such egotism. Do you think you are the only one in London with a secret? Wait until you hear what scandal is brewing before you decide that you must flee the scene."

"By then it will be too late."

"If I laid you even odds, I could still make a fortune betting that you are not the subject of this latest gossip."

Watching the people by the door, Digory realized that Lady Letitia was undoubtedly correct. Not a single head was turned in his direction.

Still a bit tense, he settled back into his seat, and a remarkably few minutes later one of Lady Letitia's cronies hurried over with the news.

"Lady Hester Hugford has run off to Gretna Green with Captain Trowbridge."

"Indeed?" Lady Letitia said mildly.

"Oh, yes, Mrs. Creighton saw them changing horses at the Green Man in Barnet, so there can be no doubt. They say her father and brothers are in hot pursuit, but the lovers have a full four hours head start, so it is quite possible that they will make it. Oh, but there is Mrs. Orlebar signaling to me. I must tell her the news."

As soon as her friend was out of earshot, Lady Letitia turned to him and said, "You must not feel bad, my dear boy, for while I freely admit that in matters of smuggling and sailing you are the expert, I will not yield the premier position to anyone when it concerns the follies of society. Therefore, you must believe me when I say you are not to worry. This mad gallop to Scotland will keep idle tongues wagging for at least a sennight, and by the time the elopement is resolved, someone else will have done something to attract the attention of the gossips. In short, my boy, you have just become yesterday's news."

"I bow to your superior wisdom," Digory said, feeling a vast measure of relief. For the first time since he had come to London, he began to think that this unlikely charade might actually succeed.

Listlessly Bethia looked at the bronze silk being displayed for her approval by Madame Verseau. "You decide," she said to Mrs. Drake, who gave her an odd look before beginning to discuss with the modiste the pattern and trimming that might be used to best advantage.

Bethia wished she had never agreed to this shopping expedition, which she suspected had been suggested by her husband, who could not understand her recurring bouts of apathy.

When Digory had done so much for her, how could she explain to him that she cared nothing for social acceptance? That with each passing day, she felt more and more estranged from "her world" as he persisted in calling it.

She had even gone to Lady Letitia for advice, but all her elderly friend had said was that men are different from women—that what is perfectly obvious to a woman is frequently incomprehensible to a man.

While Bethia could not dispute the truth of that statement, it still left her with no way to change her current situation.

"Mrs. Rendel?"

Bethia glanced up to find both Mrs. Drake and the modiste looking at her. "Excuse me, I am afraid I did not hear what you said."

"I was telling Madame about the sprigged muslin we purchased last week, and I was sure I had brought along a snippet to show her. But I cannot seem to find it. Did I perchance give it to you?"

"I do not think so, but I will check." Opening her reticule, Bethia looked inside. The scrap of fabric was not there—what was there was much worse. Instead of a handkerchief and a few copper coins, her purse now held a folded piece of paper on which her name was inscribed with bold strokes.

For a moment she could not move—could not think. Then she heard herself say calmly, "No, I do not seem to have the sample either. I am afraid we must leave it for another day." With shaking hands she pulled tight the strings of her bag and tried to think what to do.

Without even reading what was written on the note, she knew it was something wicked—something from the shadowy world where Digory had lived before he married her. The underhanded way the message had been delivered automatically precluded an innocuous note from one of her friends.

"Are you feeling all right, Mrs. Rendel?" Madame

Verseau now inquired solicitously. "You are looking a bit pale."

Without hesitation Bethia lied. "I fear I have had too much sun."

"Or too many nights dancing until the sun comes up," Madame said with an approving smile.

"Well, we have done enough for today," Mrs. Drake decreed, assisting her to her feet. "I shall instruct Little Davey to fetch a hackney for us, since I can see that you are not up to walking."

Bethia wanted to protest—to delay in any way she could the awful moment when she would have to unfold the note and read it. But at the same time, every minute she was forced to remain in ignorance was an eternity of unbearable suspense.

Silently, she allowed herself to be driven home and helped up to her room, where her dresser soon settled her on the chaise longue, pulling the curtains closed so that the light would not hurt her eyes. Then, just when Bethia thought she must surely be left alone, Mrs. Drake insisted upon laying a handkerchief dampened with lavender water across her forehead. Only then was the dresser willing to leave her alone.

No sooner did the door close behind her, than Bethia cast off the sweetly scented handkerchief and hurried to her dressing table. Opening her reticule, she removed the note and quickly unfolded it.

It was a map of Vauxhall Gardens, with a message written in block letters on the reverse side:

Mrs. Rendel—I know who your husband is and what he has done. The price for my silence is £3,000. Bring the money to Vauxhall Gardens tomorrow night. Wear a green domino and take a boat across the river precisely at midnight. I have marked on the map the place where I will be waiting. Come alone or you will regret it for the rest of your life.

That was all. There was no signature.

Chapter Fourteen

The next morning Bethia directed Little Davey to drive her to Rundel & Bridge, where she was to meet Lady Edington so that they could choose a gift for Lady Letitia—or so she told him in any event.

Instructing him to wait for her, she entered the premises alone and without undue problems, sold for a bit more than £3,000 a diamond bracelet that had come to her from her mother.

"We shall be happy to hold this back for a week or two," the clerk assured her, "in the event that you might wish to redeem it."

She did nothing to correct his impression that she had lost more at cards than she wished to confess to her husband, but it was more difficult to fool Little Davey, whose suspicions were aroused the minute she walked out of the jeweler's shop without Lady Edington.

For a moment she considered lying to him and claiming that her friend had sent 'round a note postponing their meeting, but she changed her mind when she realized that she could not under any circumstances go alone to a rendezvous with a known murderer.

Nor would it avail her to seek Adeline's help, for though Bethia had no doubt her friend would find it a marvelous adventure, two unescorted ladies were not really much safer than one woman alone.

Moreover Little Davey was the logical one to confide in, since he might possibly be persuaded not to tell her husband.

"Do not attempt to pull the wool over my eyes with more talk of presents for Lady Letitia," he said when he helped her into the carriage. "I am not such a fool that I cannot see there is mischief afoot."

"I can explain everything," she said, but Little Davey made no move to climb up into the driver's seat.

"It's not me you should be telling what's going on. Mr. Rendel is the one what needs to know about anything that's havey-cavey, 'cause he's the best one for thinking his way out of a tight spot that ever I met."

"Please trust me," she said. "There are reasons why he must not know any of this. Only meet me in the kitchen garden as soon as possible after we return home, and I promise I shall tell you the truth."

"The whole truth or only the part of it you wish me to hear?"

"I swear on my grandfather's grave that I will hold nothing back," she said.

With a grudging nod he took his place in the carriage and turned the horses' heads toward home.

"It would be better if we told Mr. Rendel," Little Davey repeated after Bethia had explained it all to him.

"He will forbid my going there," she replied. "You know as well as I do he would not allow it."

"Then it should not be done."

"In which case, my murderous cousin is free to spread slanderous gossip about me and my husband," Bethia pointed out, trying to keep her tone of voice reasonable in the face of such pigheadedness. "Besides, I have said you may tell Mr. Rendel everything. All I ask is that you wait to tell him until ten minutes after I set off for the river."

"But that means you will have to cross the Thames alone."

"Not alone. There will be a boatman. I shall not set foot in a boat that contains even one additional person, of that you may be sure."

"I still think it would be better if Mr. Rendel and I went with you."

Becoming thoroughly exasperated, Bethia said, "I do not know why you refuse to admit what is so obvious. I was told to come alone. If my cousin sees you or my husband, then he will not reveal himself. I do not know about you, but I do not intend to let him get off scot-free after he shot a man in cold blood."

From his expression she knew that the mention of the murder had struck home. Little Davey hesitated, mulling over what she had said, but in the end he was not yet ready to concede defeat.

"But the danger to you—"

"Is minimal," she said firmly. "You have seen the map, so you will know precisely where I shall be going. How hard can it be to follow at a safe distance? Even if you lose sight of me in the crowd, you know where I will be meeting my cousin, so you can easily be there at the crucial time."

"Maybe, maybe not. But tell me, what is to stop the blackguard from spotting us in the crowd? For if you've forgotten that the trap in Carwithian Cove failed because we did not think there would be a third man, then I have not. We've no way of knowing how many men your cousin may have hired this time, and we are all of us now so well known in London that we cannot hope to remain unrecognized."

"I will give you money, and you can go out right now and purchase a green domino for me and also two black dominos, one for each of you," Bethia said, feeling as if her nerves would not stand much more arguing.

"Aye, that is easily enough done," Little Davey said, "but if you did not think about disguises for us, then what other detail have you forgotten? I have learned the hard way that the best plans can go wrong just when you least expect them to." From the expression on his face, it was not hard to deduce that he did not consider her plan to be one of the best.

"But if anything untoward happens, then my husband will be there to deal with it," Bethia said. "And you yourself told me how adept he is at getting people out of dangerous situations."

Grudgingly, Little Davey admitted she might be right, but it still required another half hour of repeating her arguments over and over again before she finally got him to promise that she would have her ten-minute head start.

Which left her nothing to worry about at the theater that evening except how on earth she was going to cross the Thames in a small boat without Digory there beside her lending her courage.

It was entirely possible that Little Davey was correct when he told her she was dicked in the nob for thinking about undertaking such a dangerous errand.

With great trepidation Bethia climbed out of the hackney coach at the landing where boatmen waited to carry their passengers across the river. It was even worse than she had imagined. Not only was the water dark, but a light mist was curling up from the river, like the ghostly fingers in her nightmares.

The words she had said so blithely to Digory now came back to haunt her. *I want to find out who I am. I want to know what I am capable of.*

So easy to say when she was safe in his arms, but now the time had come to test her mettle. If she stepped into the boat that was now bobbing gently before her, she would be entering the world he had been telling her about—the world where a man's courage and cunning determined his fate, not the title affixed to his name.

It was not bravado that made her take the boatman's hand and allow him to help her down into the boat, because her terror did not abate in the slightest. Indeed, she felt more and more sick with each stroke of the oar.

But deep inside her heart was the knowledge that she could not do anything else. If it were necessary to save her husband's life, she would even cast herself into the water. In comparison, a short ride in a boat was merely a minor obstacle to be overcome.

By the time she stepped once again onto dry land, she was so proud of conquering her fear that she plunged right into the crowd, allowing it to sweep her along to the main pavilion. From that point on, however, she was on her own, and she dared not hesitate lest her fears overcome her resolution.

Circling the pavilion, she set off down the walk that led

in the general direction of the gazebo where she was supposed to meet her cousin.

Even the young bucks who were already half drunk and who were accompanied by half-naked females apparently recognized from the purposefulness of her walk that she was on her way to a rendezvous. Other than calling out ribald remarks as she hurried past, they did not attempt to accost her.

Turning down the last path that should have led to the folly, she found herself instead in a cul-de-sac that held nothing but a stone bench. With a cry of dismay, she turned to retrace her steps, only to find that her way was blocked by a man in a scarlet domino.

"Ah, my dear sister-in-law, how delightful you look this evening—so pale and wan and ethereal."

Bethia had expected one of her cousins, but when the man removed his mask, she recognized instead the notorious Earl of Blackstone.

"Cat's got your tongue? What a pity." He leered at her and took a step forward, but Bethia held her ground, afraid to let him suspect just how terrified she really was.

"I have brought the money," she said, holding out the bag.

He waved his hand negligently. "There is no rush. I have decided that I shall first claim a kiss or two—just a taste of what my bastard brother has been getting." Extending his arms, to prevent her from darting around him, he moved even closer.

Too late Bethia realized just how naive she had been. Little Davey had been right—unforeseen things had a horrible way of spoiling the best of plans. And as he had tried to point out, her plan had not been terribly well thought out in the first place.

Somewhere wandering around in the crowd—probably already at the gazebo where she was supposed to be—were her husband and Little Davey.

But unless she managed to force her way through the shrubbery, Lord Blackstone had her trapped. And if she screamed or tried to call for help, her cries would be lost among the many shrieks, squeals, and raucous laughter she could hear around her.

Which meant she had only her wits to depend on, and they did not seem at all adequate to the task.

If her husband were here, he would say it was proof that she did not belong in his world. Of course, if he were here, she would not be in any danger from the wicked earl, who was coming ever closer.

She was about to take her chances with the bushes, when two shadowy forms entered the cul-de-sac. The moonlight was strong enough for her to recognize her husband and Little Davey, both of whom were considerably larger than the wicked earl.

Unaware that they were no longer alone, Lord Blackstone said, "Come to me, my pet." Before he could grab her, Little Davey caught him by the back of the neck and lifted him half off the ground.

"We decided to join the party," Digory said. "Although if I had known who the host was, I would have forgone the pleasure."

Bethia edged her way past Little Davey and threw herself into her husband's arms.

"Did he hurt you?"

"No," she replied.

Little Davey shoved the earl forward, and he stumbled, but caught himself before he fell. When he turned around to face them, he had a gun in his hand.

"Surprised to see me back in England?" he said, his voice mocking.

"A bit," Digory replied. "I had hoped you'd drowned after you jumped overboard."

"It's not that easy to kill one of the devil's own," the earl said. "I was hauled out of the sea in a fisherman's net. I am sure there must be some cosmic significance in that."

"You would have done better to have stayed out of England," Digory said. "But the odds are good that there'll be a place for you on the next ship sailing for Macao."

"I fear I must decline your kind invitation to travel," the earl said with an insouciant smile. "Having sampled the pleasures to be found in foreign lands, I find I much prefer England."

Something was wrong here, but Bethia did not know what it was. The earl should have been at least a trifle intimidated, but instead he was acting as if this were all nothing more than a game.

"You will excuse me if I say that none of us are particularly interested in what a blackmailer likes or does not like," Digory said. "And if you think your pistol will protect you, may I point out that you cannot kill the three of us with only one shot."

"Ah, but you see, like all successful gamblers, I have an ace up my sleeve." Concealing his gun under his domino, the earl raised two fingers to his mouth and let out a piercing whistle.

There was a sound of hurrying footsteps, and a slight, fair-haired man appeared. Actually he was little more than a boy, probably about her own age, Bethia estimated.

"Ah, there you are, James," the earl said. "Let me introduce you to these charming people. Mr. and Mrs. Rendel, may I present my dearest friend, James Bartholomew, the Marquess of Baverstock."

The young man grabbed her husband's hand and began to pump it up and down. "Oh, I am so delighted to meet any friend of dear Geoffrey's. You must be very proud to know him. I myself shall always be in his debt. He saved my life once in Italy, you know, and my pocketbook on too many occasions to count. The Reverend Mr. Wooddale and I count ourselves most fortunate to have had him as our companion, for you would be astonished how many truly abominable people are to be found in all those foreign countries. Their only purpose in life appears to be separating innocent travelers from their money, and I freely admit, the Reverend Mr. Wooddale and I were both truly naive when we embarked at Dover for the Grand Tour. But once we met Geoffrey, he was able to guide us around all the pitfalls and protect us from the card sharks and others of their ilk. Is he not a truly wonderful person?"

"And now if you will excuse us, James and I have plans for the rest of the evening," Lord Blackstone said. "But before we go on our way, I believe you picked up something I dropped, did you not, Mrs. Rendel?" He held out his hand.

"No," Digory hissed in her ear, "he will take the money and still betray us."

But Bethia gave the earl the leather pouch containing the £3,000, even though she feared her husband was correct.

"If you wish to have further intercourse with me," the earl said with a smirk, "James and I are sharing rooms at the Albany."

"Do you realize how foolish you were to go alone to meet a blackmailer?" Digory asked as the hackney coach rumbled back over the bridge.

"I thought it would be one of my cousins."

"Ah, you thought it would be a man who had already tried repeatedly to kill you. Well, that certainly explains why you felt it was safe to sneak out to meet him."

"You needn't be sarcastic. I have already come to see the folly of my ways."

"Then why did you give Geoffrey the money after I told you not to?"

"Perhaps because I am desperate enough to clutch at straws; perhaps because—oh, it doesn't really matter," Bethia said. "I am too tired now to argue any more. I admit I was wrong to come, wrong to keep secrets from you, and wrong to pay off a blackmailer. It is all my fault. From start to finish, everything is my fault."

"No, I am to blame for getting you into this predicament in the first place. I should never have married you."

It was not his fault, but Bethia found she was indeed too tired to debate the matter any longer. All she wanted was to be home in bed with him.

Or better yet, back in his cottage in Cornwall where they could ignore the rest of the world.

As the days went by, Bethia discovered a sad truth about blackmailers. "Lord Blackstone is acting very peculiar," she told her husband when they were alone in bed. "He comes to all the balls, but he does not dance. It sometimes seems to me that all he does is look around the room until he sees us, and then he smiles and departs. Is it my imagination, or have you noticed it, too?"

"It is not your imagination."

"But why is he doing this?"

"He wishes to remind us that he has power over our lives. And doubtless it amuses him also to play with us the way a cat sometimes plays with a mouse before killing it."

"Well, he is making me very nervous. How long will he keep this up?"

"Until he needs more money. When his luck at the table turns, we can expect to receive another note. And doubtless he will ask for more the second time, and still more the third time."

"Will we never be free of him?"

Her husband was quiet for a long time. "If you tell Cavenaugh what is happening, he will be happy to arrange for an unfortunate accident. A fatal accident."

For a moment Bethia actually considered doing just that. Then she was overcome with shame and guilt that she had even briefly thought about doing such a wicked thing. "I do not think protecting our reputation is worth a man's life."

"Nor do I," her husband said. "So we had better hope that Cavenaugh never notices what is going on, because he might handle the problem without consulting us."

Wilbur Harcourt was in the worst predicament in his life. Very little stood between him and a cell in the Fleet. He had no money, and his landlady had stripped him of all his possessions that could be sold. Or at least she thought she had.

The first thing he had done when he had recovered enough to get out of bed, was hide assorted articles under his bed, pushing them back into the farthest corner, where she would not see them.

If she had been any sort of housekeeper, she would have discovered them, but she was in truth a slattern and a cheat, charging him an exorbitant amount for a very slovenly job of cleaning.

Unfortunately, although he was able at least to go out in public, he had insufficient means to leave London, and as his landlady reminded him every day, the tipstaves were after him.

What he needed was to find a friend gullible enough to loan him the money he needed to flee the country. Pacing back and forth in his now virtually empty rooms, he considered where best to look.

There were not many options. He could not, for example, go to any of his clubs or to the more popular gaming hells, because he was sure to run into someone he owed money to. And it had been weeks since he had received an invitation to a ball . . . but on the other hand, this was Wednesday, and there was a chance that he could gain admittance to Almack's.

But only if he still had a pair of knee breeches. With every muscle and joint in his body protesting, he got down on his knees and began to retrieve his few remaining possessions from their hiding place.

With glee Geoffrey realized that his moment of revenge was at hand. His bastard brother had come to Almack's with Lord and Lady Edington, but now the cripple was leaving early with his wife. Which meant there would soon be no one for Rendel to hide behind.

He had dreamed of this moment all through those months of exile. There had been times when only the thought of destroying his half brother had kept him going. And now that the opportunity was finally here, he would enjoy every minute of his triumph.

Waltzing with her husband was like nothing else, Bethia decided. With other men a dance was simply a pattern of steps, but with Digory it was a hint of what heaven must be like.

But as always, the music ended too soon. "Thank you for a lovely dance," he said softly, smiling down at her.

"You are quite welcome," she said, taking his arm.

Then above the chattering of the crowd, a voice rang out. "By jove, it's my bastard half brother, Digory Rendel. How the devil did a base-born smuggler ever gain admittance to Almack's?"

The sudden silence of the crowd struck Bethia like a blow, and she froze in place.

"It seems that I was wrong," her husband whispered. "My brother does not intend to bleed us dry. He prefers revenge to bank notes."

The crowd around them had quickly begun moving away, and they were soon isolated in the middle of a vast empty space. Then the murmurs started and spread like a wave. Someone snickered, and another person laughed, and the volume of noise seemed to rise in a horrible, discordant crescendo.

"Steady on," Digory said. "We shall soon be out of here."

Clutching his arm, Bethia managed to walk stiffly to their chairs, but just before they got to their seats two figures separated themselves from the crowd and stood directly in their paths. It was Mrs. Drummond Burrell and the Countess Lieven, and they were positively livid with rage.

Gradually, the crowd quieted down in eager anticipation of more bloodletting.

"We are not amused," Mrs. Drummond Burrell said.

"We must ask that you surrender your vouchers and leave at once," the countess added.

Sally Jersey emerged from the crowd to stand shoulder-to-shoulder with her fellow patronesses. "And if you are wise, you will not remain in London."

Now instead of amusement, the crowd began to grow hostile. Bethia feared that they might become violent, but a path cleared before them as they walked toward the door.

"I think we should take Lady Jersey's advice," Bethia said when they emerged into the cool night air. "I would like very much to go back to your cottage in Cornwall."

Instead of replying, her husband stopped abruptly. Looking up, she saw a man blocking their way, his face so contorted with anger, it took her a moment to realize it was her cousin Wilbur Harcourt.

"How dare you cheat me out of my fortune," he said. "It should have been mine—all mine!"

Bethia shivered and clung to her husband's arm. Her

cousin was attracting the attention of the coachmen and grooms waiting in front of Almack's.

"You should be dead—I saw your body—you are an imposter," Wilbur screeched.

"He is mad," she whispered. "Totally insane."

He began cursing, and when they tried to go around him, he scuttled sideways, again blocking their way. Oh, if only Big Davey and Little Davey were here! But her husband had instructed them to return at one o'clock, and it was not even midnight yet.

Casting her mind back at the faces she had seen in Almack's, she realized that Lord Edington was the only one of the former espionage agents who had been there, and he had left early.

It was not until Lord Blackstone came up and stood beside her that she belatedly realized how well he had chosen the time to denounce them.

"How interesting," he said. "It would seem that I am not the only one who bears you a grudge. Well, dear brother, never let it be said that I did not do you a favor."

Before her husband could reply, the earl pulled a pistol out from under his jacket and without hesitation pulled the trigger.

The noise was deafening, and at first Bethia could not believe the evidence of her own eyes, not even when Wilbur Harcourt staggered backward, then fell to lie motionless on the ground.

"Murder—murder—help me!" the earl cried loudly, casually tossing the pistol down on the ground in front of them. "Rendel has killed Mr. Harcourt in cold blood—shot him down like a dog on the street. Seize him before he gets away!"

Chapter Fifteen

To Bethia's great relief, the various grooms and coachmen just stood there, looking at the body on the ground and then at the three people standing next to it. Despite Lord Blackstone's order to seize her husband, they showed obvious reluctance to lay hands upon a gentleman.

"It is Lord Blackstone's gun," she cried out. "He is the one who pulled the trigger." Clutching Digory's arm, she said, "Tell them you are innocent. Tell them that it was Lord Blackstone who killed my cousin."

"Indeed, Rendel, tell us—we are all ears," the earl said, smiling maliciously.

"I did not shoot Mr. Harcourt," Digory said, biting off each word.

The earl turned to the crowd with a look of mock bewilderment. "Here is indeed a puzzle. The unfortunate Mr. Harcourt, God rest his soul, lies before us obviously dead. I say I did not shoot him, yet Rendel and his wife claim that I did. That is two against one, so it appears you must believe them when they say that I am lying. And yet . . . " He paused, and the crowd became even more attentive.

"And yet I would ask you to judge whether we can believe the word of Rendel, who has been passing himself off as a gentleman. Why, he has even gone so far as to marry this lovely lady, who is a great heiress. Indeed, until I recognized him in Almack's, he had successfully concealed from everyone that he is nothing more nor less than a smuggler from Cornwall."

Still the crowd did not move, and for a brief moment Bethia thought they did not believe the earl. But then he laughed and spoke again.

"And I should know, after all, since he is my bastard half brother, although I am sure I will be excused if I do not usually care to acknowledge the connection."

An excited murmur ran through the crowd, and two liveried grooms grabbed her husband's arms from behind. He could easily have gotten free, but to Bethia's surprise he stood quietly, making no effort to get away.

"No, no!" she cried, trying to pry the men's hands loose. "The earl lies!"

Fortunately, assorted gentlemen and even a few ladies began streaming out of Almack's, saying that they had heard a shot, and demanding loudly to be told what was going forth.

To her dismay, they were even quicker to condemn Digory than their servants had been. Ignoring her pleas to listen to the truth, they spoke only with the earl, and he was doing his best to excite their emotions to a deadly degree.

"What is the meaning of this?" an imperious voice rang out.

Bethia saw with relief that it was Lady Letitia. Using her cane to good advantage, the elderly lady quickly cleared a path from the doorway of Almack's to where the principals stood around the body.

As regally as if she were the queen herself—or perhaps, Bethia thought, it would be better to say as boldly as a general with an army at his back—Lady Letitia marched up to Digory and demanded to know what was going on.

"Lord Blackstone has shot and killed Mr. Wilbur Harcourt," Digory said in a voice loud enough to carry to the outer fringes of the mob.

Like an angry beast that has been taunted, the crowd surged forward, and assorted voices cried out, "You lie! Murderer! Imposter!"

Lady Letitia stopped them with a single raised hand. "Has anyone notified the watch that there is a body here?" she asked.

"I do not believe so," Digory replied.

"You, Mr. Farnall and Mr. Redvers, be so good as to see to the arrangements for having the body removed."

With obvious reluctance the two unfortunate gentlemen departed to find the watch.

"And you, Lord Jodrell, be so good as to tell your men to release Mr. Rendel."

"He is a murdering imposter," a voice cried out belligerently.

"Indeed, Major Henniker, and did you witness the crime yourself?" Lady Letitia asked. When there was no reply, she said, "Before you make any more unfounded accusations, I suggest that you think about the penalties for slander and defamation of character."

From somewhere in the back of the crowd there were mutterings of "bastard" and "imposter," but Lady Letitia ignored them. Looking around, she said, "Since there is nothing else to be done until the inquest, I suggest that you all disperse and go about your business."

By this time only one portly gentleman was foolish enough to try to take matters back into his own hands. "That scoundrel belongs in jail, and I say we take him there right now."

His attempt to rouse the mob to action failed.

"I personally guarantee that Mr. Rendel will be present at the inquest," Lady Letitia said with icy disdain, contriving somehow to look down her nose at the outspoken gentleman even though he was a good six inches taller than she was. "But if you truly wish to be of assistance, Lord Bomford, I suggest that you make it your task to see that Lord Blackstone also puts in an appearance. The earl, as I am sure you have noticed, has a regrettable tendency to vanish from London when it suits him."

A titter of laughter ran through the crowd, and Lord Bomford's face became quite red.

The earl, who had been observing the proceedings with a look of sly satisfaction on his face, now spoke up hotly. "I did not *vanish*, as you put it. My bastard brother here had me kidnapped and sold to the Barbary pirates."

Bethia felt a stab of fear. Despite his earlier lies, the earl was now telling the truth, and there was no way she or Digory could deny the accusation.

But to her surprise, the crowd was less willing to believe

Lord Blackstone when he was telling the truth than when he was lying outrageously. Instead of grabbing her husband and dragging him off to jail, everyone merely tried to get a better view, obviously not wanting to miss a single word of the duel between Lady Letitia, whom none of them dared to cross, and the earl, whom none of them actually liked.

"I see," Lady Letitia said. "So the reports we have been hearing for the last year about how you have been bear-leading Lord Keppel around Europe were quite false. You were really toiling as a slave in North Africa—languishing in chains perhaps? Tell me, for I am truly overcome by curiosity, what was the name of your owner, and did he perhaps put you in charge of his harem?"

Now the merriment of the crowd could not be contained, and it was a long time before the earl could make himself heard. "I never reached Africa," he said in a loud and angry voice. "I jumped overboard and—"

The rest of his reply was drowned out by the ensuing laughter.

"And—and—" Lord Bomford finally managed to say, "—and no doubt you were pulled from the sea by a fisherman."

His jest was received with great glee, and soon other gentlemen and ladies were likewise engaged in baiting Lord Blackstone, whose rage grew with each minute.

Lady Letitia signaled to Bethia and Digory, and the three of them managed to walk quietly away without anyone taking notice of them. But it was only when they were safely in Lady Letitia's carriage and the mob was far behind them that Bethia's heart gradually slowed to normal.

"I will never forget what you have done for us," Digory said. "I only hope you do not come to regret your very generous actions this evening."

"Don't talk gammon," Lady Letitia replied. "I can do what I please and say whatever I want, and there is no one in London or indeed in all of England who would dare give me the cut direct, or even host a party without sending me an invitation."

"I can only hope you are right," Digory said.

"You may count on it," Lady Letitia said, "not because I

am beloved by one and all, but because I know too many secrets. If I wanted to, I could destroy the reputations of virtually everyone who was at Almack's tonight. But enough of this—I must know more about what happened this evening so that we can figure out how best to get you out of this coil."

"The earl denounced us as you doubtless heard," Digory said. "And when we left Almack's, Wilbur Harcourt accosted us."

"Yes, he was apparently drunk," Bethia said, "for he started screaming at me that I had stolen his fortune. Then Lord Blackstone came up beside me, and before I realized what he intended, I saw a gun in his hand. Without hesitating, he shot my cousin."

"And did you also see the gun?" Lady Letitia asked Digory.

"Not until he tossed it down at my feet and began to shout that I had just killed Harcourt. Apparently no one else was close enough to see what happened."

"Dear me," Lady Letitia said. "This is worse than I thought."

"But I saw him shoot my cousin," Bethia said, fear squeezing her heart. "I can swear under oath that Lord Blackstone is lying. And he is not only a murderer, but also a blackmailer. I paid him £3,000 not to tell anyone that my husband is his half brother, and you need not tell me how foolish that was, because Digory has already given me a thorough lecture."

"We must assume," Lady Letitia said, "that you will be tried for murder."

Bethia clutched Digory's arm more tightly. "But I can swear on the Bible that he had nothing to do with it."

"Unfortunately," Lady Letitia said, "you will not be allowed to speak in court. As far as the law is concerned, a man and wife are legally one, and so a woman may not testify for or against her husband."

"And even if you could," Digory said, "no one would believe you. In the court of public opinion, we have already been found guilty of deceiving the *ton*, and a more heinous crime than that is scarce imaginable."

"But everyone knows the earl is a wicked man," Bethia protested. "Why, he is notorious—his nickname is Lord Blackheart. Surely no one will believe his lies."

Lady Letitia shook her head, and her expression was sad. "He is a peer of the realm, and that is all that matters."

Digory stood at the window of his room and looked out at the night, which was not as dark as his thoughts. He had been so sure that he knew the worst that could happen, but he had been wrong. By trying to protect Bethia, he had destroyed her life.

It had not been necessary for Lady Letitia to explain that the judge and jury would not believe him. From the moment the earl shouted out his accusation, Digory had known that his life would end with a hangman's noose around his neck.

Moreover, the revelations of this evening—that he was the bastard son of the Earl of Blackstone—would not be a "nine-day wonder." The ladies and gentlemen of the *ton* would never forget how they had been duped, and they would never forgive Bethia for her part in it. They would not be merciful, and he would not be there beside her to deflect some of the more vicious attacks.

And when the time came that she wished to marry again, she would discover just how vindictive the *ton* could be. Even though she had sufficient money to buy herself a husband, her choices would be limited to the dregs—perhaps a widower with too many children, or more likely a gambling man who would quickly game away her fortune.

Knowing just how helpless he was, Digory did not have the courage to go into her room and face her. She was doubtless soaking her pillow with tears, and there was nothing he could do—nothing he could say—that would alleviate her misery.

And despite his promise, after tonight she would have to sleep alone.

He heard the door behind him open and knew his wife was there. But he could not turn around and face her. He was indeed a failure in every way that counted.

A moment later her hand slid into his, and she gripped him with surprising strength.

"You were right," she said calmly. "You do not belong in my world any more than I belong in yours."

She said no more than what he already knew, but somehow hearing her words made his pain worse.

"But do you know," she continued, "I have come to realize that I do not belong in my world either, nor do you actually belong in your world."

Her words reached to the innermost part of his soul, where he had been trying to hide. Without conscious volition, he turned his head and looked down at her.

She was smiling up at him, and although there was pain in her eyes, there was no fear. "In your little cottage in Cornwall, we made our own world, and here in this room we also do not need to concern ourselves with anyone else."

Reaching up, she laid her hand against his cheek. "I love you," she whispered. "I would cross the widest ocean alone just to be with you. I will never stop loving you. You are the other half of my soul."

Shaken by the intensity of her emotions, he could not speak, could not reply.

"Do you love me?" she asked, the merest hint of uncertainty in her voice.

Finally, he managed to say, "I love you with all my heart and soul. I would willingly lay down my life for—"

She stopped him by laying her hand on his lips. "You will never die," she said, "for you will always be alive in my heart."

"Tomorrow—" he tried to say, but again she stopped him.

"Tonight," she corrected him. "We have tonight to be alone together in our own world, so do not think of tomorrow. Please! Please. Please . . . " Her voice trailed off.

He knew what she was asking, and she was right. No matter what they did, tomorrow would come. No matter how hard they struggled against treachery and deceit, they would soon be separated forever.

But they had this one night together, and no one had the power to take that away from them.

"Yes," he said softly. Then he bent his head, and pulling her close, he kissed her. Her arms slid around his neck, and her passion flared up to match his own.

After a long time, he lifted her in his arms and carried her over to his bed.

Bethia lay still, encircled by his arms, her head on his shoulder. "I do not think I will ever forgive you," she said.

Her words would have hurt, except that he could hear the smile in her voice. "For what?" he asked, stretching out until his joints popped and then pulling her closer.

"For wasting all those nights," she murmured, stroking his chest and dropping little kisses on his face and neck. "We should have done this that first night in your cottage . . . and every night since."

"Forgive me. I have been a fool."

"Most men are," she said with a laugh.

He made no attempt to dispute her statement. There were more pleasurable ways to spend the rest of this night than in pointless arguing. Besides, his wife was correct—he needed to do everything he could to make up for opportunities they had missed.

The force of her love was so great, Bethia felt as if she could surely prevent the sun from rising—as if she could by sheer will power keep the day from dawning.

But the light coming in through the window was already chasing the shadows back into the corners of the room, and on the street outside the milkmaids were calling their wares.

Bethia had not slept a wink all night, nor had her husband. They had loved each other until they were exhausted, and then they had talked of everything except what this day would bring.

"I do not want you to come to the inquest today," Digory said, breaking the silence.

"I must," she replied. "I must be there with you."

"There is nothing you can do. No one will be allowed to

testify except the coroner, Lord Blackstone, and I, and the magistrate will not believe what I say."

"I cannot bear for you to face them alone," she protested.

"And I cannot bear for you to watch."

You ask too much, she wanted to say. You cannot know the pain you are causing me.

But she could feel his pain in the tension of his body, in the words he had to force out, and she knew she had no choice. She would do what he asked, no matter what it cost her.

Lady Letitia was one of the few women present at the inquest, and as she had anticipated, Digory was bound over for trial on the word of Lord Blackstone alone.

The mood of the spectators was ugly, and the mob waiting outside was even worse. Were it not for Big Davey, she would never have made it back to her coach, and she could only be thankful that Digory had refused to allow Bethia to attend.

Just as the vehicle began to move, the door was jerked open, and Lady Letitia swung her cane up to repel the roughly dressed intruder. Fortunately, she recognized Lord Cavenaugh just in time to check her blow.

He was no longer dressed as a dandy, or even as a gentleman, and looking into his eyes, Lady Letitia could see why Digory thought him the most dangerous man in London.

"Matthew and I are going to speak with Lord Quissenworth," he said. "We may be able to persuade him to approach our beloved Prince Regent about a pardon. And if that option fails, we shall be making other arrangements on our own."

Without waiting for the coach to stop, he opened the door and swung down, leaving her to go on alone to the Rendels' residence, where Adeline was keeping Bethia company.

Lady Letitia was not looking forward to telling them about the outcome of the inquest, but Bethia surprised her. Instead of weeping and wringing her hands, she said, "I shall not let them hang Digory. If I have to kill Lord Blackstone myself to prevent him from testifying against my husband, then I shall do it."

Her determination was such that Lady Letitia could only marvel at how completely Digory failed to understand his wife's character. This was no timid little mouse who cringed at a harsh word, or hid herself away in a corner, afraid to face what life offered.

"It is clear how Lord Blackheart came by his wickedness," Adeline said indignantly. "Bethia has been showing me the letters the old earl wrote to Mr. Rendel's mother. He promised—not once, but many times—to marry her. See—it is all right here."

Taking the sheaf of papers that were shoved in her face, Lady Letitia said, "I agree that it is unfair, but I do not think the courts will be willing to hear a suit for breach of promise of marriage brought by a dead woman against an equally dead man."

"It is not only breach of promise," Bethia said bitterly. "He married her by special license, got her with child, and then informed her that the marriage was invalid because she had not secured her father's permission. That is out and out fraud, for you will never convince me that he did not plan such action from the very beginning."

Lady Letitia was about to repeat that it was indeed quite unfair, when she realized that not all the papers that had been thrust into her hands were love letters. There was also a certificate of marriage and a letter from the late earl's solicitor.

She herself had no real grasp of English common law . . . except for the part that pertained to marriage. And there were certain discrepancies in these documents that the courts might find very interesting.

Deftly, she steered the conversation away from the late earl. "Do not despair totally, my child," she said. "Even though none of us were allowed to testify at the inquest, all of Digory's friends can appear at the trial as character witnesses."

Her two young companions immediately began discussing what strategy might work in the courtroom, and they did not notice when she slipped the two crucial documents into her reticule, leaving the love letters on a side table.

Once that was accomplished, she wasted no more time. "If you do not mind, I shall take my leave now."

"Oh, must you?" Bethia asked. "I was hoping you could stay for dinner so that we can make our plans."

Lady Letitia had already made her plans, and the first order of business was to send for Digory's solicitor, but she did not tell Bethia that. There was, after all, no point in getting the child's hopes up when it might all come to naught.

So she pleaded exhaustion, and Bethia and Adeline were instantly all solicitude, reproaching themselves for not having noticed her fatigue, which was in truth nothing but playacting.

"And could I perhaps borrow Big Davey again?" Lady Letitia asked, making her voice as feeble as possible, which was not at all easy, considering that she was filled with righteous energy. "I may yet run into trouble on the way home, and my coachman is rather elderly."

Another plumper, but Bethia and Adeline swallowed it whole, even insisting upon helping her out to her coach as if she were too ancient and decrepit to walk unaided.

Ah, the gullibility of the young—it was really a crime to take advantage of it. But at least her motives were good.

As soon as they were out of sight of Bethia's house, Lady Letitia cast off her die-away airs and rapped on the roof of the coach with her cane. The coach stopped, and a moment later Big Davey opened the door, looking as if he expected to find her prostrate on the seat.

"Do you know who Mrs. Rendel's solicitor is?" she demanded.

"Aye, that'd be Mr. Kidby," Big Davey said without blinking an eye.

"Then fetch him to my house at once," she ordered. "We've not a moment to lose."

Lord Quissenworth was not happy when Cavenaugh and Edington were ushered into his office. He had a strong suspicion that they had come about that Rendel fellow, and he did not have the slightest desire to get mixed up in such a sordid affair.

Unfortunately, he could think of no way to prevent his two former agents from dumping the problem into his lap.

"There is nothing I can do," he said when they finished presenting their case. "I have no knowledge of the event—I was not at Almack's yesterday evening, and I do not believe I have ever actually met Rendel, so my testimony as to his character would be worthless."

"We aren't interested in having you testify," Cavenaugh said. "We want you to persuade Prinny to grant Rendel a pardon."

"Rendel was invaluable to you when we were fighting the French," Edington said. "You owe it to him."

Lord Quissenworth would have laughed in their faces, but he had a niggling feeling that any levity at this point would be extremely foolish if not actually dangerous. "There is not the slightest possibility that the Prince Regent will intervene," he said, keeping his voice calm despite the unreasonableness of their demand. "If it were only a case of murder, I am sure I could persuade him to commute the sentence to transportation. But I am equally certain that he will never forgive Rendel for pretending to be a gentleman. His Highness will take the deception as an affront to his dignity. So you see, there is nothing I can do. My hands are tied."

As if he had not heard a single word, Cavenaugh said, "Let me explain to you just how it will be. Simply put, it matters not what the verdict is, Rendel *will not hang*. Nor will he be transported. If he is found guilty, then he will mysteriously escape from jail and never be seen in England again. Do you understand me?"

So venomous was the look in Cavenaugh's eyes that a chill went up and down Lord Quissenworth's spine. For the first time he began to believe all the wildly improbable stories he had heard about the activities of his former agent.

"If we have to do this without your cooperation," Edington added dispassionately, "some guard or innocent bystander may be hurt. But the choice is yours."

"I shall see what—" Lord Quissenworth cleared his throat and started again. "I shall investigate the possibilities."

"Good," Edington said. "We will return tomorrow for another discussion. And you may rest assured that if you need money for bribes, I shall willingly provide whatever amount is required."

Lord Quissenworth was not reassured in the slightest. But once the other two men left the room, he was at least able to breathe again and his heartbeat slowed to a more normal speed.

For a moment he toyed with the idea of arranging for extra guards to be put on that cursed imposter Rendel. After all, what his former subordinates were demanding was totally unethical and completely illegal, and if it ever came out that he had participated—even though he was coerced—then his career would come to an abrupt end.

On the other hand, if he did not cooperate fully, he rather suspected that he would spend the rest of his life—which might be considerably shorter than the three score and ten allotted to men—looking over his shoulder.

This was clearly a case where prudence demanded that he bend a few rules, Lord Quissenworth decided, or if necessary, he was even prepared to break the law. It was, after all, morally justified since Rendel had in truth served England well in her hour of need.

A bit more thinking along that line, and Lord Quissenworth managed to persuade himself that it was nothing more nor less than his patriotic duty to rescue Rendel, the unsung hero of England, from imprisonment.

Lady Letitia did not waste any time on polite formalities. As soon as Owens ushered in Mr. Kidby, she handed him the letter written over a quarter of a century earlier.

"Do you see what caught my eye?" she asked.

"Indeed I do," the solicitor said. "If I were writing a letter like this, I would be much more specific. Something along the lines of, 'The Ecclesiastical Court of whatever, meeting on the n-th day of whenever, has ruled that the marriage of whoever, et cetera, has been declared invalid.' Yet all this Mr. Thwaite says is, 'Your marriage to the Earl of Blackstone is invalid.' In addition, I am not at all sure that a court would have dissolved the marriage for the reason herein stated, unless the father of the bride petitioned for redress. I could be wrong, but the marriage laws are not all black and white. There are a lot of gray areas in cases such as this one."

"I have one more document," Lady Letitia said, handing him the marriage certificate.

He read it swiftly, then whistled under his breath. "My suspicions have now become a certainty. The only way the late earl could have had this marriage declared invalid is if he perjured himself. The law is quite clear—a widow does not need anyone's permission to remarry, no matter how young she is."

"Then you think we have a case?"

"If we can prove that Mrs. Rendel's first marriage was legal and that her first husband was dead at the time of her marriage to the earl, then I think we may have a very interesting day in court. There is, of course, a chance that the earl had the foresight to destroy the pertinent records years ago. Or the parish church may have burned since then, or the sexton may have kept inadequate records in the first place. But I shall send my junior partner himself to Cornwall. Do you have any idea where the first marriage and the death of the first husband may have occurred?"

"No, but I can provide your partner with an escort. Big Davey Veryan will doubtless be able to supply the information you need, and in addition, he will be able to persuade even the most recalcitrant vicar to cooperate."

"I believe I will also send clerks to each of the ecclesiastical courts that would have had jurisdiction in this case, just to be sure that we are not wrong in our supposition that there was no actual hearing. And to hedge our bets, since we do not know for sure that the necessary documents still exist, I shall secure the services of the best barrister in the City and instruct him to do his best to delay the actual trial," Mr. Kidby said, "although realistically speaking, we have little chance of gaining more than a few extra days. Too many important people will be demanding instant justice."

"Or instant injustice, as the case may be," Lady Letitia said.

Chapter Sixteen

That evening Bethia delayed as long as possible, but eventually she had to retire to her bed, which was empty and cold even though at Mrs. Drake's behest the maid had brought up a pair of hot bricks wrapped in flannel.

Absolutely miserable, Bethia shivered in the dark. How could she sleep without Digory beside her? Who would chase away the nightmares that still tormented her?

He had promised that she would never again have to sleep alone . . . and he was a man of his word . . . which meant she was not—could not be—alone.

Closing her eyes, she could almost feel his arms pulling her close, almost hear his words calming her fears, and she knew he had spoken the truth.

Nothing could keep them apart. Reality was not this empty bed; reality was the two of them together forever. Immeasurably comforted by this sense of his presence, she whispered, "My love, although you are not close enough to feel the touch of my hand, and you cannot hear my words, you will always be in my heart. No matter what happens, no one can ever truly separate us."

Her sleep that night was deep and dreamless, and she woke up the next morning with no more fears. While she did not precisely bounce out of bed, at least she was able to face the day with a degree of resolution she had not thought possible the evening before.

Which was a good thing, because rather than the usual stack of invitations, there was only a single letter on the tray when the maid brought up Bethia's hot chocolate. When Bethia broke the seal and unfolded the paper, she discovered it was neither an invitation nor a note of sympathy and support.

Instead, it was a cleverly drawn caricature entitled, "The Barbarian at the Gate," and it depicted her husband dressed in knee breeches and a peasant's smock and wearing a hangman's noose around his neck instead of a cravat. He was banging on the door of Almack's, but from the window above him, the patronesses were emptying a bowl of punch over his head.

Bethia's first reaction was anger, but almost at once she began to chuckle. What the person who had sent this had forgotten was that the barbarians had been the victors— they had swept across Europe and had conquered not only the more primitive countries, but also the vast and mighty and "civilized" Roman Empire.

With mild surprise she realized she was cast from the same mold as her grandfather, and anyone who thought she had inherited nothing from him except a vast fortune was in for a rude awakening. Admittedly, he had on more than one occasion suffered minor setbacks, but he had always managed to convert apparent defeat into solid triumph.

At this moment she was not sure precisely what she could do to retrieve her husband from jail, but there was bound to be a solution if she put her mind to it. And Digory himself should be able, with the proper encouragement, to think of some way out of this coil. After all, according to Little Davey her husband was a dab hand at getting out of tight spots.

She realized that Digory would doubtless forbid her to visit him in jail, but he would also soon discover that she was not one to follow orders blindly. Although now that she thought about it, he had already noticed that character flaw when they were at Carwithian Cove. Even so, he did not yet know how stubborn she could be when the situation warranted it.

Leaving the rest of her hot chocolate untouched, she climbed out of bed and rang for Mrs. Drake.

Having ample funds, Digory had no problem paying four times the usual cost for a cot in Newgate Prison, and he thus secured for himself a private cell. The accommodations still left a lot to be desired.

It was not, however, the hardness of his bed nor the noise of the other prisoners that kept him awake, rather it was concern for his wife, coupled with no small degree of anxiety about his own fate that kept him tossing and turning until the wee hours of the morning.

When he finally did sink into a deep sleep, he was all too soon awakened by Youngblood, who arrived with a change of clothing and assurances that there were no major problems back home. "Cook quit without giving notice. Claimed her heart was too weak for her to live in the same house with a murderer. Two of the kitchen maids went with her, and they was all three roundly booed by the rest of the servants. Mr. Uppleby has already taken steps to secure replacements."

No sooner was Youngblood finished shaving and dressing Digory, than Lord Cavenaugh appeared, delicately waving his scented handkerchief under his nose until the turnkey departed, at which time Cavenaugh abandoned his role of dandy and began explaining the rudiments of the plan he and Lord Edington were already devising to free him from jail.

Before Digory could point out the shortcomings in their scheme, Lady Letitia arrived with her butler, who was carrying a basket filled with enough provisions to feed half the prisoners in the jail. "Dear boy, you look worse than you did our last morning in Marseilles," she said with a laugh, "and you cannot possibly be that hung over this morning."

To his surprise, she appeared to be in remarkable spirits—all the more astounding since she had looked every year of her age the previous day at the inquest.

Townsley came in next. He said nothing beyond a terse greeting. Remembering the months that the younger man had spent in a French prison, it did not surprise Digory that the younger man's restlessness was even more pronounced than usual.

Then Fitzhugh wandered in as casually as if he made a daily habit of strolling through jails. "Nyesmith is down at the docks, checking out the possibilities for ships," he explained. "What is your pleasure, Rendel? I suppose the colonies would be the safest, although a bit dull. On the other hand, from what I've heard, if one goes far enough west—into Kentucky or Ohio—there is still plenty of excitement to be found."

"There is quicker profit to be made in the Far East," Townsley said, "and I'm not talking about India. China cannot forever keep her doors all but shut to western traders, and there's a fortune waiting to be made in the silk and tea trade."

"Rendel already has a large enough fortune," Cavenaugh pointed out.

"And I am too old to deliberately wish for any more adventures," Digory added.

Lady Letitia took umbrage at that remark, but before she could finish scolding him for his lack of gumption, an elegantly dressed stranger was admitted by the turnkey.

The newcomer's reception bordered on the hostile until Lady Letitia introduced him. "This is Sir William Lyttcott, K.C. I have arranged for him to defend you in court."

"If it comes to that," someone muttered, but Digory could not tell who had spoken so indiscreetly.

The barrister was slender and scarcely taller than Lady Letitia, but he spoke with all the assurance of a much larger man. "I have already met with Mr. Kidby this morning. He has briefed me quite thoroughly about your case. Still and all, if you have a few moments free in the next day or so, it might not be a bad idea to go over some of the points of our defense with you before the actual trial."

"And when is the trial?" Lord Cavenaugh asked with a hard edge on his voice.

Sir William ignored Cavenaugh even while he answered the question. "Despite my every effort to have it postponed, Mr. Rendel, your trial has been scheduled for a week from today at ten o'clock."

"In truth, I would as soon have it over and done with," Digory said, not looking directly at any of his friends.

"Tut, tut," the barrister said. "Let us not welcome defeat before it actually stares us in the face. While I am well aware that I do not cut an imposing figure, my record before the bar is quite impressive. I have secured freedom for the majority of my clients, a vast number of whom were more than likely guilty."

"But I am innocent," Digory replied, "which will doubtless make your task more difficult."

"Well spoken," Mr. Lyttcott said, clapping him on the back. "I like a client with a bit of wit. Remember, you must look confident when you are in the defendant's box. Under no circumstances give any sign that you are unsure what the outcome of the trial will be."

"Oh, I shall have no trouble with that. I have every confidence that I shall be found guilty and sentenced to hang."

"Balderdash!" Sir William said, his cheerful demeanor not wavering in the slightest. "I have had years of experience at the Old Bailey, and even I would not wager a farthing on the outcome of any trial, no matter how obvious the case might appear to be. Too much hinges on the judge, don't you see, and even they are unpredictable. The most lenient can be harsh because his morning tea happened to be brewed not to his liking, and the strictest stickler for proper procedure can ignore every objection from the prosecutor because the day is fine and he wishes to shed his wig and robe and escape for a drive in the country with his mistress. No, no, my dear fellow, the law is indeed capricious, and Lady Luck can easily smile on us."

"Or just as easily turn her face away," Digory pointed out.

"Too true," the barrister said, "but you will find that in judicial matters I am luckier than most."

His words provided little comfort, and once the barrister departed, Digory exerted every effort to send his other visitors on their way also.

Unfortunately, he had not had five minutes alone before he heard the sound of the key again turning in the lock. Feeling quite put upon, he shouted angrily, "No more visitors!"

But the door opened anyway, and his half sister, Lady Cassie, entered. "Really, Digory, it is too bad what you have done."

At least she was accompanied by her husband, which did

little to improve Digory's mood. "It needed only this," he said, feeling a strong urge to pound his fists against the stone walls surrounding him.

"You did not even let us know that you were coming to London," Cassie said indignantly, "and then, as if that were not bad enough, we were obliged to read in the paper that you were in jail, awaiting trial on a charge of murder! Why in heaven's name did you not send for us at once?"

"I did not send for you because I did not wish to have your reputation ruined by association with a condemned murderer," he said, "as you could have easily figured out for yourself before you came on this fool's errand."

But Cassie was not willing to listen to reason. "It is all quite ridiculous—" her voice broke, and before he could stop her, she threw herself weeping into his arms. "You could never shoot a man down in cold blood—never! They are fools to listen to Geoffrey. He is out-and-out evil."

"Really, Cassie, if you must soak someone's shirt, let it be your husband's." Digory tried to detach her, but she clung like a limpet. "You should have kept her at home," he told his brother-in-law. "She does not belong here."

Richard Hawke smiled and shrugged. "She would have come with or without me. And in any event, I had a mind to find out how you managed to get yourself into such a mess."

"I was fool enough to ape my 'betters,'" Digory said. "The rest followed as night follows day."

Again he heard the jangle of keys in the corridor, and a moment later his wife stepped into the cell.

For what seemed like an eternity she just stared at him. Then she said in a voice that betrayed no emotion, "I had not realized what comforts were provided for prisoners."

With a strange noise that was halfway between a laugh and a sob, Cassie pulled free of his arms and wiped her eyes with the handkerchief her husband held out to her. "You must be my sister-in-law," she said. "I shall never forgive Digory for not inviting us to the wedding. You would think he was ashamed of me."

Digory did not bother trying to deny the accusation, but

Cassie and Bethia now ignored him, chattering away as if they were bosom bows.

He was, in fact, more than a little astonished. Not that the two women were getting along so well—he had thought they would like each other. No, what was puzzling him was that his wife looked as if she had not a care in the world.

"I returned a pair of books to Hookham's on my way over here," he heard her say, "and it was vastly amusing. You would have thought I was that monster Napoleon, so fast did everyone flee the premises."

Her words touched off his temper, which he had thought was well under control. "What the deuce do you mean, you went to Hookham's? Are you entirely witless? You could have sent Little Davey—you could have sent a maid—you should have known what kind of a reception you would get—"

"Indeed I did know," she said, staring at him with a rather cool expression on her face, "for you have certainly warned me often enough. If they discover you are not a gentleman, they will ostracize me, you said, and they have certainly done just that. If they know you are a bastard, they will taunt me and call me names, you said, and indeed, I have heard any number of epithets this morning, half of which I have not even understood. But you neglected to mention the caricatures. I received this in the morning post, and there are more in all the shop windows."

Reaching into her reticule, Bethia pulled out a folded piece of foolscap and handed it to him.

He unfolded it and stared down at the drawing, angry at himself that he had failed to protect her from such things.

Removing it from his grasp, she held it out to Cassie. "Rather droll, do you not agree?"

"I find nothing amusing about it," Digory said.

"But you see," Bethia said, a rather smug smile on her face, "they forgot one thing, namely that the barbarians succeeded in storming the gates." Coming over to him, she slid her arms around his waist and looked up into his eyes. "Do you seriously believe that we shall let them hang you?"

"We?" he said, fear roughening his voice. Surely Cavenaugh and the others had enough sense not to involve her in their plotting.

"We," Bethia said. "Those of us who love you and those of us who call you friend. Am I not right?" she said, turning to Richard Hawke. "Will you allow them to hang him?"

"No," Richard said, "you need have no worries on that score. If Digory is found guilty, we will contrive to smuggle him out of jail and then out of England. I have two ships in port at the moment, so it will not be hard to arrange."

"There, you see," Bethia said. "This is all for the best. Now that the worst has happened, just as you predicted, you will have to accept what I have been telling you all along."

"And what is that?" he said, stroking her hair.

"That I care not a fig what any of them think or say or do. The 'ladies' and 'gentlemen' of the *haut ton* have no power to hurt me because their opinions do not matter to me."

He started to point out that she could not leave England with him because she was afraid of the sea, but almost as if she could read his mind, she said, "When you are beside me, I am not afraid of anything—not the deepest ocean, not the densest fog. You must accept that I am going with you, for if you try to slink away without me, I shall simply follow you. And I shall find you, even at the ends of the earth."

Bethia had never before had occasion to be inside the Old Bailey, and she found it was far smaller than she had imagined. The spectator's gallery was packed, and the only empty seats were the ones around her and Adeline and Little Davey. As far as she could tell, that was the only positive benefit of the *ton*'s desire to ostracize her and anyone else connected with her or her husband, who was even more thoroughly isolated in the defendant's box.

"Look there," Adeline said, speaking directly into Bethia's ear and pointing at someone below them. "Is that not odd?"

At first Bethia thought her friend was directing her attention to Lord Blackstone, who with his cohorts around him was sitting behind the prosecutor, but then Adeline said, "I was wondering why Lady Letitia did not join us today."

Shifting her glance, Bethia saw that Digory's barrister had been joined by Mr. Kidby and Lady Letitia. The solicitor was handing over some papers to Mr. Lyttcott and the two of them began an intense conversation. A few minutes later, Mr. Kidby and Lady Letitia took seats directly behind the barrister.

"Whatever do you suppose is going on?" Adeline asked. "And what on earth could those papers be?"

Bethia could not answer, but in her heart she prayed for a miracle, which no longer seemed totally impossible because Lady Letitia was smiling quite smugly.

A few minutes later, everyone rose to their feet and the judge entered and took his place behind the bench. The last murmurs died down, and everyone listened intently when he asked the question, "How do you plead?"

Before Digory could reply, Mr. Lyttcott rose to his feet and said, "With all due respect, my lord, I must point out that my client, Digory Anderby, Lord Blackstone, alias Digory Rendel, cannot be tried by this court since he is a peer of the realm and thus can only be tried before the House of Lords."

For a moment there was stunned silence, then the courtroom erupted with noise as everyone tried to talk at once. The judge banged his gavel repeatedly but to little avail. Only his threat to have the room cleared of spectators succeeded in quieting the mob.

Through it all, Mr. Lyttcott stood quietly, a faint smile on his face. When he could finally be heard, he said merely, "If I might approach the bench, my lord?"

The judge nodded, and the barrister took the papers Mr. Kidby had brought and handed them over to the judge, who started reading them.

It seemed a lifetime of unbearable suspense to Bethia, but it was probably only ten minutes before the judge raised his head and said, "As this court has no jurisdiction to try Digory Anderby, Lord Blackstone, this case is dismissed."

The judge rose to his feet, but before he could take a

step, a voice rang out. "You lie! He is nothing but a bastard! I am the rightful Earl of Blackstone!"

It was Geoffrey, the erstwhile Lord Blackstone, and he was livid with rage.

"I beg to correct you," the judge said with a look of disgust on his face. "It would appear that you are nothing more than the illegitimate offspring of a bigamous marriage."

"You lie, you lie!" Geoffrey shrieked. Reaching under his jacket, he pulled out a gun and aimed it at the judge, who immediately ducked down behind the bench. "It is all a plot to deny me my heritage!"

All Geoffrey's supporters were now scrambling over each other in their attempt to get away from him as fast as possible, which made it impossible for the bailiffs to reach him—not that they were exerting any particular effort to apprehend the onetime earl, who now leveled his pistol at Digory.

"You are the imposter, and I am the rightful earl," Geoffrey cried out. "I will see you dead at my feet if I have to hang for it myself!"

To Bethia it seemed as if nothing could save her husband, and she would have thrown herself from the balcony onto the madman below if Little Davey had not caught her arms and held her back.

The shot and the scream were simultaneous, and Bethia felt her heart stop beating. But to her astonishment, her husband did not fall down nor did he seem to be the least bit discomposed.

Indeed, it was Geoffrey who was now screaming and clutching his right arm to his chest. "You've broken my arm," he wailed.

"And I shall break your head if you don't stop sniveling," Lady Letitia said, holding her cane up ready to strike him a second time if that should prove necessary. "Bailiff, I suggest that you retrieve the pistol this scoundrel was attempting to use. I would not be at all surprised to discover it matches the one that was used to murder Mr. Harcourt."

Digory could not fault his friends for wanting to celebrate the splendid coup that Lady Letitia had engineered, but it was getting later and later, and the revelry showed no sign of abating. As much as he liked his friends, he could not help wishing that they would all go home and leave him alone with his wife, who had scarcely moved a step away from him since his release from custody.

"Do you suppose they will notice our absence if we slip out?" he murmured now.

"Do you suppose I care if they do notice?" Bethia replied, smiling up at him.

"Then after you, m'lady," he said, his heart nearly bursting with pride that she loved him above all others.

"I suppose we shall have to give a ball," Bethia said while he was brushing out her hair.

"A ball?" Digory asked blankly, his mind on other, more delightful activities.

"Well, we could, of course, have a Venetian breakfast first, but there will be so very many people who will be scrambling to secure an invitation—after all, you are now the darling of the *ton*—that I really think we should have the ball first, followed perhaps by a musical evening. Then perhaps a few dinner parties, opera parties, a breakfast or two—I must see what dates are still free."

He stopped her chatter by kissing her neck. "Do you know, my dearest love, I have no interest in such entertainments."

Turning around, she stared up at him, wide-eyed with astonishment. "But how can you not care about your standing in society? How is it possible for you not to care what other people think?"

For a moment he thought she was serious, but then he saw the twinkle in her eyes. "Are you mocking me?" he asked with pretended gruffness.

"Mocking you?" she said with a saccharine smile. "But my lord, ever since we met, you have not missed a chance to point out to me how important the opinion of the *ton* is, and how I must do nothing to jeopardize my reputation. Now that you are an earl and thus have unlimited entrée into the highest levels of society, I made sure that you would—"

His laughter interrupted her. "I admit I have been a fool."

"And do you acknowledge that you were wrong to squander even a moment of our time together?"

He pulled her to her feet and wrapped his arms around her. "Kiss me, and you may have your ball and your Venetian breakfast and anything else your heart desires."

"All I want is to be with you in your little cottage in Cornwall."

"I am afraid there are two problems with that."

He could feel her stiffen in his arms, and her eyes were worried.

"I see," she said, trying unobtrusively—and unsuccessfully—to extract herself from his embrace.

"The first problem is that I now am the owner of an estate in Cornwall, which has been shockingly run down by the previous owner. I cannot shirk my obligations to my tenants."

She relaxed, and a faint smile began to play around the corners of her mouth. "A not insurmountable problem. I am sure I can adjust to the role of lady of the manor. And the second problem?"

"I am afraid that once you cease your foolish prattle and allow me to carry you off to my bed, I shall not willingly let you out of my embrace for days and days."

"Perhaps even weeks?"

"I promise to do my best," he said, picking her up in his arms.

"And as I have already ascertained, your best is quite good indeed."

"I love you," he said with no more levity.

"Then cease your 'foolish prattle' and show me just how much," she said with an impish grin.

It was all worth it, he realized. Every moment of pain he had suffered—every slight and indignity he had endured—it had all brought him to this point. He had spent years wishing that his father had treated his mother with the respect and honor that she deserved, and yet now, if he had the power to go back in time and change whatever he wished, he would alter nothing.

Because all of the events of his life had conspired to

bring him to this place and time, and Bethia was now so firmly entrenched in his heart, it was impossible for him to imagine life without her beside him.

"You are crying," she said wonderingly, reaching up to brush a tear off his cheek.

"I have never been happier in my life," he replied, carrying her over to the bed and laying her down gently.

"You will be a wonderful earl," Bethia said. "Everyone will come to admire you, I am sure."

He laughed out loud. "What do I have to say to persuade you that I don't care a fig about the title or about anyone else's opinion?"

"Why," she said looking up at him innocently, "you do not have to *say* a thing . . . "

Taking her meaning, he quickly lay down and wrapped his arms around her and pulled her close.

"And as for me," she said, "I shall exercise great restraint and forbear to point out to you that you have been insisting since the day we met that I should care about such things."

He silenced her with a kiss, and after a few more moments, his darling beloved wife abandoned all thoughts of restraint.